Drama City:

By

Larry Moon Jr.

Copyright ©2011 Larry Moon Jr.

All rights reserved. No part of this book may be reproduced in any form without written permission from the publisher, except by a reviewer who may quote brief passages in a review to be printed in a newspaper or magazine.

This is a work of fiction. It is not meant to depict, portray or represent any particular real person. All characters, incidents, and dialogues are the product of the author's imagination and are not to be construed as real. Any reference or similarities to actual events, entities, real people, living or dead, or to real locales are intended to give the novel a sense of reality. Any resemblances are purely coincidental.

ACKNOWLEDGEMENTS

First I would like to give thanks to God for allowing me to defy the odds. Please continue to use me as an instrument to do your will. I appreciate the undying support from all of my readers.

I would like to give a special thanks to my kids, Kamari Moon, Larry Gross, Kaila Young and Cahir Moon; my mother Sheila Green, my sister Carolyn Moon, Danita Richardson, Conrad Richardson, Cailah Richardson, Camiyah Richardson, Veronda Hazelton, Brittany "Pooh Bear' Gross and My Granddaughter Malai , Barbara Johnson, Kevin Dickerson and the Dickerson family, James Bates and family, Latoya Young, Delores Hinnant, Tia Hinnant, Patricia Forbes, Uncle Fred, Patrice Forbes, Nicole Hinnant, Michael Hinnant, and the entire Hinnant Family, Tyrone Ragland, Clara Miller, John Lyons, Carolyn Moon, Keisha Hill, Michael Lindsay, Tracy Press, Damon Wilson, Tony Young, Otis Forbes, Marcellus Green, Curtis Spivey, Marlin Moore, Renee Beach, Donyelle Rosborough, Kim Daughtry, Ms. Earles, Mr. Butler, Mr. Jones, Mr.Brisbane and the entire staff at RSC; Keia Gross and family, Earl Johnson, Sean Johnson and family, The entire Malik family, James R. Jeter, The Ultimate weapon Group, Artavia Gadson, Arjhane Beach, Zaire Beach, Ajayla Beach, Marjhay Tomlinson, Antionnay Forbes, Larry Moody, Gerald Rich, Corey Rich, Ernie Davis and family, Burnis Cole, Michael Richardson, King Ragland, Mike Lomax, Barry Saunders, Mike Saunders, Doug Butler, Kim Nelson and Family, Marlin Moore, Linwood Pippens, My Extended fellowship; The Slade Rhythm Band, Mike Speaks, Thank you, Ghetto Princess Publishing for recognizing the potential of Drama-City and Shalleice Hudson for your ground work and loyalty, , Merchant Holloway, , Guy Raspberry, Marlon Stuckey and Family, Tameka Baylor and Family, Erica Pitts, Chiquita Moon, Haywood Warner, Ms. Mclean from the U.S. Parole Board, Vincent Haskell, Rashawn P, Christina Blake, Keisha Troublefield, Reggie Johnson, Eddie Paige, My former colleagues at Double Decker

Tours, Chariots For Hire, Khaleem Washington, Eric Murray, Reico Welch, Gregory Blue, Delores and James Hinnant, Sidney Stevenson, Aunt Tracy, Madonna Belton, Lovely Flower, My grandparents May you rest in peace The Hot Biscuit coalition My Aunt Denise Moon, My Uncle Reginald Moon and last but not least Sulaimon Yusaf Malik a true friend and fallen soldier Rest in Peace. If I have failed to include you in my acknowledgements charge it to my head and not my heart! Thanks for your support.

CHAPTER 1

"Ya'll bumped!" Darryl Jenkins yelled through the slight quietness of the recreation room at the Central Facility (that housed violent and non-violent offenders in Lorton V.A.). "We have ten books so ya'll can't have but three," Darryl continued bragging about the spades game that he and his boy, Timothy Johnson, were winning against their long time comrades Cliff Porter and Tony Young.

"You two bammas are cheatin, so you can charge those push-ups to the game," Cliff said absent-mindedly. "Bamma" was the slang word they used to describe an outcast or someone not up to date in fashion, but in most cases, the word was a natural part of conversations.

"This is the type of shit that causes bloodshed on the streets, nigga," Tim said in a hostile tone. Tony looked up to find Tim standing over him.

"Why are you directin' your frustrations at me? You scared of Cliff?" Tony asked.

Tim reached out and grabbed Tony's throat. "I got a very sharp knife. I'm not scared of nothin that breathes this penitentiary air. Damn Skippy, I'm serious about mine."

Cliff looked around, "Well, get 'em like Mike Tyson got a piece of Holyfield's ear," he said before he ran out of the recreation room laughing.

Tim was a slim, tall, muscular brother with wavy hair and hazel eyes. He had a typical poise about himself that most women found attractive and the only thing that was wrong with it was that he knew it.

Every inmate at Lorton had an obtrusive story to tell. Some of them spoke of fame, hardships and broken homes, but mostly, their stories revolved around narcotics. None of their stories ever really held verbal sentiments of desire for change. These young brothers were caught up in a garden of misconception for acceptance, which was originated by the generation before them. They were fed the misconception that they would not be accepted. If they were not wearing what the in crowd wears, then you were considered a bamma. For most of the drug dealers in Lorton, the aforementioned was the case. So to pacify their need to be accepted, most of them resulted to a life of selling drugs on the streets. After money, came the desire and the greed, and for the most compulsive ones came a drug habit; a habit that prevented them from keeping or maintaining all of the worldly items that they had acquired through selling drugs.

    For a lot of the older inmates, heroin was their drug of choice. Heroin swept through the city in the late sixties, picking up those who chose to sample and enchanting those who came back for more. The ones who weren't fortunate enough to sustain from its grasp, were carried into the wave of the nineties with a vicious dope habit, which in turn defeated their original purpose of getting into the drug game in the first place (to make money). But for Timothy Johnson this was not the case. Tim liked to smoke a little weed, but as far as other drugs was concerned, the only thing he could see in it was money and easy access to automobiles, televisions, clothes and whatever else the dope fiends stole to fence off for narcotics.

    Tim was at the highlight of his drug dealing career, when one of his runners caught a petty dope charge and turned him in; in return the runner's charge for possession with the intent to distribute heroin would be dropped. Luckily, Tim never trusted anyone enough to include them in his personal business affairs. Therefore, no one knew about the apartment complex or beauty salon that he owned which was in his mother's name. He also dealt with a Dominican named Sol who traded him counterfeit currency for U.S. currency. Sol would give Tim a hundred thousand dollars of counterfeit money for twenty five thousand in U.S. currency and in turn Tim would sell the hundred thousand dollars' worth of counterfeit money for fifty thousand in U.S. currency. The way he figured it, he was making a twenty five thousand dollar profit for transferring the counterfeit money.

When the narcotics division tried to pursue Tim for questioning, he evaded them for weeks. They finally tracked him down when he was on his way to drop off ten thousand dollars' worth of drugs to one of his runners. Tim initially fled, but after six miles and a shootout, Tim was caught and charged with possession of a controlled substance (two counts), discharging a firearm while eluding police, and reckless endangering the lives of others. He was facing life without parole if he took the case to trial and lost.

After weighing all the options open to him, he decided to take the plea agreement that was offered by the District Attorney and Prosecutor. His plea agreement stated that he could get sentenced up to thirty years. The judge gave him twenty years non-mandatory, which meant that he would be eligible for parole in twelve years, but his good time rewards could bring him as close to eligibility as nine years. Normally, this would have been a federal case due to the amount of drugs found, but since Tim ditched most of the drugs, they couldn't tie him to them.

*****

Rhonda Warner wasn't feeling like her usual self; she was filled with a lot of emotions that she hadn't felt since the beginning of her six year marriage. She was self-confident and alluring. She had a five year old son name Roland and he was the center of her world. Melvin Warner was her husband, a thirty year old stock broker and a very simple man. He wasn't into wining and dining and he very seldom presented her with surprises or romantic tactics.

Rhonda was slim with wide hips that always called for a double take whenever she would pass the conspicuous eyes of her co-workers and the inmates at the Lorton reformatory. Her eyes were brown and she developed full lips from her mother's side of the family. She was 5 feet 7 inches tall and she weighed a hundred and thirty five pounds.

"Wake up little man. You had a long night, but it's time to get ready for school now," she said as she pulled the blanket from Roland's comfort.

"Can I go to work with you today mommy?"

"No baby, there's a lot of bad guys at my job."

Roland stared at his mother for a second, "They don't like kids my age?"

Rhonda was caught off guard by the question, but she needed a quick response or else Roland would sense the evasiveness."

"Honestly, I am afraid that some of the guys at the job have done bad things to kids your age, not all but probably a few."

"You can come to school with me mommy, there's no bad guys there."

"Maybe another day sweetie! Now, let's get ready to go."

As Rhonda exited Roland's room, she inhaled at the thought of her son wanting to spend more time with his mommy. She then went into the bathroom and prepared herself for another long day at work. After preparing breakfast for Roland and Melvin she went to her bedroom and kissed Melvin on the forehead and told him that breakfast would be on the stove once he awakes. He smiled, asked about the time and went back to dreamland. Rhonda was glad that he didn't wake up because she had been feeling guilty about her actions toward him. She had become distracted lately.

The weather report predicted that it would be slightly breezy with a fifty percent chance of showers, so Rhonda grabbed her umbrella and jacket then called for Roland to do the same. Rhonda opened the door to her 2001 Nissan Xterra by remote.

"Mommy, will I ever learn to drive?"

"Yes honey, when you are sixteen."

"When will that be?"

"Soon enough baby. Don't rush time. Life is short enough as it is."

*****

His eyes gazed nonchalantly at the ceiling in the dormitory oblivious to his surroundings.

"Come on, what's your answer," Cliff said while nudging Tim. "What would you do for a slice of the devil's pie?"

"I would have to know exactly what a slice of the devil's pie consisted of!" Tony said. "Or at least, what consequences and rewards are involved."

"Why do you always have to turn my conversation into an intellectual forum?"

"I'm not. I just needed to know the temperature of the water before I jump in." Tony replied.

"Well, to my understanding the temperature in hell is one thousand degrees, so answer my question."

"The question is this!" Tony looked around cautiously as he spoke trying not to look informal, "What would the devil do for a slice of his own pie after I stick my .357 magnum in his face and confiscate it from him?"

5

Cliff frowned at first, but he couldn't help but laugh at Tony's remark. Every now and again they needed humor to pacify the burning guilt of the responsibilities they'd left in society.

Cliff and Tony were trying to compete on an intellectual level to show that not all jail dudes have a limited vocabulary.

*****

The chill in the air competed with the beautiful sunny skies as Daryl, Cliff and Tony played basketball in the recreation yard. Luckily for them, the more games they played, the higher the temperature seemed to rise.

After the third game, a correctional officer (C.O) entered the recreation yard and informed Tim that the nurse wanted to see him at the infirmary. He was escorted by Officer Warner, a correctional officer whom he had several conversations with in the past. They had discussed everything from investments, to politics, to materialism and responsibility. Tim was surprised to see that Officer Warner knew so much about stocks and bonds. "My husband is a stock broker, therefore he keeps me abreast." is what she explained to him. Tim wondered if he would ever get the chance to pick up where he left off in their conversation, but he never saw her much so he took it for what it was; a chance to be in a female's presence.

As Tim stepped passed the security booth and was patted down for weapons or contraband, he glanced at Officer Warner and noticed that she was even prettier than the last time he saw her. As they walked the compound side by side, Tim imagined that he and Officer Warner were walking down the aisle to the altar. There were a few inmates standing around having idle conversations, so Tim included them in his day dream as witnesses to his imaginary wedding.

As he turned to Officer Warner, he said "Yes."

The weather report predicted that it would be slightly breezy with a fifty percent chance of showers, so Rhonda grabbed her umbrella and jacket then called for Roland to do the same. Rhonda opened the door to her 2001 Nissan Xterra by remote.

"Mommy, will I ever learn to drive?"

"Yes honey, when you are sixteen."

"When will that be?"

"Soon enough baby. Don't rush time. Life is short enough as it is."

*****

His eyes gazed nonchalantly at the ceiling in the dormitory oblivious to his surroundings.

"Come on, what's your answer," Cliff said while nudging Tim. "What would you do for a slice of the devil's pie?"

"I would have to know exactly what a slice of the devil's pie consisted of!" Tony said. "Or at least, what consequences and rewards are involved."

"Why do you always have to turn my conversation into an intellectual forum?"

"I'm not. I just needed to know the temperature of the water before I jump in." Tony replied.

"Well, to my understanding the temperature in hell is one thousand degrees, so answer my question."

"The question is this!" Tony looked around cautiously as he spoke trying not to look informal, "What would the devil do for a slice of his own pie after I stick my .357 magnum in his face and confiscate it from him?"

Cliff frowned at first, but he couldn't help but laugh at Tony's remark. Every now and again they needed humor to pacify the burning guilt of the responsibilities they'd left in society.

Cliff and Tony were trying to compete on an intellectual level to show that not all jail dudes have a limited vocabulary.

*****

The chill in the air competed with the beautiful sunny skies as Daryl, Cliff and Tony played basketball in the recreation yard. Luckily for them, the more games they played, the higher the temperature seemed to rise.

After the third game, a correctional officer (C.O) entered the recreation yard and informed Tim that the nurse wanted to see him at the infirmary. He was escorted by Officer Warner, a correctional officer whom he had several conversations with in the past. They had discussed everything from investments, to politics, to materialism and responsibility. Tim was surprised to see that Officer Warner knew so much about stocks and bonds. "My husband is a stock broker, therefore he keeps me abreast." is what she explained to him. Tim wondered if he would ever get the chance to pick up where he left off in their conversation, but he never saw her much so he took it for what it was; a chance to be in a female's presence.

As Tim stepped passed the security booth and was patted down for weapons or contraband, he glanced at Officer Warner and noticed that she was even prettier than the last time he saw her. As they walked the compound side by side, Tim imagined that he and Officer Warner were walking down the aisle to the altar. There were a few inmates standing around having idle conversations, so Tim included them in his day dream as witnesses to his imaginary wedding.

As he turned to Officer Warner, he said "Yes."

Her expression brought him back to reality. Tim realized he was caught up in his daydream.

"You remind me of my jeep," Tim flirted.

"Is that so?" the officer responded. "Well just what color is your jeep?"

"It's a luxurious cocoa drop top."

She glanced at Tim to see if she had his full attention. "Did you drive it luxuriously or did you just dog it out?"

"A little of both, sometimes you have to be gentle and sometimes you have to play rough."

"Are we still on the same page, Mr. Johnson?" Officer Warner interrupted, appearing slightly unnerved at Tim's advances.

"Yeah, but you've got to be careful because if you are reading a book and you never turn the page, you may find yourself reading the same thing over and over again. That's sort of like running in place."

Tim knew that there was an equal attraction on both of their behalves but he had to be careful with this woman because she had a lot of class. He could spot class a mile away, hiding under massive debris and rubble.

Tim and Officer Warner entered the infirmary. There were a few nurses and physician assistants roaming the hallways. Tim noticed that the halls were especially shinny and he wondered why the orderlies never tried to give the floors in the unit the same shine but then again, he knew that the standards for maintaining the inmate facilities weren't as high.

As he waited for his number to be called, he observed an inmate stealing hypodermic needles from a room adjacent to where he was sitting. He immediately went into action by seizing Officer

Warner's attention; not because he was in on the scheme, but because he respected every man's hustle. Even though he had done his part, he could not warn the guy who was in the room, that the doctor was coming. Tim was quick on his feet.

"Excuse me Doc. Who do I have to see so that I can schedule…..." Before Tim could finish the inmate stepped towards the hallway. Despite Tim's efforts, the doctor was well aware of the fact that the inmate did not belong there.

"What the hell are you doing?" the doctor screamed at the inmate.

"I ….. I'm trying to find the bathroom," the startled inmate responded.

"The hell you were!" the doctor rebutted.

The disruptiveness of their confrontation invited nurses and a few of the other medical staff to see what the commotion was.

"What's going on Dr. Brenner?" one of the assistants asked urgently.

"I just observed this young man exiting the x-ray room, claiming that he was looking for the bathroom." Before the doctor could continue with his allegations, the inmate had moved swiftly behind him and grabbed him in a choke hold while brandishing a homemade knife. The room was filled with utter chaos as one of the correctional officers called a code blue emergency. The inmate, named Rabbit, was totally unaffected by the screams and pleas of the physicians and nurses.

"Your job is not to be a police, it is to give inmates medical attention and you can't even do that!" Rabbit screamed at the doctor who was trembling in his grasp. "I was minding my own business and you made my business your business, so you'll have to see firsthand, what happens to Good Samaritan's."

Tim knew what was about to happen with this scene so he whispered to Officer Warner and she understood completely. Tim told her that it would be best to let the emergency response team (ERT) handle this situation.

The sight of so many correctional officers made Rabbit lose his focus. In a panic-stricken state, he quickly pulled Dr. Brenner to the pavement and stabbed him with the homemade knife repeatedly. Blood spurted from his neck and body area fluently.

The nurses were screaming at the sight of violence that had occurred before them. They usually dealt with situations such as this but they never had the displeasure of viewing the actual assault.

After Rabbit assaulted the doctor he took visual inventory of the room. The Lieutenant and the Warden had arrived along with an entourage of correctional officers.

"Drop your weapon, it's not worth it," the Lieutenant said. In a flash, Rabbit turned and ran towards a window in the infirmary wing. He leaped at the window head first, but to his dismay it didn't break. Rabbit fell to the floor in excruciating pain and went into an unconscious state shortly thereafter.

The Lieutenant's name was Jerry Cooper. He had seen his share of situations, but this was one of the oddest one yet.

"Get this man a helicopter," Lieutenant Cooper said in reference to the still-bleeding Dr. Brenner. "And find out what happened and which nurse saw it."

Dr. Brenner was airlifted by helicopter to Fairfax Hospital where he underwent surgery and received forty-two stitches for his stab wounds. Rabbit was treated for a minor concussion then was escorted to the segregation unit while further investigation was ensued.

CHAPTER 2

The following morning Tim woke up and reminisced about the day before. He didn't concern himself with the assault that he witnessed because this was nothing new to him. Instead, he focused on something that had been stolen from him the very moment he left society. Something that at times didn't mean anything to him because he had forgotten what it felt like, but something that meant everything to him at this moment because of a recent encounter. It was the feeling of affection from a woman.

Since being incarcerated, Tim only had the emotional gratification that receiving letters gave him. The visits he was allowed only frustrated him because of the setting, but things were different when he talked to Officer Warner yesterday. On the way back from the infirmary, Tim and Officer Warner had ventured into each other's thoughts, peeling away secrets and building trust.

Tim woke up for chow call feeling no closer to freedom nor any further from insanity. His cell mate was still asleep so he tapped his bed and asked him if he was going to breakfast. Tim proceeded to move about the room in a quiet fashion so that he didn't disturb his cell mate. He washed his face, brushed his teeth and just as he turned towards the door he saw a shadow breeze by in a sneaky manor. He laughed to himself because he assumed that it was Tony or Cliff trying to pull a prank on him. His cell was dark because he had not turned on the light and no sunlight was seeping through the window because the sun had not begun to rise. Tim stood beside the door as two people walked pass him. Just as he was about to grab one of them and turn the prank around, he heard a voice say, "Should I hit him in the neck?" The other voice whispered, "Just get him good."

Tim weighed his options. He knew that it was two of them and one of him and he couldn't get to his knife. He didn't wait around to see if it was a prank, instead he ran out of the cell and stood by the tier so that he could see who his assailants were.

The door to Tim's cell opened and he watched as the two inmates looked out of the door. Tim was not surprised at whom they were, but he was surprised that they had the heart to enter such a rowdy dormitory to assault someone with enough inside connections to run a correctional drug gang. The two assailants quickly emerged from the cell nervously then left as quietly as they arrived.

Tim was sort of impressed as he thought about it. The two fools were smart enough not to chase after him as he fled, but they were dumb enough to put themselves at risk by revealing who they were. Tim had dropped out of college, but he was smart enough to figure out why this whole scene had occurred. It was because of Rabbit. Now, he had to find out what provoked the two fools to believe that anything else happened other than what really occurred.

Tim quickly went to Cliff and Daryl's cell and summoned them to the common area. The common area was the main area in the dormitory where inmates often congregated to play card games and board games. He told Cliff to wake Tony up also. Once every one was present, he explained the situation. He also gave graphic details of what occurred in the infirmary with Rabbit and the doctor. He included why he thought that Rabbit may have sent a letter saying that he snitched.

"I tried to be a decoy to the best of my ability, but Rabbit was moving like a zombie," Tim explained.

"Man, fuck the bullshit!" Darryl said. "That nigga know that you don't get down like that. I guess he's just trying to compensate or get some gratification because he fucked up."

"Well, he will not get any gratification at the expense of my life or health," Tim responded hastily.

"Are you sure that it was Rah-Rah and Peanut?" asked Cliff.

"Are you scared of a little drama? "Tony stated rhetorically.

"I wasn't talking to you I was speaking out loud…I like the way my voice sounds," Cliff retorted jokingly.

"Look, it was them, and if I can help it, there will not be any drama. But if I can't help it, somebody's going to get hurt real bad. I have to look into this a little deeper. Then and only then will we retaliate," Tim said with certainty.

*****

Linda Anderson looked into the mirror in her bathroom. She saw her reflection for only one moment before she began to look pass her attractive face and features. She began to seek refuge within her soul's intellect, not ignoring the fact of who she once was and who she had become. Linda was reminiscing of being free and irresponsible, but those days were long gone because now she was in her own prison and she had plenty of responsibilities.

Linda and Tim were engaged months before Tim went to Lorton and she's been his backbone for the past seven years. Linda eyed the mirror with fear in her heart. She was taunting herself for being what Tim wanted her to be. "Why do I have to wait for his call?" she asked the mirror rhetorically. "He left me out here all alone, but he thinks that he's in control. Well, he's not in control of shit but his mouth."

The house that Tim bought for the two of them was a two bedroom mini mansion. It had two bathrooms and an enormous kitchen that revealed a glass floor. Tim also bought Linda a Nissan Maxima which she exchanged for a Pathfinder.

The house was located on the outskirts of D.C. in Clinton, Maryland. Tim chose this location because he didn't want to live in the midst of the lifestyle and people who helped him acquire his wealth.

Linda stared at the letter that she'd written Tim two months prior. For so long, she didn't have the courage to send it. Linda felt dependent on Tim for so many reasons. He was strong willed, always able to find a path through the toughest storms, and she admired his integrity.

He was able to make the weakest link stronger in various ways and he was a fighter.

Linda had finally found the strength to break free from the hold that Tim had on her; she was ready to write him off.

Tim and Linda met at a club called The Mirage in Southeast, Washington, D.C. and even though Tim did not usually frequent clubs (let alone meet woman who did with the intent of seeing them more than once), he saw something in Linda that caused immediate attraction. Linda was light brown with short hair that she had dyed red, she had hazel eyes and she weighed a hundred twenty pounds, her height was five feet four and she navigated her frame with full confidence.

After briefly getting acquainted they exchanged phone numbers. Tim did not give her his cell phone number or his pager number, but he gave her his home phone number instead. This is something he never did before. He was very impressed that she wasn't easy and she wasn't going to the hotel with him or anyone else after the club scene which was usually the protocol for most people after meeting someone new at The Mirage.

After a week had passed, Tim wondered why she hadn't called him. He scolded himself for not giving her his other phone numbers in addition to his home number. He did not want to phone her out of fear that it was an incorrect number, and if that was the case, then his ego would have been shattered.

After becoming annoyed and anxious, Tim decided to call Linda. He did not get in contact with her the first time, so he called continuously until he finally reached her. She was glad he had called and she explained to him that she had lost his phone number. After conversations with each other night after night, they discovered they both had a lot in common. They shared the same interest of hobbies and they both didn't have any kids. Once they started dating, they became inseparable.

Linda often wondered what type of occupation Tim had that allowed him to keep up with all of the latest fashions, ride in a nice car and bathe her with spontaneous gifts. Tim would tell her that he helped his mother run her small business. She felt guilty for her notions of suspicion so she alleviated any further probing.

As Linda sealed the letter that would bring closure to such a meaningful relationship, a tear drop had fallen from her eye. She smiled for a moment as she recollected a distant memory. For someone on the outside looking in, it would have appeared to be a tear of joy, but Linda was on the inside looking out. She knew all too well that those were tears of pain; a pain which had driven her to let go of the past and venture into the future.

Linda couldn't build up enough courage to mail the letter herself, so the next day she asked her friend Ronald to do it. Ronald was more than happy to oblige her. He had been there for Linda and he had shared her pain and pleasures for the past six months.

Linda and Ronald met at a bowling alley in Forestville, Maryland. She had explained her relationship with Tim and her desire to wait for him. Ronald respected her decision, but applied his finesse towards her vulnerability.

"I just want to be a friend," he said. But after a while, their friendship transformed and he gave her an ultimatum. In the end she finally chose Ronald. Tim gave her caring words and emotional support, but Ronald gave her love and affection. Tim was too controlling, even from prison, so Ronald's laid back nature won her over in the end.

As Linda brought herself out of a daze, she began to remove all of Tim's pictures from the wall and mirror. She was no longer feeling like a prisoner, but she could feel an emptiness swelling inside her; an emptiness that refused to be ignored.

The phone rang and Linda reached to pick up the receiver. She knocked over a picture of her and Tim. The picture fell and shattered, but she barely noticed

"Hello," Linda said.

"Hey baby," the voice responded on the other end.

"Hey Ronald. Did you mail the letter?"

"Yes I did my princess. I was tempted to open it but you deserve your privacy."

"I'm not trying to keep anything from you, Ronald. As a matter of a fact," Linda continued, "I am about to call Tim's mom and arrange for her to pick up the engagement ring that he gave me."

"Okay, you handle that. I am going to go to the grocery store so I can prepare a gourmet dish for my Princess tonight."

"I am looking forward to it, Sir Ronald," Linda responded. They both hung up.

As Linda stepped back from the bed, she stepped on a piece of glass. When she looked down and saw the shattered picture frame, she cried. It was her and Tim's engagement picture; the one they had taken while in Cancun for a week.

CHAPTER 3

"Stephan.... Bradley.... Washington," the C.O was adhering to a daily protocol that had created both tension and relief inside the Lorton reformatory. He was delivering mail to the inmates. Normally he would go from room to room, but today he was not physically in the mood.

Tim waited patiently until he heard his name before he grabbed his mail. He attempted to walk away, but heard his name once again. He looked at the return address and noted that the first letter was from Linda, his fiancée; the second letter had no name on the return address, just the words "a special friend" written in bold face letters. Out of curiosity Tim decided to read second letter first.

Dear Special Friend,

I know you are wondering who I am. I'll give you a clue, and when you figure it out you can come and claim your prize. I am someone who should remind you of your jeep. I was reading a book, but I never turned the page until we crossed paths; I must have been reading the same page over and over. Have you figured it out yet? Hope to see you soon.

Yours Truly,

So Far,

But So Close

Tim was astounded. He knew who it was, but did not expect her to make the first move. Now that she has, he began to flourish in the thought of what could have motivated her to this extreme. Tim began to open the second letter, and thought it was odd that Linda hadn't sprayed this letter with perfume. Tim opened the letter and began to read.

Dear Tim,

I really don't know where to begin.

I have experienced so many lonely nights, distraught visits and unwanted feelings since you have been away. I have also experienced an enormous amount of romantic times, special embraces, and unspeakable love while you were here. Somewhere along the line, the distance that has been created began to feel much stronger than the love that used to keep me afloat.

I am writing this letter with all respect for you, so that there will be no hard feelings. I have chosen to move on with my life. I have a friend who has been supportive in my time of need and I understand that this is a choice that I will have to live with. Feel free to call me if you need anything.

Love Always,

Linda

Tim was awe struck. He staggered back for a moment as a tear drop fell from his blinking eyes. He realized that he was still standing in the day room where curious eyes roamed freely, but his emotions had no remorse for his surroundings. "That bitch is going to pay," he said as he turned and headed for his cell.

Once Tim got to his cell he paced back and forth while uttering profane statements directed at Linda. Of course, Linda could not hear him, but the walls that surrounded him for many years could.

Tim stayed in his room the entire evening. When Daryl and Cliff visited, he explained the situation, and they knew that he needed some time alone to soothe his pain, Tim reached into his locker, grabbed his walkman and tuned into Sade's "Love Deluxe" album.

*****

The Lorton reformatory consisted of six separate compounds. Minimum facility housed non-violent D.C. inmates, and at that time, a few violent ones that have completed the majority of their sentence. For the most part, however, the inmates incarcerated at the minimum facility were parole violations, drug abusers and petty criminals.

The Medium facility housed inmates with minimal violent histories, parole violators and inmates who were waiting to go to minimum or half way houses. Inmates whose sentencing ranged from three to nine years and five to fifteen years non-mandatory (sentences) were usually housed here, unless there were disciplinary problems.

Youth Center inmates usually were younger adults who were sentenced under the Youth Rehabilitation Act. The Judge would normally give them a lengthy youth act sentence. If an inmate had a ten year youth act sentence, he would not necessarily do the ten years. The board would give him a sufficient set off so that the inmate can get his GED or take up a trade. The Classification Board would ultimately determine the inmates release date, but the remaining time on any sentence would be completed on parole.

In some instances, there were older inmates still completing youth act sentences. Most of them had violated their probation terms. The youth act benefits can be promising if successfully completed. Once an individual completes the terms of a youth act sentence, they can have the charges expunged from their criminal record.

The Occoquan facility was a dwelling for violence and doing hard time. There were frequent robberies, murders and mayhem amongst the compound. Inmates who were housed here were doing lengthy sentences. Most of the inmates were younger dudes with eighty years or better. There were guys who were serving three life sentences as well. It was once said by those who served sentences at this institution, that once you enter this world, which they called Vietnam, your life would never be the same.

The facility housed parole violators who had high custody level points, meaning they were in maximum security. Those who refused to abide by the rules and procedures and continued to be a disciplinary problem were often transferred to the Maximum Security facility, which was a twenty three hour lock down institution. This facility housed a lot of the violent criminals who couldn't maintain while being incarcerated. In addition, this facility housed inmates who had been stabbed and refused to snitch, leaving the institution no choice but to place them on involuntary protective custody.

The sentences often being served in Maximum Security were lengthy as well. Although all of the facilities remain in the past, there were many scars left behind to show the history of Lorton. The last of the facilities to be closed is the combination of all the facilities rolled into one as far as the inmates are concerned.

There was a time that the inmates could get food and clothing packages sent from home. This was also a memory. The society that lived outside of this correctional reformatory had often signed petitions and rallied to close the institutions. Years and years passed with no progress, finally, as a result of the frequent murders and threats to the environment, the Lorton community was finally granted its request to close Lorton's` Correction Reformatory. The only remaining institution was Central facility. A lot of inmates were transferred out of the other institutions on separate occasions to Central or federal institutions.

*****

Tim woke up to an empty sound flowing from his walkman. The tape had stopped and he was trying to figure out how long it had been since he dozed off. Tim started to day dream for a moment. He thought about Linda and all of the special times that they shared. He thought about other woman who offered their love, but was denied by him because of his loyalty to her.

There was a knock on Tim's cell door just as he began to gather his hygiene items. He ignored the first two knocks, but as he heard the person's footsteps begin to walk away, he opened the door.

"Tony," Tim said in a low voice

"Damn, slim are you playing possum or what?" Tony said with excitement. "Look man, you cannot do your time like this."

"I had to get me some rest, Joe. I am going through a transition," Tim replied.

The name Joe was used frequently and sometimes subconsciously. It was a slang word.

"I got a letter from Linda," Tim said.

"That's good. Is she coming to visit you this weekend?" Tony inquired.

"No. I doubt if she's ever coming again…she left me."

"Damn. First Austin Powers loses his mojo; Now this."

"That shit ain't funny, nigga," Tim said in an irritated tone.

Before Tony could state his claim the cell door flew open and the correctional officer announced a shake down. The officer asked Tony and Tim if both of them slept in the cell; Tony said no and Tim said yes. The officer asked them both to step out of the cell while it was being searched.

Tim told Tony to exit the unit because he knew that Tony was known for carrying drugs and knives on his person. The both of them fortunately did not get patted down by the officer, because Tim also had a joint of weed in his sock. The officer told Tim to enter the cell and Tim responded in a casual tone.

"I guess I get to be handcuffed, huh?"

"Be careful what you ask for, handsome," the officer replied. "Were you surprised?"

"I was more ecstatic than I was surprised."

"Is that right?"

"Yes, that's right Officer Warner."

"You can call me Rhonda for now."

Officer Warner was pretending to shake his room down. She wanted to talk to him and at the same time see what his living conditions consisted of. Tim loved the fact that he could call her by her first name.

"Do you mind if I ask you what's so special about me, that of all the things to do, and all the people in your life, you were thinking about me enough to put it on paper?" Tim said.

"Well, I feel like special people need special attention."

"What's so special about me?"

"When we talked the other day, I realized that you were intelligent and isolated to a certain degree. You don't like to start confusion, but you will finish it to protect yourself or love ones. I know that if I choose to become better acquainted with you, I might be playing with fire. But it's a risk I'm strongly considering," Officer Warner explained.

"Damn, I'm worth the risk, huh? And it sounds like you have me down in a nutshell. You could write a biography on me," Tim said as he laughed. Officer Warner stared at him until she realized that it was not an appropriate setting.

"If I wrote your biography, where do you suppose I would fit in?" Officer Warner asked.

"I guess that you would fall into the middle of the book, close to the end," Tim responded.

"Why is that?"

"Because I would have to tell you my life story, I would fill up at least twenty chapters taking you from my childhood up until my incarceration; and that's just telling you the things that I think you are capable of handling. You will come in close to the ending, after I have been betrayed and trampled over by those who misuse the word love to benefit their own selfish motives."

"This biography may be very interesting," Officer Warner said.

"You should know. You are the author, I am just the subject," Tim replied.

Tim and Officer Warner's eyes locked into each other exploring. There was no doubt about it; they had both found compatibility in conversation and they were both willing to share personal information. Officer Warner exited Tim's cell and went to several other cells to perform a shake down. She was not looking for contraband, but she made it seem that way to avoid suspicion.

As Officer Warner visited other cells a few inmates attempted to solicit a conversation. She was good at sending messages of disinterest through her body language. Therefore, most of the inmates were discouraged.

Several days passed and Tim began to really open up to Officer Warner. He told her that his fiancé left him and slowly, Office Warner began to fill Linda's void.

CHAPTER 4

The following morning, Tim, Daryl, Cliff, and Tony gathered on the recreation yard. It was a big day for them because it was visitation day. Although Tim was not getting a visit, his three colleagues were.

Tim had set up some transactions of marijuana and heroin so that Daryl, Cliff, and Tony could smuggle it in out of the visiting room. As they gathered, each individual greeted each other. Daryl thought that maybe the visits were off because Tim had given each one of them the low down a week prior, and usually there's nothing said after their initial meeting.

"The reason why I called for a meeting is because some plans have been changed," Tim said.

"Damn slim, you are slipping. You use to be the penitentiary Frank White," Daryl replied.

"Yeah nigga, you are losing a lot of brownie points around here. First you let shit slide with Rah-Rah and Peanut, now I guess the business is getting shaky," Cliff added.

"Nah, Quick Draw McGraw, I am smarter than the average hustler therefore, I know when to bat-up and when to let up. I know when and where to handle my business, so if you will allow me to get to the business at hand, I will be obliged to do so," Tim said hastily.

"Today is the big day. Everything I said last week remains the same except for one thing. There's going to be more weed and much more blow than I expected, so we will probably have to do this again tomorrow. There's going to be an ounce of weed in each balloon, and you will get one balloon a piece. There's going to be an additional balloon with two separate balloons inside of it, one of the balloons is going to have pure heroin in it and the other one is going to have some Bonita cut in it. You will get one of those each also. Ya'll can't be in there bull shitting. The heroin balloons are worth at least fifteen thousand dollars each, once I cut it and bag it. They should be calling your names for visits within the next half an hour, so I will see you all later. Don't forget to get that shit off you as soon as you get to the unit, and then take it to the safe spot."

They shook hands, and then departed. Tim headed towards his dormitory. He had a mission to fulfill, but first, he had to make his rounds. He stopped at the officer's booth; this was part of this plan. He talked to the CO for at least thirty minutes then continued to walk to his dormitory.

Tim gathered his sweat suit and tore some of his sheet so that he could make a hand wrap. He then reached behind his mirror and got his homemade knife. Once he tied the wrap around the knife, he continued to tie what was left of the wrap around his arm. Once he was satisfied with his grip, he practiced hand motions, swinging the knife inward and outward. He knew that anyone in his crew would have loved to carry out this mission, but he felt he would not have gotten the revenge that he was seeking unless he handled it himself.

Tim looked in the mirror, speaking to him.

"They think I have gotten soft, man. I am a cold blooded killer and a gangster and a lover. I am all that and a bag of commissary," Tim laughed at his own words. He exited the dorm with his hands in his pants and quickly walked towards the back of the mess hall. He waited patiently.

Tim reached in his pocket to make sure that his mask was still in place. As he waited, he began to fantasize about the time that a crew of dudes from Northwest D.C. tried to take over one of his operations in Southwest. They had succeeded in confiscating forty pounds of marijuana, but they were not satisfied. They even tried to sell the weed to customers on the same block afterwards. Tim told his crew not to worry about it, because violence would bring heat on his operation. His crew backed off even though they disagreed.

Two weeks later, Tim decided that the crew from Northwest should have sold most of the drugs by now. Tim plotted and waited. He brought an old model Caprice classic, tinted the windows and tested its durability. After he was satisfied, he went to his stash house and got his AK-47 assault rifle and two .45mm caliber guns and placed those inside his holster. He then went to the spot that had been taken over and watched the rival crew's every move. He knew who had the money and who had the drugs and guns. Once the crew left, he followed the car with the money. He did this for two days. On the third day, not only did he follow the car with the money, but he tied his rivals up and tortured them until they told him where the money was. He confiscated approximately twenty-two thousand dollars. Before he left, he shot four of the five dudes in the head, leaving one alive to tell others about the horrific experience.

Afterwards, Tim went to the crew's other stash house and repeated the same act. This time he confiscated three Uzi's, one Beretta, and two pounds of marijuana. Before he killed the rivals he stated that they had done a good job selling his drugs and if the circumstances were different they would have made some good team members. One of the rivals survived the ordeal, but ended up paralyzed. Though the victim witnessed everything, it all remained a secret. Tim kept the guns for his private collection, but he distributed the money amongst his crew members and never told them where the money came from.

Tim was brought back to the situation at hand by sounds of laughter. He peeped around the garbage can which obstructed anyone's view of him and spotted his culprit. He made sure that his knife was strapped tightly, and then he proceeded to walk behind Rah-Rah at a safe distance. There were a few inmates coming and going to different institutional programs that were provided on the weekend, but other than that, the compound was relatively isolated. Just as Rah-Rah approached the corner of the walk way that lead to the recreation yard, Tim picked up his pace, bringing the distance between the two to a minimum. Tim then put on his mask and quickly turned the corner almost at the same time as Rah-Rah.

Rah-Rah heard footsteps and attempted to turn around. Before he could confront Tim, he was on the ground pleading and struggling. Tim pulled him behind the tool shack and started stabbing him in the neck and the upper body.

"What did I do?" Rah-Rah began to scream. "Stop man, help! Somebody help!……. Shit!.....Shit!" His cries went unheard. Tim continued to stab away until he heard nothing.

"Say something, Nigga." Tim got up and looked at the bloody mess that his sweat suit now entailed. He lifted his sweat suit carefully over his head and revealed the institutional uniform that he wore beneath his sweat suit. Before he discarded the knife, Tim spat in Rah-Rah's face. Tim stepped from behind the tool shack and quickly blended in with the quietness of the compound. He then headed towards his dorm to continue his conversation with the C.O.

CHAPTER 5

The visiting hall was crowded with familiar faces. The chairs were set up in rows and aisles. The inmates were allowed to embrace and kiss their visitors in the beginning of the visit and at the end, and even though further touching was not allowed, the inmates usually found a slick way to get around that. They usually cut holes in their pants and encouraged their visitor to wear dresses with no under wear for easy access. Then they would get another inmate to block, while they had sex. They would in turn block for the other inmate. Cliff and Daryl entered the visiting room nonchalantly.

Cliff stepped towards the officer's desk first, so that the officer could document his shoe color and style and log him in. His shoes were documented just in case there were suspicious of him switching shoes with his visitor. The officer also checked for watches and jewelry. Tony and Daryl indulged in the same routine while absorbing their surroundings. They had to make sure that it was safe for them to make a move. Afterwards, they were each directed by the guards to sit in assigned seats.

Cliff was directed to his seat first, followed by Daryl, then Tony. They couldn't always be sure that they would know their visitors, because Tim often switched them so that emotions would not obstruct anyone's judgment. He also didn't want the guards getting familiar with females who smuggled "the goods" as he called them.

Cliff, Daryl and Tony were in a good spot to move the goods. They laughed and pretended to be deeply involved with their visits. Cliff was kind of upset because he had to spend an entire hour with what he called "A big black Zulu broad." In his mind, he cursed Tim and promised to pay him back, but for the moment he knew he had to make the best of it. He put his pride aside and indulged in conversation.

"Why are you staring at me like that?" the female said who was visiting Cliff.

"First of all, what's your name?" Cliff asked.

She smiled. "It's Tonya."

"Well Tonya, I am staring because I have the honor of sitting before a beautiful black queen and I am trying to figure out where I would begin to start making love to you because you are a lot of woman."

"What?!" she stated in shock.

"I am not talking about making love to you physically, but mentally. When I tell you to hand me the goods, do it swiftly ok?"

Tonya was totally taken by his calm façade and his ability to switch gears in the conversation. As soon as she got the opportunity, she handed Cliff the balloons and just as quick as he got them he turned around to make sure that he could make a move. Cliff lifted his shirt up, stuck his hands downs his pants and reached back towards his ass so that he could stuff the balloons. He made sure that he had greased his anal area before going on the visit.

Daryl and Tony used the same method as Cliff, but unlike him they weren't able to get both of the balloons. Instead they got one each, which would allow them to come back for the others the next day. Afterwards, they all sat anxiously indulging in meaningless conversation awaiting the conclusion of their visit. As soon as Cliff heard the officer call Daryl and Tony's name, he knew that his name would be called next to confirm the ending of the visit. Daryl and Tony only stood up and began to hug the other two females, while Cliff looked around and attempted to be evasive.

Tonya grabbed Cliff's arm and pulled him up, hugging him tightly while Tony and Daryl laughed at him uncontrollably. There were hugs, kisses, and tears shared as visitors departed the visiting room. Cliff, Daryl and Tony waved their visitors good bye and waited in line to be strip searched.

Daryl and Tony stared at Cliff, both laughing.

"What the fuck do you two bammas find so hilarious?" Cliff said in a sharp tone.

Daryl continued to stare aggressively then he smiled and said, "You had a nice little honey slim, so cut the big boy act." Then Daryl looked at Tony and they both giggled.

"That's alright," Cliff said, "As long as she pays like she weighs, her big ass could be three hundred more pounds."

The line that led to the inmate shakedown room was moving slowly, so Cliff thought about trying to sneak out without being searched. He quickly dismissed the notion because he did not want to risk any suspicion if one of the officers caught him. He considered the fact that they would have given him a real thorough pat down and strip search under the assumption that he was trying to elude the shakedown for whatever reason.

Cliff, Daryl and Tony entered the shakedown room one at a time. One waited for the other afterwards until all three were reunited on the small walk, which lead to several dormitories.

"Man, I don't know what's going on with those CO's in the shakedown room," Cliff said disgustingly.

"I know what you mean," Daryl said, "Because if I had a sweet job like this, I would not be worried about what's under nobody's nuts and definitely not what somebody is trying to smuggle in their ass. I would get the easy money and call it a day." They were referring to their encounter in the shakedown room. The inmates were required to strip themselves naked, open their mouths, squat and spread their butt cheeks and lift their bottom of their feet as a precaution to bringing contraband or illegal items in from visitation.

"I guess that is why we are the crooks and they're the cops, huh?" Daryl stated sarcastically. As they headed down the small walk, they were confronted by a homosexual named Yummi.

"I see that you gentlemen are in order to have your little naughty deeds removed," Yummi stated.

"As a matter of fact we are," Cliff said as he motioned Yummi to a door that lead into one of the dormitories. Yummi was one of Tim's stash confidants. Even though Tim did not permit any of his crew members to involve themselves with homosexuals, he knew that the homosexuals in Lorton pulled rank with the officers and most of them were reliable informants. Therefore, they were decreasingly harassed.

After Cliff, Daryl, and Tony gave Yummi the balloons, they left the dorm and headed towards the mess hall. Surprisingly, the officers on the walk began to run toward the ball field while other officers came out the dormitories informing the inmates who were going to and from chow that the compound is closed.

As the correctional officers shuffled recklessly trying to clear the compound, some of the inmates followed the officers trying to see what the disturbance was about. Tony and his two comrades walked towards the entrance of the ball field but were directed by a correctional officer to report to their unit.

"Man, I saw the helicopter. Someone must have gotten hit for faking." Daryl said. He was referring to a stabbing. When an inmate is stabbed the compound is put on lock down status, and depending on the seriousness of the assault, the individual is transferred to the local hospital by way of helicopter. As the three headed back towards the dorm, they noticed an officer was at the gate which was located on the hollow walk. The correctional officer was doing a routine shakedown.

"Ok, I need to see your hands and check for bruises," the officer instructed as each individual approached his post."

"Man, what happened," Daryl asked.

"Somebody got stabbed real badly by the ball field. I don't know if he made it," the officer explained. There were sounds of loud conversation approaching as Daryl, Tony and Cliff began to walk away from the officer after being frisked. Tony turned around and asked one of the inmates, Trey, what happened. Tony greeted Trey by hitting his fist lightly.

"Did somebody get hit?" Tony asked Trey

"Yeah, that dude Rah-Rah got smashed. I don't know what happened, but I think he just got added to the Lorton body count," Trey answered.

After a few minutes had passed, Tony, Daryl and Cliff let Trey and his friends go ahead of them.

"Damn, somebody got Rah-Rah before me," Tony said as he imagined the culprit's satisfaction.

"If you were serious about your business then you would have gotten to him first," Cliff stated aggressively.

"Man, let's get to the dorm before they try to give us the beef," Daryl demanded. They headed towards the dorm as quickly as possible to avoid any suspicion or false accusations. They may have been over reacting, but in Lorton, it's best to be safe than sorry.

*****

He was frustrated and annoyed as officers escorted him in the wake of the night. He listened to the silent crackling of the floors with each step that he took towards what he knew would be a long night. There were two correctional officers on each side of him who stared at him intensely.

"Man, what the fuck is going on?" Tim demanded.

"We'll tell you when we get there," one of the officers replied.

"Hit three," the other officer said in his walkie-talkie to the officer who was in the booth. After the door opened the officer handcuffed Tim and proceeded to escort him to the lieutenant's office.

Once inside the lieutenant's office, Tim's eyes inventoried the different plaques and awards that decorated the office. He wondered what his life would be like if he would've chosen the career that they had chosen. This would surely be a better place, he thought to himself, but in reality he knew that most inmates thought this way and that's what probably landed them in jail.

The door to a room that was directly across from where Tim was sitting opened. It caught him off guard because he realized that he was already in an office but he wasn't aware of any additional offices. A correctional officer walked towards Tim, opened door and un-cuffed him while directing him to go into the other office.

As he entered the smaller office, he noticed that it was almost empty. There was a computer, phone, and a few books on the shelves, but other than that the office was plain Jane.

"Mr. Johnson, my name is Lieutenant Baker and if I may, I'm going to get right down to business because I don't believe in beating around the bush." Tim nodded as he looked up towards the lieutenant.

"There was a young man who was stabbed repeatedly on the ball field today and he lost his life before he even left the compound," the lieutenant said while eyeing Tim.

"What does that have to do with me?" Tim asked.

"I have a reason to believe that you may know what's going on."

"And what's your reason for believing that?" Tim asked. The lieutenant reached under his desk and pulled three envelopes out and asked Tim to pick one.

"Man, I'm not about no games," Tim said.

"Neither am I, but I've got three notes here that says you're the man and one even says that if you're not removed from the compound then you'll be dead before sunrise," the lieutenant responded.

"I'm not worried about no note because if they were really goin' put in work, you wouldn't have a note. Instead, I would be dead, bandaged up or charged with putting a good ass whippin' on somebody for fakin'," Tim retorted.

"I need to check you for scars," Lieutenant Baker said.

"They already did."

"Well, I have to check you again," Tim paused for a second, and then he realized that no matter how long or to what extreme it would be, the lieutenant would get the search that he demanded.

Tim stood up and began to undress starting with his shirt. He displayed his upper body and hands to the lieutenant. The lieutenant nodded in approval then directed Tim with a hand notion to be seated.

"I'm quite sure you know the routine Mr. Johnson. I have a note which threatens your life, so I have to place you on involuntary protective custody."

"This is bullshit! You mean to tell me if I don't like a person for whatever reason, I can actually drop a note threatening him and my problem is resolved?" Tim said enraged by the lieutenant's comment.

"We just have to take safety precautions while investigating the matter. It'll just be for a few days."

Tim's anger couldn't be hidden. In fact, he made no attempt to hide it, but he knew that this was a no win situation. He also knew that he had a fresh batch of heroin and weed on the compound and he had to get to it as soon as possible, so he wanted to get this ordeal over without further delay.

"Okay, lieu, I understand your position," Tim said. He also noticed the relief in Lieutenant Baker's eyes, the relief of not having to result in trying to physically restrain Mr. Johnson.

The rest of the night was long, but full of re-evaluating instances for Tim. He thought about having it all and then having nothing. He toyed with the thought of being all alone with Officer Warner and giving her the love that has been stored inside him for so long.

Tim sat up on the end of his bunk for hours listening to sounds that probably existed throughout his incarceration, yet he never took notice. He heard the walls and floors crackling and he heard the keys of correctional officers' jingle endlessly.

Before long, he heard the sound of freedom. It came in the form of a voice that was so familiar to him.

Tim listened to the conversation as the officers were preparing to change shifts. He knew that it wouldn't be long before they counted the inmates, and he hoped that Officer Warner would discover his presence without him having to attract her attention.

The wait to be discovered seemed endless. Tim began to doze off, but the sound of a knock on his cell bar brought him back. For a moment, Tim thought that Officer Warner had realized that he was in the hole. He heard the knock again, but this time louder.

Tim paused for a moment then he heard a voice whisper.

"A...Eleven cell, next door," the voice whispered. Tim wasn't aware of his cell number but he was certain that the shallow voice was talking to him.

"Yeah, what's up?" Tim responded.

"This is little Donnell, do you have anything to read?"

"Nah, I just came in not too long ago."

"Well, I have a little something to read, but you have to be careful because this is some deep shit," Donnell chuckled.

Tim thought that it was ironic that he knew Donnell, yet they had never spoke a word to each other besides an occasional, "Hey." Tim knew that Donnell was notorious and Donnell respected Tim in the same manner.

"Eleven cell," the shallow voice of Donnell's whispered again.

"Yeah?"

"I don't like to converse with the walls because they don't talk back. Plus, I can never get them to tell me their name. So, since you can talk back, I need to know who I'm conversing with."

"This is Tim."

"There are a few Tim's in here. Is there any particular reason why I should know who you are just from your voice? Look, man, nothing personal, but I have a few enemies on the compound so I have to protect my well-being."

Tim paused for a second and smiled to himself. "Trust me slim, we're not enemies. I know this because one of us would be off the compound if this was the case," Tim said assertively. The entire block got quiet momentarily, then Tim continued, "But for the record this is Tim Johnson."

"Ah man, what's up slim? I basically run this shit down here so let me know what you need," Donnell said in an ecstatic tone. "What a fly nigga like you doing in here anyway slim?"

"Man, they're trying to put me with that move that happened earlier with Rah-Rah," Tim said.

"I heard the officer talking about that earlier but I didn't really trip because that fake dude had it coming to him," Donnell said.

"I got my ass covered though. I guess a few bammas felt a sudden need to drop notes on me so that I could be removed from the compound. But as soon as the investigation is done, I'll be out," Tim asserted.

"I might as well let you know that Rabbit was in here spreading rumors that you let him get caught, or should I say, drew heat to him while he was trying to make a move in medical."

"Man, Rabbit was in there fumbling and I did what I could do, but he messed up," Tim explained.

"Where is that knuckle head anyway?"

"Rabbit likes to flash his little weenie at officers when they pass, preferably nurses, so they put him in isolation. But before he left he made a lot of female enemies," Donnell said.

The segregation unit was usually chaotic and filled with disruption, but for some odd reason it had recently become subtle.

The cells were rather small, but there were also cells that housed two inmates. Very seldom would the cells be occupied by two individuals, because it would cause confusion amongst the inmates.

"Hey Tim, here's the book I promised you. It's a poetry book called *Moonlighting*. The author did time here, but he changed his life around. He probably was a misdemeanor case who was born with a silver spoon in his mouth and decided to run a red light then got busted. I tell you one thing though, that nigga can write," Donnell said humorously.

Donnell handed Tim the book through the cell bars. Tim absorbed the enchanting decoration while visually inhaling the name of the author. He looked the book over carefully trying to remember the face of the author whose name was so familiar to him.

"Larry Moon jr....Larry Moon ...Moon," he whispered to himself. "Man I know this dude. He went to the feds for trying to bring drugs into Occoquan for one of his so called buddies who turned his back on him," Tim said to Donnell, but really to himself.

"The book is nice. I guess change is possible for those who want it," Donnell added.

Tim lay back on his bunk, content with having a non-fiction book to read, by someone who could really feel his pain and identify with his condition. After fifteen minutes had passed, Tim heard footsteps that alerted him of the fact that an officer was either counting or making their rounds. He sat up on his bunk, but as the footsteps got closer he rose to his feet and went to the front of his cell. As their eyes met, Tim was confronted with a joyful feeling.

Officer Warner stopped at his cell and smiled. She was happy to see him, but disappointed that she had to see him behind the bars. She lifted her hand up in a writing motion which silently told him that she'll write him a short note. Officer Warner was aware that eyes and ears were usually listening, so she wanted to be as discrete as possible.

They both were in the mist of appreciating the beauty of having the privilege to accompany each other, even if this short interaction was non-formal and non-verbal.

Tim went closer to the bars as Officer Warner began to walk away. The only thing that kept his eyes, heart and soul from physically following Officer Warner was the cell bars, but emotionally he was side by side with her.

Tim stared for a moment longer, and then he turned toward the center of the cell taking inventory of the wear and tear of generations of D.C. prisoners. Tim sat on his bunk wondering how many inmates were killed here. He wondered about the sons of fathers who never made it home from Lorton. Then strangely he began to regret his dirty deed.

*****

The next morning, Daryl headed towards the recreation yard where Cliff, Tony and himself had planned to meet the day before.

"Man, what's going on?" Daryl asked.

"Their trying to say Tim had something to do with that stabbing last night," Cliff responded.

"That's bullshit, because Tim wouldn't have made a move like that unless Rah-Rah came at him first," Tony added.

"We know that, but these people ain't concerned about that, they just want to get their man," Cliff stated.

"We have to take care of business as planned. They should be calling you and Tony to visitation soon," Cliff said to Daryl.

"Man, I'm ready," Daryl responded.

"Okay, I have to go holler at a few people and find out who can handle getting Tim what he needs while he's in the hole," Cliff said in a low tone.

Each crew member's spirits were visibly down. They were so used to having Tim's guidance and strength to lead them, that they had become dependent upon him to a certain degree. Tim had prepared his soldiers for situations like this. However, it was hard to prepare specifically for a certain situation, because different events come in different shapes, forms and fashions.

"Man, I'm ready," Daryl responded.

"Okay, I have to go holler at a few people and find out who can handle getting Tim what he needs while he's in the hole," Cliff said in a low tone.

Each crew member's spirits were visibly down. They were so used to having Tim's guidance and strength to lead them, that they had become dependent upon him to a certain degree. Tim had prepared his soldiers for situations like this. However, it was hard to prepare specifically for a certain situation, because different events come in different shapes, forms and fashions.

CHAPTER 6

Cliff headed towards the dormitory where he knew that he really had no valid reason for going towards, except for what he believed to be a choice that any good leader would make, and a choice that Tim would be proud of him for making.

There were two individuals standing by the doorway that led to eleven dorms. Cliff adjusted his eyes so that he wouldn't have to walk all the way to the dorm if the person he was looking for was actually one of the inmates standing by the doorway.

He continued to zoom in on the vague figures that stood before him until he spotted who he was looking for.

"Hey Yummi!" he yelled. "I need to holla at you."

Yummi turned around and headed towards Cliff. As soon as he got within three feet of Cliff he said, "I knew you would come back for momma. I saw the way you looked at me."

"Nah bitch, it ain't dat type of party. I have some business to handle," Cliff said in disgust.

"What kind of business could you possibly have that concerns me, other than parking your car in my pretty little garage?"

"Tim went to the hole, so first of all I need to know who I need to holla at to make sure he's straight, and second of all, I need to get the dope from you."

"I can help you with the first issue, but the last one is a no-can-do because my instructions were to deliver them to no one but Tim." Just as Yummi got the last word of his sentence out, he felt a fire strike him; a burning flame that was so intense upon his face he spat blood.

Cliff hands moved so swiftly that he surprised himself, but he knew that Yummi's response would be firm unless he had taken immediate action. The slap was sudden but effective. Cliff grabbed Yummi and pulled him to the side of the dorm where they were out of view from the other inmates. Cliff then ripped Yummi's homemade shorts, licked his own fingers and pulled his penis out while stroking Saliva on it. He bent Yummi over and rammed his penis into Yummi's anus. The scream was loud until Cliff covered Yummi's mouth.

"I'll teach you a lesson you'll never forget," Cliff said as he penetrated. "And if this gets out to anybody, there's no place that's safe for you to go," Cliff pushed Yummi away after he climaxed. He saw tears running from the homosexual's eyes, but wasn't sure if they were tears of joy or pain, because during the assault, he could've sworn he felt Yummi moving in enjoyment.

Cliff had never experienced any sort of homosexual activity, but his spontaneous decision was driven by the urge to prove his leadership capabilities. Tim had once told him that to be a leader, you have to be prepared to persuade others (at any given time) that it would be to their best benefit to give you what you ask for or suffer the consequences. However, deep down inside, Cliff knew that Tim wouldn't have condoned the unspeakable act of taboo that he just indulged in.

Cliff reached towards Yummi and startled him. "I just need your t-shirt so that I can wipe myself off." Yummi was terrified. He had heard stories about Cliff, but every encounter had been passive until this most recent. Cliff, on the other hand, was embarrassed because he knew he would have to live with this for the rest of his life.

Cliff began to rid himself of any physical reminder that this incident ever occurred. He used Yummi's t-shirt diligently wiping away the guilt and the unsanitary feeling that plagued his penis.

"Now, who do I need to see to get my man Tim a survival kit while he's in the hole," Cliff said aggressively.

"You just let me know what it is you want to give him and I'll handle it," Yummi responded.

"First of all, I need those balloons, but I'll give you something nice for yourself until Tim gets out."

"Okay, I'll have the goods ready for you after the count."

"And I'll have everything ready for you to send to Tim."

They both nodded in agreement while Yummi straightened his torn and wrinkled clothing. Yummi began to walk away, but stopped in his tracks and turned towards Cliff who had already begun to walk in the other direction.

"Cliff, did you notice that I didn't put up a fight?"

Cliff turned around with a look of disgust on his face. "Bitch, don't flatter yourself. You know you couldn't win." Cliff turned around and walked away. After a few seconds, Yummi did the same.

As Cliff walked towards the north side of the compound he felt relieved that he had did his part, but somehow he couldn't dismiss the filthy feeling that came along with the act he'd just committed. He stopped for a moment and inhaled his surroundings. Cliff noticed that inmates were moving about with their daily routines as if they were normal citizens in society, living productively. There were guys going to and from visitation while others sat on trash cans or steps that led to the dormitories indulging in idle conversation. Cliff continued to walk freely towards his dormitory as if the world existed only because he was in it. Each step he took brought him closer to the dorm where he knew a long hot shower would be the order of the day. He knew that he would have to meet Daryl and Tony on the ball field in an hour or so. Therefore, he wasted no time once he got to his dorm.

Cliff was relieved. No one was in the shower, so he rushed to his room to gather his bathing kit. Once he entered his room he kicked his shoes off and undressed, exchanging a robe for the clothes that he had on. After getting prepared, he exited his room and went to shower away a bad memory.

*****

Tim sat on his bed mesmerized by what he was reading. He couldn't believe the strength that engulfed the poetry book called *Moonlighting.*

It was as though the author based the poem on Tim's life. Tim read through several poems until he came to a specific one that wouldn't let his eyes or fingers go pass. It was called *Aftermath*, and the more Tim read it, the more convinced he became that he had to get out of jail soon. *Leaders manipulate others into following in directions that are unfamiliar.* He was a leader, and this was a mantra he lived by. He had twisted this statement up so many times, and he knew exactly what he meant even though others struggled with understanding how they should interpret it. Tim laughed quietly while he read the poem again.

Aftermath

As my eyes journey through the peephole of my past,

The warfare I've seen; the aftermath!

Walking unfamiliar streets create a permanent void,

You must keep in mind that even though I was free,

The streets ventured a premeditated penitentiary.

Those who laugh first often cry in the end,

Then pray to God for forgiveness of their sin.

I often regret this road I chose, feelings

Cold as ice, thoughts hot as coal,

Looking for life in all the wrong places,

Death will replace this lust for thy hatred.

I've tried to speak while reaching my plight,

I've failed at teaching a snake not to bite.

Now that I've been bitten, my family hurts,

Another statistic predicted by experts

Who've never seen through the eyes of a guy?

Who lived to tell the hell of life that passed me by.

Not really watching the steps that led my path

Falling six feet deep into this aftermath.

"This dude has written the doctrine on my life in one poem," Tim said to himself. He folded the top of the page so that he could mark the page that he was on. Before long, Tim was beginning to get restless. He smoothed his pillow and bed sheets out by wiping his hand gently across both garments. Tim was about to lie down when he heard footsteps moving toward his cell. He was about to hesitate with his movement, but followed his first instinct which was to step towards the bars.

Before Tim reached the bars, someone tossed a brown bag into his cell. He tried to question the detail worker, but he wasn't acknowledged. There were several inmate detail workers cleaning the floors at this particular moment, but they were all busy. Therefore, Tim's pleas for conversation went unanswered. Tim grabbed the bag and sat on his bunk. He opened the bag then he slowly inventoried its contents. There were two novels, two pieces of fried chicken, a soda, and a letter that said page 14.

Tim grabbed the first novel. Flipping the pages quickly, he realized that he passed page 14, so he flipped backwards until he reached page 14. There was nothing to be found as Tim turned the book upside down trying to produce what was missing. He realized that whatever he was looking for was probably in the other book, so he placed the book that he was holding on his bed and grabbed the other book. Before he could turn five pages, a letter fell from the book. Tim looked at it momentarily as if it was snake getting ready to attack. He bent over and grabbed the note while curious to see what the contents entailed. He felt relieved as he opened the letter and began to read.

Hey Stranger,

I'm working on getting you a detail position so we can converse more. I also heard about the allegations and note dropping against you, so you have to be careful about who you talk to and what you talk about. So far, you're just being held up for safety measures which could last indefinitely. I've been thinking about you a lot. How can I not? Don't worry about responding to this letter; as a matter of fact it should be in the toilet as soon as possible.

Keep ya head up!

Tim was surprised, but impressed. Officer Warner had proved to be the solider that needed no persuading. He knew that he had to play his cards right or else lose the card game. There was no doubt in his mind that Officer Warner was trying to be down with him.

After a few minutes of daydreaming, Tim grabbed the bag off of his bed and reviewed each book. Then he carefully placed them back in the bag and shoved them under the bed because he wasn't a big fan of dramas; he preferred westerns.

Tim sat on his bed listening to other inmates hold frivolous conversations in distant cells. He knew that there had to be a way out of this misery besides death and he knew that finding his way out would be harder than finding his way in. For now the only escape would be through the doors of dreamland, so with that thought, Tim curled in his bed and searched for his escape.

Not long after he dosed off, Tim was awaken by a gentle touch. He was startled initially, but his fears were quickly erased by the sweet smile of attraction that Officer Warner had on her face.

"So we meet again," Tim said.

"You need to wake up if you want to be on my work detail," Officer Warner added with a huge smile on her face. Tim rolled over on his side hesitantly at her remark. He didn't want it to appear as if he was overly excited.

"What time is it?" Tim asked.

"It's time for you to get up and get to work if you don't want to be boxed up in this cell," Officer Warner said.

"Okay, you said the magic word."

Officer Warner instructed Tim to come to the officer's station as soon as he got ready. When she turned to leave she stopped for a moment, turned around to face him and blew a kiss off of her hand. Tim was ecstatic, but he kept his cool long enough for her to exit his cell. Then he started singing to himself while he washed his face and brushed his teeth. "Gonna betcha he don't love you…like you know I love you. Gonna betcha he would never do, all the things I'll do for you," Tim whispered the song passionately.

Officer Warner left Tim's cell door open, and for a moment he felt as if they were at home and she was waiting for him to fix her breakfast in bed. He daydreamed for a moment, but soon realized that time was valuable. Therefore, he put his fantasy on hold and quickly headed towards the officer's desk.

"So what's my position title?" Tim asked while smiling.

"You're a detail worker. Your job is to sweep and mop the hallway and clean the counselor's office as needed," Officer Warner responded.

"Nah, what I'm saying is what my professional title is? Am I some kind of Floor and Office Technician Analyst?"

Officer Warner's face lit up in amusement as she began to laugh hysterically. Then she realized what was actually missing in her marriage. It was laughter and fun. Her husband was beginning to become tiresome and she began to long for some intimacy, warmth and humor in her life. Officer Warner laughed until she almost cried and looked deep into Tim's eyes as if she could see the pain and agony that plagued his life; the life of living in Washington D.C., which had recently been given the nickname Drama City because of its reputation for violence. Tim allowed her to stare for a moment then he took control of the conversation.

"I thought you were working in the dormitory. What happened?" Tim asked.

"I'm still working in the dorm. The regular officer assigned to this block is on vacation, so I'm stuck here for two whole weeks," Officer Warner replied.

"What a coincidence...I'm stuck here for a few weeks myself," Tim said.

Officer Warner smiled once again, but this wasn't her usual smile. This time her smile was exotic and non-discrete. She was letting Tim know that her attraction for him was no fantasy.

Tim stepped forward and grabbed her hand. He became so emotionally trapped in the moment that his movement was more impulsive than desirable. Tim began to pull her closer to him, ignoring his surroundings, as well as Officer Warner's hesitant gestures. He knew that his judgment was impaired by this sudden arousal, but at that moment it didn't matter.

"The timing for this is all wrong," Officer Warner insisted.

"There's never a perfect time for anything, but some things are worth making time for," Tim said as he looked into her beautiful eyes. Tim pulled her even closer and kissed her lips gently. He knew that he didn't have to worry about anyone intruding because he was the only inmate on the floor and she was the only correctional officer working in the disciplinary unit. However, Tim also knew that he couldn't treat her like a one night stand, so he continued to kiss her but not on the lips. He kissed her hands first, her forehead, and he noticed that she was more aroused than she had previously appeared to be.

"Can you show me the office that I'll be cleaning?" Tim asked.

"Okay, but only if you promise to be good."

"I'll be especially good."

Officer Warner had never before entertained the thought of cheating on her husband until she met Tim Johnson.

As soon as they entered the counselor's vacant office, Tim began to visually inventory his surroundings. He took notice of the spacious little office and he appreciated every inch of it.

"Your job in here consists of emptying the trash, sweeping, mopping, and dusting," Officer Warner explained. Before she could fully finish her sentence, Tim was caressing her lips with the magic in his own. She was utterly speechless as Tim gave her more intense feelings in a moment's time then her husband gave her in years.

Tim began to kiss her gently on the neck, while unbuttoning her shirt. Once her shirt was spread open by the movement of his hands, he noticed that she was wearing a sky blue open tip bra that fully exposed her perky nipples. He squeezed one of her nipples gently and she jumped as if he had startled her. She'd actually forgotten that she was wearing her open tip bra and she felt embarrassed because it probably appeared as if she was prepared for this occasion. On second thought, she considered the fact that first impressions were always the best impressions.

Tim removed his hand from her nipples slowly then directed his hand towards the chair that was positioned behind the counselor's desk in the office. Tim attempted to unfasten her pants once she was seated but she resisted.

"You don't have to worry, you're in good hands," Tim said.

"I'm quite sure I am, but this is not safe. You don't even have protection," Officer Warner stated.

"You're absolutely right. That's why I want to make love to you my way. Just relax baby." With that said, Tim slowly unbuttoned her pants, placing her dispatcher radio on the desk. He noticed that she had on g string panties that matched her open tip bra. Tim thought about removing her underwear, but then thought against it. He was feeling sexy, so he moved her underwear to the side with his finger exposing her pussy to the wonderful world of Tim Johnson. He could see the wetness of her pussy walls as he prepared himself for an unforgettable experience. Officer Warner sat back and closed her eyes until Tim told her that he wanted her to watch. Her husband was never this adventurous, she thought, as she did what Tim demanded.

Tim took his time with her clitoris, sucking, licking, and slurping in places that she never knew existed. She began to moan loudly. She was no longer in control of this situation. The more he licked, the more she begged for him to enter her.

"Fuck me, Tim…Please make love to me."

But Tim didn't oblige her immediately. He stopped for a moment and looked upwards into her crying eyes.

"What's wrong baby?" Tim asked.

"Nothing is wrong because you're beginning to make it right," Officer Warner responded. Tim gave her a long, sexy stare, and then began to untie her work boots. After he untied her boots, he rubbed and stroked her feet slowly, and gently slipped her big toe into his mouth. Officer Warner was truly taken by his romantic character. Tim was what she had been missing, and what she wouldn't forget. Her eyes were closed as she wallowed in the erotic pleasures that overwhelmed her.

With her body language, she spoke silently and urged Tim to continue.

Tim didn't ignore her silent gestures. He began to rub her pussy while he continued to suck her toes.

As her moans became more intense, there was no outlet for the room to breathe. In fact, it seemed as if the walls were sweating as Officer Warner tried to hold her composure. Tim pulled away, releasing the connection that his tongue had to her pussy.

Swiftly, Tim pulled her pants down to her ankles. He was in awe of such a sexy sight. Officer Warner was completely his and the thought of her being married never crossed Tim's mind as he began to kiss her neck and rub his erected rod on her leg.

Tim kissed Officer Warner until he could no longer stand the wait. Eventually, he stopped in mid-kiss to put the condom on that

Officer Warner had given him earlier in the brown bag that came to his cell. There was a note inside that said, "Act as if you don't have a condom, I like to role play." Officer Warner smiled and winked her eye to acknowledge that she was satisfied with Tim's efforts to play by her rules. Once Tim put the condom on, they both were very aroused by the intensity of his foreplay.

Tim began to lick her gently on the neck, and without warning, slid his dick into her unmercifully while covering her cries with his mouth. He slid in and out of her with long passionate strokes, but the passion didn't last long because Tim's tolerance level was low. He hadn't had sex since he paid for a conjugal visit with a crooked C.O. about six months ago.

As he exploded in the condom, Tim's eyes rolled in the back of his head, and he dropped his entire body weight onto Officer Warner, leaving her laughing while rubbing his back. As they both lay there, Tim was startled by the sudden sound of Officer Warner's walkie-talkie. They were both embarrassed initially, but their fears were soon erased by intimate kisses.

Officer Warner couldn't believe that she put so much trust in someone that she barely knew, but Tim made her feel wanted and adored. She never even considered the fact that falling in love with someone other than her husband would have a significant ripple effect on her son Roland. She thought about a messy divorce and what her friends would think; she shook off her obscene notions and realized that a few minutes of pleasure didn't constitute a lifetime of devotion.

"I need to get to work," Tim said.

"Is that a question or statement?" Officer Warner asked.

"Which ever you prefer," Tim stated seductively.

"Well, I prefer for it to be a question so that I can say no. On the other hand, if it's a statement, then I would ask, 'Haven't you worked enough for one night?'"

"Yeah? Is that right? In that case, I would reply, 'There's plenty more work where that came from,'" Tim said as they both smiled with delight. Afterwards, Tim started to move spontaneously. He helped Officer Warner get dressed while he got himself together.

Officer Warner grabbed him by the hand and escorted him to the supply closet where all of the cleaning supplies were stored at. She didn't intend on allowing Tim to start his detail job immediately; she just wanted him to be aware for future reference.

Tim stepped into the supply closet and took notice of how well arranged it was. He asked a few questions concerning several chemical cleansers then he pulled Officer Warner in closer and gave her a deep kiss goodnight.

"Will I see you tomorrow?" Tim asked.

"Yes but It'll be strictly business."

"I'm always strictly business...even when I'm at play."

The walk back to Tim's cell seemed to be very short. It was as if the cell had started walking to meet him halfway. He thought about Janet Jackson's song, "Funny how time flies when you're having fun," and began singing. Officer Warner started laughing as his melody encouraged her. When they reached his cell, the bars were slightly ajar from the locking mechanism that kept the cell gate locked. Tim didn't hesitate as he walked through the cell gate. He knew that he was very fortunate to have experienced such a wonderful night of pleasure and to turn around and acknowledge Officer Warner's departure would dilute the moment because he would look pass her smile and see her lips kissing her husband's lips which would lead to a sleepless night of envy.

CHAPTER 7

The loud noise of laughter woke Tim up from a deep sleep. The smell of breakfast mixed with perspiration made Tim dubious about eating this morning. In fact, Tim was used to cooking his own meals in the dorm and sometimes paying the officer on duty to order carry out food from a restaurant. Tim lay in his bed while trying to retrieve the passion of the night before. Even though he was capable of exploring his thoughts vividly, there was nothing like the real thing. Therefore, he rested his mind in hopes that the next encounter with Officer Warner would come much sooner than later.

Tim pulled the sheets back and revealed his muscular body. He knew that even though he was confined to his cell, that didn't limit his ability to be active. The water from the sink was lukewarm as Tim rinsed his face cloth then began to wash his face.

Tim brushed his teeth afterwards and started smiling in the mirror acknowledging the whiteness of his teeth. He heard the day shift detail workers approaching each cell distributing breakfast trays. He heard complaints and grunts from several inmates in different cells. Most of them were complaining because the food on their tray was scarce while others complained about the quality of their food.

When the detail worker who was distributing the milk and eating utensils finally reached Tim's cell he could see the disappointment in Tim's eyes. He knew that inmates who were in the hole for their first forty eight hours were usually on edge.

"Man, I would've preferred my breakfast before my drink," Tim said.

"Well, I'm doing the milk and utensils so how were you going to eat without utensils?" Tim shook his head in agreement as the detail worker looked around nervously then handed Tim a brown bag. Tim quickly tossed the bag under his bed and proceeded as if the transaction had never taken place. Then he waited for the other detail worker to deliver the breakfast trays.

Once he got his tray and opened it, he was surprised that he didn't hear a lot of racket or further complaints from the other inmates in the cell because the trays consisted of two biscuits and one sausage. Tim sat the tray on the bed and bent down in a squatting position to retrieve the brown bag that he had under the bed. This bag was a little heavier than the first bag he received and that alone aroused his curiosity much more. Tim unfolded the bag and smiled at the first thing he saw. He knew that his soldiers would find a way to make sure he was straight.

Tim reached in the bag and fumbled around the large sack of weed. After he realized that it was almost impossible for him to retrieve the other contents from the bag without removing the large sack, Tim grabbed the sack of weed out of the bag. He noticed that there was a large piece of tape wrapped around the sack. The tape held two bags of heroin to the sack of weed.

Tim didn't use heroin, but he could surely use the canteen that the heroin would bring. Once Tim set the sack under his pillow he continued to search through the bag. There were a few fish sandwiches, a pornographic book, and a note. Tim laughed as he flipped through the book. *If they only knew*, Tim thought to himself, referring to the officers who were none the wiser about what his package really entailed. Tim set the book down and began to read the note:

Hey Slim,

Everything is straight out here. I just need you to hurry out. \If not, I will continue to oblige your every need.

Tim laughed out loud. He knew that Cliff would be the one that took control and he was glad that he had taken extra steps to guide Cliff and show him how to be a leader.

Tim knew that a good joint of weed would put him right where he needed to be, but there was nothing imaginable that he wouldn't risk for the ultimate high that Officer Warner has given him. Plus, he needed to stay focused just in case the lieutenant sent some of his fellow officers to question him.

*****

Tim's knock on his neighbor's wall was almost silent, so he knocked again. Finally, he heard a voice say, "What's up?"

"I have something I want to send you," Tim said.

"Okay, let's have it," Donnell's shallow voice responded.

Tim reached through the bars and extended his arm until he felt Donnell's finger.

"Reach your arm out a little further," he said to Donnell.

"Man, my arms are not as long as yours you need to extend your arm a little further." At that moment, Donnell felt Tim's hands grab his own and give him a small package. There was a moment of silence between Tim's cell and Donnell's cell and Tim assumed that Donnell was probably examining what he had sent. Donnell knocked on the wall to acknowledge that he was more than okay with what Tim had given him. Tim gave him the heroin and a sack of weed with a note that said, "I give this to you in exchange for the *Moonlighting* book." Tim sat on his bed holding the *Moonlighting* book, that had, over time, given him hope and a new outlook on life.

As he had plenty of time to his self these days, Tim had been working on a few loop holes that he found in his case and he believed that based on those discrepancies the courts would rule in his favor. If in fact the courts ruled in his favor, he would be replaced within four months. Therefore, he prepared himself as if he was leaving tomorrow.

*****

Several weeks passed and Tim was still in solitary confinement. However, he was not as uncomfortable as other inmates because he was a detail worker. He had special privileges. Tim was allowed to come out of his cell every night to clean and some nights there was nothing to clean so he was allowed to watch television.

His relationship with Officer Warner had become very intense and each night he learned more about her. Tim continued to make love to Officer Warner whenever she asked and he initiated it when she was reluctant to. He was falling for her deeply, but she had already fallen for him.

Tim sat in his cell waiting for his daily duties to be assigned to him by the shift officer. While waiting, he browsed through a few of the immaculate poems that lie dormant in the *Moonlighting* poetry book. He came across a particular poem that held him captive. It was short, concise and straight to the point. He smiled as he read it.

The life I'm In

The life I'm in has days and nights but these

Days and nights are not too bright.

Conclusively, I feel free but reality has a hold on me.

The loud sound of noise and silent crackling of floors,

Often awakens me to slamming jail doors.

As dusk turns to dawn and the night ends

The shine I often reminisce of loved ones left behind

This routine is continued again and again and

This explains the life I'm in.

Tim felt as if this book filled a void in his soul that had been given to him the day he was sentenced. He wanted to share his thoughts with anybody who would listen. He thought about Donnell, but quickly dismissed that notion because he figured that Donnell had given it to him for a price that meant pennies to Tim. But still, Donnell has to be aware of the power that this book held.

*****

Cliff, Daryl, and Tony sat facing each other in the mess hall. They were very careful and choosy about whom they allowed to sit at a listening distance from them.

Their mission had been accomplished in the visiting room and now it was time for them to map out their plan.

"Here's the deal," Cliff began. "I've taken care of Tim and I will continue to see to it that he's straight until he gets out. I haven't received any word from him, so I take it he trusts us to take care of business. You two have been just as busy as I have these last few days so I think that you deserve a break. Puff a little and take a load off your feet, but don't get too twisted because you never know which way the wind may blow."

"I have one question," Daryl leaned over and said in a very subtle tone. Cliff didn't respond, but his body language said what's up. "Who the fuck died and made you the king of the Lorton cartel?"

"No one put me in control," Cliff responded defensively, "But I'm the one who took control because contrary to popular belief, when the chips are down, I'm the one who's going to go hard for my soldiers. But since you think you're capable of guiding this sinking ship then you steer us to shore."

Tony looked at Daryl. "So...What do we do next Captain Save-a-Ho?" Daryl remained silent.

"Just like I thought," Cliff smiled. "We'll lay low for a few days then bag up the goods. When we get back to the dorm, I'm going to give you something nice to give to Yummi for stashing the goods," Tony nodded in agreement. Just as Cliff attempted to continue, he heard a loud scream then he saw what appeared to be ketchup splash on Tony's face.

Neither one of them was ready for the horror that awaited their eyes as each one of them turned around in sync to witness the bloody massacre. Stabbings were frequent in Lorton but this one was no ordinary stabbing. This dude had a shank that was made from a lawn mower blade. He was very persistent in not allowing his victim to move while he plunged the blade inward and outward at a very rapid pace. Cliff, Tony, and Daryl knew that it was vital that they get away from this scene immediately. They couldn't afford to be suspects or witnesses for that matter. Tony turned around for a second and was mesmerized at what he saw. The assailant was holding the C.O.'s at bay while he repeatedly stabbed the life out of his victim.

Cliff grabbed Tony by the arm. "Come on fool, you act like you never saw any drama before." Tony turned to face Cliff then vomited on the table that was adjacent to him.

"Damn slim, I might need to get you to a doctor." Cliff laughed while grabbing Tony and pulling him towards the door. The other inmates were moving along nonchalantly. Some had stopped what they were doing to be nosy. Others seemed to act as if nothing happened. Daryl, Cliff, and Tony continued to walk towards the ball field once they exited the mess hall.

So many unfamiliar faces hurried past them. Neither one of them stopped to chat nor converse; they kept in stride. Once they reached the recreation Yard, Cliff noticed that he was being stared at by eyes that were reluctant and willing at the same time. He was annoyed, but something told him that he had to be quick on his feet to elude any preconceived notion that Yummi may have had.

"Hey Yummi," Cliff yelled through a gang of homosexuals that were conversing with Yummi.

"Yes Daddy?" Yummi responded sarcastically. Daryl and Tony looked at each other inquisitively because it was not like Yummi to act out; especially with the warning that Tim had given him awhile back.

"My niggas are off limits to you bitch. So respect them as you do me whenever you conduct business with anyone of them or you'll answer to me," Cliff said. Tony thought about those cold, vicious words and wondered if Yummi was just taking advantage of Tim's absence. "And I'm not your daddy, bitch, so wipe that smirk off your face before I turn that smile up-side down."

Cliff lifted up his shirt and revealed a medium sized shank and Yummi knew that he had to get serious or get hurt. Cliff looked passed Yummi's shoulder gazing at the other homosexuals. "What happened between us was business, so you need to put that behind us."

Yummi glanced in the direction that Daryl was standing, then nodded.

"My man Tony is going to come by your dorm later and give you something nice for yourself. Plus I need for you to make sure Tim has what he needs," Cliff said in a calm voice.

"Look nigga, I don't work for you and I'm a sorry bitch that don't take kindly to too many orders. Furthermore," As Yummi's face snapped back from the intense slap that Cliff enforced, nothing else came out except for the words that transformed into saliva.

Cliff quickly grabbed Yummi's throat, "I'll kill you, funky bitch."

Daryl took a few steps towards Cliff. "Man chill out. We have some business to handle and we don't need any unnecessary heat on us."

Cliff knew that Daryl was right and he knew that he had to show his gratitude later to Daryl for doing the thinking for him while he was in a hostile state. He let Yummi out of the noose that he had him in. Yummi was in complete terror as he backed away from Cliff, unsure about whether he had Cliff's permission to do so or not.

"Man, let's get the fuck away from these gumps," Tony demanded.

The other homosexuals were standing at a distance. Some were confused, while the others were embarrassed that they couldn't help Yummi. As Cliff, Tony, and Daryl walked away, Daryl started teasing Tony.

"Man...I'm glad you stepped up to the plate and redeemed yourself because just a minute ago you threw up at the sight of blood. Now I know we can't send you on a hit, cuz you'll probably stab the dude then spit up on him."

"Yeah, that'll really kill him," Cliff said, agreeing with Daryl humorously.

"Man, I've been in the midst of warfare my entire life because I was born and raised in Dodge City. It was once said by Chuck

Brown that D.C. don't stand for Dodge City, but I'm here to tell you that's a lie because I've been ducking and dodging my entire life. Lorton is no different, because almost everyone who was causing others to duck and dodge is here locked up, too." Tony stated his claim.

"I guess you're right," Daryl said. "The reason I chose to duck and dodge was because the roller raids were always hot on my trail, but as far as drama, I always tried to be on the other end of the barrel." oller re' was pig latin, it meant rollers, a slang word for police. Somewhere along the line, the phrase was turned into Roller raids by those who misinterpreted the pronunciation.

"Man, we don't have time for this, I'm my brother's keeper bullshit," Cliff said cutting their conversation short. "We have some business to handle so let's roll."

They passed the homosexuals who were now standing at the front of the ball field entrance, but no one glanced in their direction. As Daryl, Cliff, and Tony proceeded, they saw the correctional officers clearing the compound. They knew that it was probably because of the stabbing in the kitchen.

*****

The room was somewhat dark with the exception of the sun light that the rusted window allowed seeping through its structure. Tim smelled the scent of religious oil which he attributed to Donnell trying to conceal the smell of marijuana smoke. Tim listened as the sound of jingling keys assured him that a C.O. was probably making rounds. A few seconds afterwards the officer was at his door.

"Mr. Johnson, I need you to gather your things and come with me," the correctional officer demanded.

"Where are we going?" Tim asked, knowing he wouldn't get a direct answer.

"You'll know when we get there."

"I'm on detail, but I work nights. Is there any particular reason that I should be working overtime?" Tim was trying to manipulate him into revealing his reason for wanting to see him.

"Don't go, Tim, they're trying to incriminate you!" Donnell yelled from his cell.

"They can't make something exist that ain't there," Tim responded.

"Well...keep your guards up and be sure you bob and weave because they're heavy weight contenders," Donnell said, referring to the correctional staff in general.

Tim was sure that they probably wanted to question him about the stabbing. But on second hand he considered other reasons. Maybe someone dropped a note implicating him and Officer Warner. But no one knew he assured himself.

"Do I need to bring my stuff with me?" Tim asked.

"Yeah you do," the C.O. responded "And I would appreciate if you stop asking so many questions."

Tim didn't grab any other items besides his *Moonlighting* book and his address book. He snatched the sheets and blankets off of the mattress and threw them in the corner of the cell. Then he walked towards the front of the cell where the officer was waiting to handcuff him.

"Are you just going to leave those blankets and sheets lying there?" the officer said.

"Man...it sounds like you already know the answer to that, so let's go champ!"

66

The C.O. laughed and told Tim to turn around so that he could handcuff him with his hands in the front of him and not the back. As Tim exited the cell and walked down the small tier, the officer whispered in his ear that he was being escorted to R&D (receiving and discharge). Inmates have to come through R&D to be processed into the institution, when their being released, transferred to another facility, or still dealing with a legal matter in court.

Tim felt a certain wave of impatience run through his body because of the officer's comment. The thought of going to R&D was the last thing on his mind. As they approached the front desk that led them to the entrance of the disciplinary unit, the officer sitting at the desk asked the officer that was escorting Tim, "Is this the inmate that's getting released today?"

"Yeah, I have to take him to R&D immediately," the officer responded.

Tim's mind was really racing now.

"Did you say that I'm getting released?"

"Uh huh that's what they told me. Damn they didn't tell you your own release date?"

"I wasn't expecting my case to be reviewed this soon. Plus I thought that my lawyer would've contacted me once he received the outcome of my motion."

Tim was getting released, but the procedure required him to be handcuffed.

The ride to R&D was very short. Tim hadn't seen anyone that he could've given a message to for any of his comrades, but he knew that he would write them. Therefore, he dismissed the extra effort of relaying a message. Once they arrived at R&D, the officer helped Tim from the van. They both stood at the door waiting for the R&D officer to come and open it.

"Hey Tim what's up?" a voice yelled from a distance.

"Man, I'm gone Joe. They overturned my case...Tell Cliff, Daryl, and Tony that I'll hit'em in a few days." The door opened and Tim stepped into what would be the beginning of a whole new world for him.

The way Tim's sentence was designed, he was charged for several counts of endangerment which enhanced his mandatory minimum. But once he got those additional counts overturned, that would put him pass his release date which meant that they had to immediately release him. Tim watched as several inmates scrambled to collate paperwork and laminate inmates Identifications. He thought about the money that was being saved by the government because they allowed the inmates to work. He thought about all the years that he'd lost here that couldn't be replaced. Then he thought about Linda, but he quickly replaced those thoughts with thoughts of Officer Warner.

Dressed in blue polyester pants and a matching blue chambray shirt, Tim wiped the lint from the last institutional outfit that he vowed to wear. After processing the necessary paperwork for releasing an inmate, the officer asked for Tim's signature. Soon after, Tim was directed to the entrance by the officer so that he could be escorted to the jail for release. Once an inmate is released, he's escorted to D.C. jail then allowed to go free from the parking lot.

"Hey! You forgot your book!" the inmate who was working in R&D said while inventorying the title of the book. He noticed that the name of the author looked familiar but he was unsure.

"Thanks slim, this is my blueprint. I can't leave this.." Once they got back to the van Tim was still awestruck. He laid his head back and listened to the tunes that were playing on the radio.

CHAPTER 8

As Tim awoke, the van was driving pass the congressional cemetery. The small street led directly to the rear of the D.C. jail where some of the employee's park their vehicles and where inmates are detained and processed.

Tim thought about the first day he was escorted through the gates of D.C. jail during his pre-trial proceedings. So many years had passed since then; seven to be exact. When he left the streets, it was 1993. Now, he was being welcomed into the new millennium of 2000.

Tim was eligible for parole ever since last year, but he had a few disciplinary infractions that warranted the parole board the obligation of giving Tim an eighteen-month set off date. However, his most recent legal victory squashed the remainder of his front number, allowing him to go free. He was still a parolee and would be for fourteen years.

Tim would eventually fight another legal battle after a few years to get his mandatory minimum sentence reduced, but he would have to show the parole board and the courts through his success that he's worthy of maintaining a productive life if he's allowed to get off parole early.

It was the beginning of August and the fall weather began to slightly brush in. Tim inhaled the beautiful sight of freedom as the officer stopped the van and allowed him to get out.

His feet absorbed the feeling of treading different, more earthly soil. "Have a good one, Mr. Johnson," the officer said while pulling off.

Tim noticed that the van had stopped for a moment, and then he saw what appeared to be someone talking to the officer who had just dropped him off but couldn't make out who it was. Then the van pulled off, only to reveal a sexy short female correctional officer.

Tim looked in awe as the woman walked towards his direction. He noticed that her name tag revealed the same last name as his. He thought about shooting her a corny line about Johnson and Johnson but quickly dismissed the thought. She swayed pass him only taking a slight glance and he realized that it was probably because he still had on his Lorton outfit.

Tim hadn't had the opportunity to tell any of his family or friends that he was coming home and he was glad. He would rather exercise the element of surprise.

Tim's mother lived on 16th and D Streets S.E. and that was right around the corner from the jail by which he stood. He felt like taking a long walk, but he wanted to get out of that Lorton outfit.

Tim started walking, letting freedom blast him from every direction possible. His eyes searched his surroundings diligently, noticing the different makes and models of automobiles that were driving to only they knew where. Tim had walked several blocks and was approaching his mother's house at a rapid pace then he paused for a moment and noticed that his brother's Astro van was parked out front; the one that Tim purchased for him months before he was arrested; the one that he had threatened to repossess as a result of his brother Calvin turning his back on him when he went to jail.

A few months after Tim's arrest, Calvin supposedly heard a calling from his higher power, so he vowed to change his life. He was listening to the radio when they were doing the Guns for Funds Sweep that allowed anyone who wanted to turn in a firearm to do so in exchange for cash - no questions asked. Calvin quickly turned his guns in, went to the nearest 7-11 store and placed the money in a receptacle for Jerry's Kids. From that point on, Calvin gave his life to the Lord.

Tim had been bitter at Calvin for all these years because Calvin wouldn't visit him even though he had the transportation that Tim bought him. It was ironic that through all of the changes Calvin endured, he never took the Astro van back, even though he knew that the proceeds to buy the van came from illegal money.

Tim felt the tension building within as he climbed each step towards his mother's house. Somehow, the lavish feeling of being free allowed his hatred to momentarily subside. Tim stood at the door, gathered his thoughts and rang the doorbell. He heard a voice that was very familiar. It sounded like a person was speaking from a distance.

"Just a minute," Tim heard his mother say.

"I got it, Ma." another voice exceeded hers. Before Tim could prepare himself, the front door sprang open. It was Calvin. He looked different, Tim noticed. He looked more mature and confident. Although, Tim was happy to be home, the resentment he had towards Calvin was too deeply rooted for him to look pass.

"Welcome home Tim," Calvin said. Tim stared Calvin in the eyes coldly.

"Even if I thought you meant that I wouldn't be able to eat with this tongue if I said anything other than, fuck you sucker," Tim breezed pass Calvin and left him standing at the door.

Tim walked through the dining room into the kitchen and peered through the fiber glass casing that surrounded the back porch of his mother's house. He watched his mother as she trimmed the hedges of the small bushes that were divided on both sides of the path that led to the back gate.

"Let me help you with that, Ma."

"No I got it Calvin," she said as she looked up in awe. It wasn't Calvin, it was Tim. She was so excited that she dropped the tool that she was working with, jumped up and gave Tim a big hug.

"You've put on a few pounds," she said while turning Tim around in a circular motion. "You don't have to worry; momma is going to help you keep up that natural look of health."

"Did you talk to Calvin?" she asked.

"Ma, we haven't talked to each other in years, why should it change now?"

"You haven't talk to him, but he has been speaking very highly of you ever since you left."

"He turned his back on me after all I did for him."

"Tim, the boy changed his life around. Give him the benefit of the doubt."

"Yeah but…"

"I don't want to go to my grave with you two holding on to asinine resentment. I won't be able to rest."

"I'll think about it when the time comes, but now is the time for me to gather my welcome home committee," Tim laughed and hugged his mother again and walked back up the steps towards the back porch. His mother followed closely behind asking him a variety of questions.

Shannon Johnson, Tim's mother, was a middle class hard working woman who raised her two kids to the best of her ability. She was a single parent ever since Tim was sixteen and Calvin was thirteen. Now, Tim was thirty and Calvin was twenty-seven and she was still the sole provider emotionally, mentally, and physically.

Terrance Johnson left Shannon fourteen long years ago and though it was difficult in the beginning, the experience eventually gave her incredible strength and the utmost respect from her peers.

Tim and his brother had seen their father on numerous occasions after he left. He had become a wino and Tim despised him, but Calvin would initiate a conversation with him even though Tim warned him against it. Tim was always the stubborn one who stuck to his own set of principles and Calvin was more of the kind-hearted humanitarian type. Terrance would never offer them anything. Instead, he would try to manipulate them into leaving him a few bucks, promising to pay it back when he got paid. Tim knew that he didn't have a job, but in the beginning he and Calvin would fall victim to their father's cunning ways; fortunately, that didn't last for long.

One day, Terrance asked them for some money and embarrassed them both in front of some friends from school. Tim denied his father, but Calvin was willing to give it to him just to make his father go away. Tim wasn't having it, so he pulled Calvin away as Calvin reached in his pocket to get a few dollars for Terrance. Terrance became angry and pushed Tim. Tim ran around the corner only to return with a four by four stick and pounded Terrance until blood surfaced and covered his entire face. Tim had earned a lot of respect not only from his father, which they never saw again, but from a lot of his peers at school.

Shannon had been the one never to turn her back on her kids. She scraped and cleaned hospitals while going to school to be a registered nurse. Family members helped her occasionally, but for the most part she was on her own.

Calvin was her baby boy so she kept him close. Tim, however, couldn't stand to see his mother struggle, so he hit the streets and helped her as much as he could. There were times that he would stay out all night selling drugs and give his mother everything he made. Sometimes she was reluctant to accept it because she knew where the money came from, but the choice she made was persuaded by their conditions.

It seemed like the money Tim brought home increased every week. His mother eventually became frightened because of the large amounts of money that he brought home, so she stopped accepting it. But that didn't stop Tim. He would just save up a lump sum, then put it in her pocketbook or pay some of the bills himself only to write her a letter informing her that such and such bills were already taken care of. Tim would also provide his brother with school clothes and spending money. He had become the man of the house, but Tim rarely enforced any rules; he just wanted to make his family happy.

Tim sat on the couch admiring what his mother had done to her house since he left. His mother was pacing back and forth from the dining room to the kitchen calling family and friends to let them know that Tim was home.

"So how is your business doing Ma?" Tim asked purposely interrupting her phone conversation. She put one finger up that told Tim to give her a minute, and then she hung up the phone.

"Baby, that's your creation, not mine. As ya'll young bucks say it, 'I was just holding it down'."

"And you held it down unquestionably. That's why you are now the proprietor."

"I only did what you would have done for me or Calvin."

"Correction…I would have done it for you, but not for that coward that you call my brother."

"Baby, you have to stop seeing everything in black and white because it's going to be those shaded areas of grey that bite you on the ass."

"And what is that supposed to mean momma?"

"I'll tell you when the time comes. Now, go upstairs and put on something presentable. I'm going to take you shopping."

Tim fumbled in his pocket until he found what he was looking for. He pulled the small business card out with his lawyer's number on it and called him. After a few rings, he got a voicemail recording. He quickly left a message, clicked the phone off until he heard a dial tone, and called his parole officer. His parole officer answered the phone and acknowledged a few available dates that Tim could come in. He wasn't really sweating Tim because Tim had quite a while to go before his parole would be terminated. This parole officer respected the fact that Tim called him as soon as he got home. They both agreed on the following week.

Tim went to his room. As soon as he opened the door, he smiled at the joyful sight. Everything was still intact; his Michael Jordan poster stared at him along with his posters of Janet Jackson, Phyllis Hyman and his favorite go-go band Rare Essence. Tim opened his walk-in closet and was surprised at all of the clothes that he had brought and left at his mother's house. Tim knew that his mother would reserve his room for him because he had a lot of stuff. Tim kept a lot of his casual attire on one side of the closet separate from his sporting wear. He started browsing through his casual clothes, searching for something to wear. He peeled back several suits from the hanger admiring his own taste. His fingers slid pass the silk Armani suit, and the plaid Gucci slacks with the matching vest. He accidentally stepped on a pair of his crocodile Giorgio Brutini decks and as he stopped to place the crocks back in order, he noticed a pair of brand new 996 New Balance running shoes. He had forgotten about those. He grabbed them, went to his dresser drawer and rummaged through a few items until he found what he was looking for - a grey sweat suit form a local clothing store called DDTP. Tim decided to keep his first day home simple and comfortable. After gathering his soap, towel, lotion, and other essentials, Tim took a half-hour shower.

*****

Officer Warner, known to her good friends and family as Rhonda, sat at the wooden desk flicking her ink pen. She cursed herself for not providing Tim with a way to contact her and she was just as angry with him for not volunteering his personal information just in case something drastic occurred. She thought about going to his case manager, but she couldn't think of a good excuse. Then her paranoia got the best of her. *Maybe he doesn't want to be found,* she told herself. *I was probably just another female he used to pass his time way.* Her self – talk was overwhelming. Her emotions were causing her to be trapped without a lifeline. Rhonda finally came to the decision of going to Cliff or Daryl if she hadn't heard from Tim within the next forty eight hours.

Rhonda and her husband, Melvin, had been living separate lives ever since she became more intimate with Tim. She suspected that Melvin was seeing someone and for Melvin, the feeling was mutual. The only reason that Rhonda was reluctant to file for a divorce is because of their son Roland. She didn't want him to go through what she went through when her parents got divorced.

Over time, Rhonda made sly comments toward Melvin and started slacking up on her good night kisses and talks with him. Although the distance between the two had started developing way before her infidelity, the intimate relationship she shared with Tim helped create the distance way more than it helped to minimize it. The phone rang just as she was about to make her rounds.

"Disciplinary Unit, Officer Warner speaking."

"Did you say Officer Warner?" the voice on the other end asked.

"Uh huh," she answered.

"Oh, I must have the wrong number. I'm looking for Mrs. Johnson. You see, I fell in love with her the moment I laid eyes on her and we were supposed to have renewed our vows, but I think that she's leaving me."

Officer Warner was confused. She'd received prank phone calls before, but this was the weirdest.

"So…what do you want me to do? You need to go after her if she's your heart."

"I want to, but I have one problem."

"And what's that?"

"She didn't leave me any way to get in contact with her."

This was getting crazy. She wanted to say, *"Can't you see she doesn't want you dumb ass?"* but she couldn't fix herself to be that obnoxious. She listened as he continued.

"You see, it's this other man in her life named, Melvin…." he stopped because he couldn't hold his laughter in.

"Tim you are sick, you know that?! I didn't even recognize your voice. Where are you?"

"I'm riding with my mother. We have some business to take care of."

"Were going shopping!" his mother yelled over his voice.

"That's nice," Rhonda said.

"So when can I see you?" Tim asked.

"Can I come pass your mother's house when I get off?"

"Sure you can."

"About what time?"

"My normal shift is midnight to eight, but I'm working until midnight tonight, so I can come pass around one o' clock."

"I'll be waiting for you," Tim said.

"Me too!" Tim's mother screamed. "I'll be waiting to meet you!" Tim said good bye and hung up.

It wasn't hard for Tim to get the extension to the Disciplinary Unit. He already had the number to Control. He called and pretended to be an insurance rep. Then he asked for the extension in which he could find Mrs. Rhonda Warner. It was easy as pie.

*****

There's no telling when an inmate is going to become violent and stab another inmate while doing time in the Lorton reformatory. This was the reason you had to always expect the unexpected and be prepared to defend yourself if need be.

Cliff sat in his cell waiting for the correctional officers to go to each cell and do a body inspection. The compound had been locked down for an hour because an inmate was stabbed fourteen times and the assailant had escaped the scene of the attack. The officers checked for marks, bruises, and anything that may indicate that the individual had been in a physical altercation.

Every now and then, someone would drop a note that would give the officers a place to start searching for a suspect. In this case, however, there was no note. The officers had to earn their pay today.

Cliff had taken control of what he believed Tim had left him in charge of. Daryl and Tony put their trust in him, and business was booming. Cliff had plenty of money, plenty of commissaries, and plenty of power.

Two weeks had passed since Tim had been released and Cliff needed him to handle his end of the bargain. Cliff, Daryl, and Tony received separate letters from Tim with pictures enclosed informing them that he was doing fine and he would keep in touch weekly. The letter he wrote to Cliff was a little more personal and informative. He told Cliff that he was going to keep the visits coming as long as Cliff handled the money appropriately.

The money was in his grasp, but the drug supply was low Cliff thought to himself. He knew that once the clientele went dry, it would take a while to rekindle, because somebody else would pop up with some good heroin and take over. He didn't worry about the weed, because that would sell regardless. He knew that he couldn't rush Tim.

A good leader is always patient, whether in peace or at war." He heard the words that rolled from Tim's lips as if he were there lecturing him this instant. He waited for the officers to come to his cell; they were in the cell next to his. He also sat patiently waiting for further instructions from Tim.

*****

Two weeks had passed and it was almost as if Tim had never left society. The demise of his empire had surpassed the test of liability verses assets and his mother was worthy of the glory. She had changed the name of the apartment complex from Crown Tower to Johnson Gardens and upgraded the living conditions, adding a medium size swimming pool, convenient daycare center and central air conditioning along with central heating. She also expanded the beauty Solon creating more Solon booths to be rented, which brought in plenty more revenue.

As he reviewed the bank statements, Tim couldn't believe the growth and stability that his establishment was built upon. There were mostly deposits and very little withdrawals. That alone told him that both businesses were generating a lot of profit and they were at the stage of further expansion. But for now, he knew that the best thing for him to do was to let his mother show him the pros and cons of running a business because he was never shown how to keep a business afloat.

A long time ago, Tim's friend Sol just told him that he needed a legal front for his illegal lifestyle. Tim had the money, the opportunity, and the motivation, therefore, he proceeded. Shortly after he went to jail, his mother had come through with what he knew no other female in his life at the time was capable of. The beauty Salon was called Braids R' Us, located on Florida Ave, N.W. The apartment complex was located on Suitland Rd. in Suitland, Maryland, just across the D.C. line.

Tim sat at the dining room table writing letters to Cliff, Daryl, and Tony. He decided to send Donnell a few pictures also. He had taken a lot of pictures all week; a few of himself, but most of those whom he had never met. He knew that Donnell wouldn't care because he was in the hole. Tim had taken pictures of females standing on the corner of Talbert St. in the alleys of Sursum Corda projects and certain historical landmarks that was sure to put a smile on any Washingtonian's face. He kept Donnell's letter brief.

What's up soldier?

Thanks for the "Moonlighting" book. Remember, death before dishonor.

Yours truly,

Tim

He added a fifty dollar money order to the letter. There was no need for him to send his comrades any money, but he flooded their letters with plenty of pictures. He informed Cliff that he was sending a heavy load down to Lorton this weekend. He laughed as he pictured Cliff's reaction, wondering if he was talking about some big girls like last time or a heavy load of drugs.

Tim sealed each letter up and called Rhonda on the cell phone that he brought her for his calls and the staff at her son's school only. He had introduced her to his mother and Shannon really took a liking to Rhonda. He was blessed to have two thorough bred soldiers in his life.

Rhonda was under the assumption that Tim was spoiled by his mother. She heard them refer to the businesses as "ours" but she thought that it was natural for a mother who loves her son to make him feel equally employed. She wondered why Shannon treated Tim so special when Calvin was the youngest son. She thought it to be strange that Tim never spoke to Calvin in her presence nor did Calvin initiate a greeting. Not even with her. She would have to ask Tim about that, she thought to herself.

Her cellular phone rang. "Hey boo," she said.

"How do you know I'm not a mad man stalking you?" Tim stated sarcastically.

"Well, if you are, I wish they made more mad men like you because you are one sexy mad man."

"Yeah? Well just how sexy am I?"

"You're…..too sexy for your jeans……too sexy for your hat," Rhonda couldn't hold the note she was singing in and the laughter interrupted.

"Where are you, baby?"

"I'm going to pick Roland up from school. It's my day today."

"Good. I get to meet him today?"

"No, you don't. You know the deal. Not until I'm completely separated from Melvin."

"I know, I know. I have some business I have to take care of, anyway, so call me tonight."

"Okay Tim. I love you."

"What did you say?"

"Bye Bye."

They both hung up.

Tim sat for a minute, than he picked the phone back up. He dialed a number and the phone rang three times. "Hello," a shallow, but sexy voice said.

"Are you alone, sexy?" Tim asked.

"It all depends on whether you mean emotionally or physically?"

"I guess he's not there. It's obvious that you don't even recognize your own man's voice!" Tim demanded.

"Stop playing so much, Ronald. When did you make it back from your trip?"

"This ain't Ronald, this is Tim. Get up. I'm on my way over."

Linda was speechless. She quickly came to the conclusion that he was trying to pull a prank.

"Are you serious, Tim?"

"I'll show you in about twenty five minutes."

Tim knew that it would take a little longer than twenty five minutes to get to Clinton, Maryland, but he wanted to keep her anticipating his arrival.

Linda was awe struck. Things were moving slow, but steady with Ronald and her, but it hadn't been very long since she decided to leave Tim. Her feelings were still there and she couldn't deny it. She anticipated a complicated battle between love and integrity; a battle in which love could easily win. The reality of it all started to kick in. Linda paced back and forth in her bedroom, and she realized that she had to put some clothes on because she was dressed in her night gown.

She opened her dresser door and grabbed a pair of sweat pants and a Nautica t-shirt. Her hair was all over the place, she thought, so she wrapped her hair in a ponytail and tried to look relaxed. It didn't work. She was still nervous as hell. Linda walked downstairs and looked out of the living room window. No sign of Tim. She began to think that Tim's visit was a joke until she saw a pearl white Camry pull up to the drive way of her house.

She was mesmerized as she watched Tim step out of the car dressed in a raven black velour Gucci suit. She was immediately reminded about why she had fallen so deeply in love with him from the start. It wasn't the money, even though that was a plus. It was his whole aura. He had class, style, and grace. He was a cut above the rest.

The doorbell rang. Linda didn't want it to appear as if she was anxious so she stalled for a moment and waited for him to ring the doorbell again. He didn't, he just waited patiently. Linda looked through the peep hole before she opened the door and wasn't surprised to see his cool, calm, and collected demeanor. Linda opened the door slowly. Tim barged his way in. She was frightened by his entrance because he was huffing and obviously upset.

"Where the fuck is he?" Tim demanded as he pulled a big black gun from his waist.

"He's gone out of town for a week!" Linda replied frantically.

"You're lying, bitch."

"No, I'm not Tim!"

"Why should I believe you?" he cut her off. "Matter of fact, get your hands up in the air. And you might want to close your eyes, because this might get ugly." Linda closed her eyes, "Please don't do this." Before she could finish her sentence, she felt a liquid substance squirting on her forehead. Then she heard the violent chuckle coming from Tim as she opened her eyes only to see him squirting water from the big black water gun. Her head felt lighter as she collapsed on the sofa. Tim grabbed her and kissed her forehead as he continued in a laughing frenzy.

"You know I wouldn't hurt your pretty ass," Tim lifted her up and spun her around slowly eyeing her figure.

"That nigga must not be on his J.O.B, because you were a little thicker than this in the back when I went to jail. What kind of a name is Ronald anyway?" Linda looked at Tim, still shocked. She didn't answer him as she figured that it was a rhetorical question. She simply smiled.

Tim knew that Ronald wasn't there once he called and heard Linda's response. The scene he displayed was all a part of his grand entrance. The longer they were together, old feelings returned and it felt as if Linda and Tim could pick up right where they left off. They talked about old times and they shared plenty of smiles. They were sitting on the sofa reminiscing. Linda had warmed up some leftover chicken from Boston Market and Tim, being the romantic he was, broke off a tiny piece and fed it to Linda. She fell right in line and they started feeding each other small portions of chicken.

"I'm sorry, Tim," Linda said looking directly into Tim's eyes.

"For what?"

"For leaving you like that."

"I guess you had needs and I couldn't fulfill them," Tim said not giving her the eye contact that her eyes demanded.

She grabbed his chin gently turning it so that his eyes would face hers. "You are quite forgiving, but I don't buy it." He tried to turn his head, but she gently turned it back so that she could see into those hazel eyes and search for forgiveness. Tim knew what she wanted. Her eyes were so demanding.

"Okay. My whole world was shattered. Is that what you want to hear?"

"No…it's not about what I want to hear. It's about what you were feeling. It's about giving you the closure you deserve."

He looked down at his Gucci loafers then he kicked them off. "When I got your letter, I sensed that something wasn't right because I didn't smell any perfume. Once I opened it and read it, I almost fainted. It was unreal to me." A tear fell from Tim's eye, but he continued. "I couldn't eat…I couldn't sleep…I didn't want to go to recreation or watch television. I was angry, annoyed, and frustrated…I cried. It was hard for me to understand losing you to the elements of time. But, I had to respect your decision because you were honest with me and you didn't just up and leave." Their eyes were equally leveled now.

Tim initiated the first, very passionate, kiss. He kissed her violently and caressed her breast gently, arousing her desire to be penetrated. Each kiss was defined by the moisture that developed between her legs. Tim moved his hand from her breast and slowly rubbed his hand between her legs. She moaned as she looked at the red light blinking on the phone, which indicated that someone was calling. She turned the ringer off the minute she hung up with Tim because she didn't want Tim to answer the phone out of spite. The light had stopped blinking, but she had a set of blinking lights of her own going off inside her mind and Tim was the cause of it.

Tim laid her down on the fluffy imported carpet and slowly undressed her, starting with her shirt, then her sweat pants. She was beautiful and sexier than ever, Tim acknowledged to himself. Her red hair complimented her hazel eyes and her figure complimented his touch. Tim started at her breast and worked his way down to her stomach, licking gently and enjoying the taste of her flesh. He wanted more of her in his mouth, so he took her underwear off. Then he lay down on the carpet and pulled her towards him allowing her to sit on his chest. Tim gripped her clitoris between his lips while slurping and massaging it with his tongue. She was moving in rhythm, moaning, and breathing aggressively all at the same time.

"Damn Tim, this feels good. You better not leave me again," she said in a moaning frenzy. Tim almost made a sarcastic remark, but he refrained. As he became more explorative, causing her orgasm to surface, she leaned over him. "Oh God...oh shit! Tim please...I'm cumming!" The taste of her orgasm blended perfectly with his erection. Linda collapsed on top of him, but Tim wasn't having it. His blood was flowing in all the right places. "Uh Uh, no you don't. You're not going to run out of gas on me because you got a little nut."

"Just give me a minute, baby," she responded.

Tim lifted her up and started kissing her breast and licking her abdomen. He was hard as a rock. Tim pulled her legs around his waist and entered her. He was standing up and he pulled her to him with long hard thrusts.

"Oh my God!" Linda said. Tim knew it was coming, but he didn't want it to happen yet. Linda was a talker while having sex. She couldn't help it. But, her moans would always excite Tim, causing him to ejaculate prematurely.

"Fuck this pussy...This is your pussy, Daddy ...Oh God, yes...hit my spot...yes, hit my spot baby!"

Tim uttered a loud moan. Linda chanted a few vulgar curse words. They both collapsed on the sofa.

*****

The biggest event at Lorton occurred at the end of the summer. It usually happened a little earlier than August, but this year there were a few administrative difficulties. The Family Fair was held every year and each inmate was allowed to invite no more than three adults and four children, however, sometimes there were exceptions to this rule. The fair was held on the ball field. It was not required for an inmate to have visitors attend.

The match making game was a high commodity at the fair. If someone introduced you to their sister, you would have to introduce them to yours or either introduce them to your girlfriend's girlfriend and vice versa. That's how the game was played. There were often go-go bands invited and groups who had been practicing for weeks while housed at the facility, who were given slots to perform and showcase their talent.

They had a coupon system set up for food. The inmate's family members would have to purchase coupons that would be used for buying food or drinks. The concession stands served fried chicken, BBQ chicken, coleslaw, macaroni and cheese, hot dogs, ribs, greens, minced beef and rice. There were several other stands that sold popcorn, candy, and slushies.

Family Fair Day was the day that a lot of inmates would use to not only visit with family, but to get their freak on. Drugs would be smoked right there on the field and a lot more drugs would be taken back to the compound to be packaged and sold; all this done right under the officers' noses.

"This is the big day slim," Tony said to Daryl while sitting in the bleachers on the ball field at the fair.

"Yeah, I reckon so kinfolk. I just hope that Tim ain't set us up with no big bamma country broads," Daryl said.

"Well, if he did, I reckon you got your slang all tallied up for 'em sir," Tony said. They were being sarcastic. "What you think Cliff?"

"About what?"

Cliff wasn't paying those two clowns any attention. He had other things on his mind.

"You need to loosen up," Tony demanded. Cliff ignored him as he eyed a sexy chocolate female that fit the description of Gloria. Tim had set it up and he talked to her twice before today. She said he would know when he saw her because she would be wearing a pair of jeans, a pair of sky blue and white lady Jordan's and a sky blue and white lady Jordan t- shirt; and boy was she wearing it well.

"Damn who is that?" Daryl asked.

"That's all me, sucker," Cliff said as he stepped from the bleachers.

"Gloria," the young lady said as she turned around and smiled.

Cliff almost fainted. Gloria wasn't all that bad, but she was nowhere near the dime piece she claimed to be. She had a lot of bumps on her face and her teeth were crooked.

"Hey Cliff, damn you look good," Gloria said.

"You do too, but you lied to me." Gloria put her head down as if she was embarrassed.

"You said that you were a dime piece, but shit, you're a twenty piece," she lifted her head up then she gave him a hug and a kiss.

Cliff forced a passionate kiss back. "Where is Tasha and Jackie?" Cliff asked.

"They're on the way. They move too slowly for me." Cliff turned around and told Daryl and Tony that their bunnies were on the way. Tony and Daryl were laughing hysterically at Cliff. They started licking their tongues and making faces whenever Gloria would turn around with her back facing them.

"You might as well brace yourself champ. If that's the dime piece, you can only imagine what we're working with," Daryl said while eyeing the ball field for any signs of Tasha and Jackie.

"Okay I got a deal for you," Tony laughed at his own remark. "I'm going to pull some of these threads from my shirt and we'll let Cliff hold them. Each of us will draw a string and whoever gets the shortest string gets Tasha, okay?"

"Okay, but only one problem."

"What's that?"

"Cliff is not going to hold the strings. He thinks he's too cool for that." Tony paused for a second as if he were contemplating. He knew that Daryl was right.

"Okay, we'll let Gloria do it." Before Daryl could protest, Tony was off the bleachers giving the small pieces of thread to Gloria.

"Hold these for a second," Tony said. Cliff was looking at him with agitated eyes.

"Come on Daryl," Tony urged.

Tony grabbed a piece first, then Daryl. Tony looked at his string, then Daryl laughed. "I got you, sucker."

Cliff looked at both of them, then at Gloria. "Come on, boo. Let's get away from these nuts."

Someone yelled Gloria's name and when she turned around it was Tasha.

"Wait up for me, Tasha" a voice said not trailing far behind her. Daryl looked at Tony and Tony looked at Cliff.

"Damn," Cliff said in a low tone.

"What did you say baby?" Gloria asked Cliff.

"Oh nothing, I thought I dropped something."

Tony dropped his string and Daryl waved his at Cliff. They didn't care who was who out of the two females, because both of them looked very attractive and classy. Tasha was short and well-rounded from the hips down. Jackie was tall and complete from the lips to her hips. Both had faces that could arouse any modeling photographer's camera.

Tony grabbed Tasha's arm, and Daryl put his arm around Jackie. Their day at the fair was like a day in the park. They all took pictures, ate home style meals and exchanged laughs, kisses, and hugs.

There were a couple of public restrooms located at the far end of the ball field. Daryl looked towards that direction and noticed that couples were taking turns going in and out of the restrooms. He whispered in Jackie's ear and Jackie whispered in Tasha's ear. Cliff had already pinned the move. They all took turns in the restroom, neither one of them lasting no more than nine minutes, except for Tony, who lasted for about nine and a half minutes.

After a long day of fun, the fair was finally coming to a conclusion. Fathers were hugging and kissing their sons and daughters. Husbands were embracing their wives, and boyfriends were caressing their girlfriends.

"This was enjoyable. Did you put the package up?" Cliff asked Gloria.

"Yeah I took care of it" she promised.

"When will you get it?" she asked.

"Not soon enough" Cliff replied.

Daryl, Cliff, and Tony hugged and kissed their visitors one last time before joining the long line that was forming for the inmates to be strip searched.

*****

Officer Gerald Ludlow was working over-time. Not literally, but financially. He was getting double over-time pay today for virtually doing nothing. "Clean that area over there!" he yelled to his crew of inmates who were cleaning the ball field after the fair.

Officer Ludlow walked passed two inmates standing not too far from the small tool shack. "You two need to find something to do," he demanded. Then he walked behind the shack as if to secure the area of any possible contraband. He picked up a small twig and brushed the bushes back and forth. There it was - the Neiman Marcus bag. *Whatever you do, don't look in it.* His mind was challenging him again. *You're getting paid five hundred smack-a-roo's, what do u care!* It wouldn't stop. He heard some laughter in the distant shadows of the ball field.

Officer Ludlow grabbed the bag and headed for his duty van. He placed the bag under the seat and returned to oversee his work crew. His part was almost done. All he had to do now was make sure the bag got to the laundry room and put it in Cliff's laundry bag.

One of the officers who worked at control allowed Gloria to enter the facility with the bag, all courtesy of Tim, who paid him a thousand dollars in cash. There were two ounces of heroin and three pounds of marijuana in the bag.

CHAPTER 9

The smell of pancakes, eggs, and a few unidentifiable aromas filled the air. The bed felt comfortable to Tim. He was treading on familiar turf. The bed should feel comfortable. After all, he was the one who bought it. He flicked the remote control trying not to let his mind wander, but he couldn't control his thoughts. He thought about Ronald contributing to the death of his love right here in the very bed that he lay.

Yes, he was treading on memorial turf. He smiled.

Linda stepped into the dark doorway and walked towards Tim. She was fully naked with a pair of knee high black boots and a rose in her mouth. She knew how to please him.

She had a large silver plate with a rounded top to conceal its contents. When she lifted the top, smoke rose in the air.

Tim was fascinated at the arrangement. Fruit surrounded the plate, and in the middle were the pancakes, steak, eggs, and portions of grilled chicken.

Linda sat on the bed beside Tim, placed the plate down, then went to the kitchen to fetch drinks. She returned with two glasses filled with orange juice. Linda sat the drinks down as well, then sat on the bed and hand fed Tim. After assuring Linda that he had plenty, she put the plate on her nightstand table and handed Tim his orange juice. Tim placed the half-full glass of orange juice back on the nightstand after he consumed a reasonable portion of it.

Three days had passed since Tim first came to visit Linda. He had called his mother and gave her a message to relay to Rhonda, telling her that he had to go out of town for some important business and that he'd be back in a few days. Three days and Tim had illuminated Linda's life again. They made passionate love, played scrabble, and talked very little during the whole three days.

There they sat, out of energy, but totally fulfilled. "Love is the strongest of forces," he said in a low tone.

Linda kissed Tim on the forehead. "What did you say baby?"

He turned to face her. "I said love is the strongest of forces. Sometimes a person can be so lost in love that once they find their way out, they become lost outside of love. Then they began to trick themselves into thinking that they don't want anything else to do with love because love hurts. But after a while, they begin to miss that good ole' feeling of love, so they let their guard down and began to welcome love again. But this time it doesn't feel the same," he wiped a tear and continued "But you settle with it in hopes of finding that desired feeling that you once encountered when you first found love." This time it was her tear that he wiped. "Some things are irreplaceable. They can't be forged or falsified because the owner of it knows every function and detail. You are the sole owner of my love it knows nothing else but you."

"Am I yours?" he asked. Her tears were flowing more rapidly now.

"Yes you are the owner." He kissed her deeply.

"Baby, there's something I want you to know," Tim said. "I've meet someone recently. Her name is Rhonda. I thought that I was in love with her, but I was just trying to fill the void that you left. I couldn't because your love can't be replaced. I'm going to call her right now and let her know that it's over and I'm going to turn the speaker phone on so that you and the whole world can hear it okay? I don't have anything to hide. But if I'm willing to do this, then you must be willing to put your mistake behind you and tell Ronald the same thing."

Linda nodded in approval. Tim switched the phone over to speaker and started dialing. The phone rang a few times.

"Hello," a sexy voice answered.

"Rhonda, this is Tim."

"Where are you? I thought that you would be home by now. I miss you." Linda frowned, she was getting jealous. Tim rubbed her hair.

"I'm at Linda's house," he said reluctantly. Rhonda's whole demeanor changed.

"What the fuck are you doing over there?" Look Tim. "I don't have time for no motherfucking games. That bitch wasn't there when your heart was broken in two. As a matter of fact, she caused it and I healed it!" Rhonda was furious Tim put his hand over Linda's mouth.

"Look Rhonda, I thought that I could replace her, but I couldn't. I still love her and I'm trying to do the right thing instead of trying to play both sides of the field-" The phone line went dead. Tim looked at Linda. Linda grabbed the phone.

"Let me show you how to do this. Let me find out that you're getting soft on me." Linda dialed the number and put the phone on speaker.

"Hello," the voice on the other end sang.

"Ronald."

"Hey baby!"

"Good morning," she responded. Remember when I used to tell you how Tim and I use to go places and do things?"

"Uh huh."

"Well, he's back in my life and we've been going places and doing things for the last four days……but we never left the house."

"Is that why you haven't answered my calls?"

"No hard feelings?"

"But we're engaged."

Tim couldn't take this pitiful dude no more. "Well, chump, Linda and I were engaged when you stole her from me."

"But I -" Tim cut him off.

"If you're done sobbing we have business to attend to, sooooo if you want her back, come on over and fight like a man. I'll be waiting." This time Linda hung up.

"That wasn't fair" Linda said.

"What?"

"You got to add fuel to the fire, but I didn't," Linda said in a hostile tone.

"Do you want me to call Rhonda back?"

"No, I'm just trying to ruffle your feathers."

"Oh, I'm a chicken now?"

"No boy," she stared into his eyes.

"You're my tiger." They kissed and fell back on the bed holding each other.

*****

The sun was shining. There was a slight breeze lingering. It felt like late September, yet it was the end of August. Cliff kept a steady pace as he walked from the laundry room with his laundry bag towards his dormitory. He spoke to a few dudes that he knew, but he still remained focused on his mission. His heart was pounding because this was the first time that he had to transport the goods in this manner. He didn't know the exact amount of goods that he was carrying, but he knew that it had to be a lump sum because of how Tim set it up.

As Cliff got closer to the dormitory, relief got closer to his heart. As soon as Cliff got to the front door of the dormitory, however, a correctional officer emerged. "Damn," Cliff said under his breath.

"Hey, Mr. Porter, let me see what you got there," the officer said. Cliff's heart was racing as he slowly opened the laundry bag. The officer looked in it, and then he dug deep.

"Damn boy, you got a mighty big load here." Cliff was about to bolt. The officer pulled his arm out of the bag satisfied that Cliff was not in violation. He allowed Cliff to walk a few steps. "Hey! I almost forgot. Let me pat you down." Cliff obliged him then he headed through the door towards his cell.

"Damn, I must have gotten the wrong bag," Cliff said to himself. When he got to his room, he sat the bag on his bed and placed his sign in the small window of the cell door so that no one could see. Satisfied that he was secure, he reached in the laundry bag. There were a lot of clothes on the top, and when he got to the bottom of the bag, there was nothing there.

"Shit," he cursed. He started to rummage through the laundry more forcefully. It wasn't until he grabbed a t-shirt that seemed to be wrapped up in layers that his fears started to subside. Cliff unrolled the t-shirt and bam! There it was. A large zip lock bag of marijuana. He unrolled another t-shirt.....then another...then another. There was enough marijuana and heroin to supply the compound for months. The goods had been stashed well. That's why the officer didn't detect them.

Cliff's mind was racing. He had to put the goods in the stash spot, but not before he bagged up at least five hundred dollars' worth of weed and a thousand worth of heroin so that Daryl and Tony could pass it out to a few of their runners.

Cliff quickly separated a sufficient amount of weed and heroin from two of the large zip lock bags. Then he rewrapped and folded each package and removed two of the ceiling tiles, carefully stashing the goods. Afterwards, he folded the smaller bags in which he had placed the small amount of the weed and heroin in. He patted his waist to make sure that they were secured, then he removed the sign from his cell window. Cliff bopped to a tune coming from his walk-man as he headed out of the dorm to deliver a package to Daryl and Tony who were waiting for him on the ball field.

*****

Linda woke up. The sun was beaming in her eyes as she attempted to fight the effects of the fun she had the night before. Last night involved plenty of drinks, music, and sex. Linda hadn't felt like this since she first experimented with alcohol in junior high school. Her feet were cold as they were not being sheltered by the satin sheets that typically comforted her. She felt the soreness between her legs and she smiled at thoughts of the night before. She turned over to touch Tim, but there was nothing there to comfort her tender touch. Maybe he was in the bathroom.

"Tim," she spoke. "Baby, are you going out?" She heard nothing. Her head was pounding with each word she spoke. She turned over and noticed that there was a note on the nightstand. She felt a sigh of relief. With her head still throbbing, she reached over and grabbed it.

Dear Linda,

I had a wonderful night, but the truth is you're just not my type. Have you ever heard the saying that what goes around comes around? Well, that's what I'm feeling as I write this letter. Either way, whatever you're feeling right now is only half as bad as how I felt when I received your letter. Good riddens. Oh, and don't bother calling Ronald he doesn't want you either.

This had to be a joke, Linda thought. She picked up the phone and dialed Ronald's cell phone number. A recording came on, "The party that you are trying to reach is not accepting calls from this number, Thank You!" She was furious. She couldn't believe Tim had manipulated her like this. She couldn't believe she allowed it to happen. She had tears in her eyes.

"I'm gonna make you pay for this Tim Johnson," Linda vowed.

*****

With the sounds of Luther Vandross whispering in his ears, Tim cruised through the streets of Temple Hills, Maryland. Tim had found out Ronald's last name through some of his and Linda's mutual friends. He contacted Ronald and placed a friendly wager that he could get her back. Ronald agreed that if Tim scored, then he would cut all ties with her and let Tim have her. Tim agreed. But, little did Ronald know, Tim didn't want her. He just wanted sweet revenge.

Tim dialed Sasha's number to thank her for posing as Rhonda when he called. Sasha was Tim's cousin. He then called Rhonda and told her that he was back in town and that he wanted to see her when she got off work. She agreed. Tim hung up the phone and continued to feel the vibes that were swimming through the speakers. Then he realized that he was supposed to meet with Sol today. He dialed Sol's number and Sol told him to come to his new shop. Tim rummaged through his glove compartment, grabbed a pen and wrote down the directions. "I'm on my way," Tim said.

Tim looked at his watch. It read 10:00 am. "Perfect," Tim murmured.

Sol's shop was not too far from where Tim was. Tim drove off of Suitland Road onto Marlboro Pike. After a few minutes, he saw the building that read Sol's Automotive Accessories. He drove around the store towards the rear of it just like Sol had instructed. He noticed another smaller building connected to Sol's shop. As

Tim drove closer he saw a figure standing by a commercial truck. It was Sol. Tim beeped his horn and waved. Sol motioned his finger to the female that he was talking to as if to tell her to give him a minute. He walked to Tim's car quickly and gave him directions where to park. Tim parked the car, checked himself in the mirror, and proceeded to Sol's shop.

"Hey buddy. How the fuck are you?" Sol said. Tim was well aware that anytime you were in Sol's presence and there were no females around or corporate lawyers, Sol had a profanity extravaganza.

"What's happening Sol? You look good," Tim said.

"Well I pay my taxes, I pay child support, and I run a pretty legit business with no stress. I ought to look good." He looked at Tim and smiled.

"What the fuck are you doing driving a Camry? Those cars are for sissies."

"It was a gift. I couldn't keep it if I wanted to because Linda will be looking for me to be driving it. That's the only way she'll be able to spot me. I gave her the boot."

"I used to like Linda," Sol said. "I'll tell you one thing, whoever gave you that fucking Camry is not a good friend and I would cut them from my will if I were you. You would probably want to put old Sol in their spot instead." Sol nudged Tim's arm, urging him to follow his lead. "I want you to know that I'm proud of you Tim."

"Yeah...for what?"

"Because you kept your good name. There's so many fucking little rats these fucking days that it makes doing business extremely hard. These little pricks wouldn't know the meaning of loyalty if it squatted over them and shitted right on top of them. But not you comrade; you looked your consequences right in the eye and stuck your dick right up its ole caboodle."

Tim was listening, but the majority of his attention was fixed upon Sol's variety of different automobiles. As they walked through a room full of busy mechanics, Sol stopped and asked one of his workers if he knew Tim. When the guy nodded "No," Sol said, " You wouldn't fuck know him. He's a cut above the rest."

Tim noticed gold Lexus SC430 convertible, a black BMW M3 convertible, and a Mercedes Benz E320 4matic station wagon. He was ecstatic. Tim looked on the other side of the platform and noticed a red Ferrari 358 spider and a summer blue Aston Martin Lagonda. He was impressed.

"Sol, you have really been handling your business."

"Get the fuck outta here," Sol said.

"No, I'm serious, man. I respect your hustle," Tim said.

"Don't try to flip it on me. You're the man of the hour, and to prove it you, see that Lexus convertible over there?" Tim nodded. "That's yours. I'm going to get the paperwork together for you."

"Man you're crazy. How the hell am I going to vouch for a Lexus SC430 convertible and I just got out of jail?"

"It's easy. I'm contracted with a certain game show. This game show gives contestants on the show prizes like this as consolation prizes. Therefore, whenever I sell one of these bad boys to someone who wouldn't normally be able to explain to the authorities where they got the money to buy such an exquisite automobile, it shows up on the computer as a consolation prize. So you have no excuses. The car is yours."

They walked into Sol's office. "Tim. Did I ever tell you the story about one of my unfaithful workers?"

101

"No. But I'm dying to hear it."

"Okay! One of my workers comes into my office and says, 'Boss, Teddy needs to leave work. He's having a problem with his feet.' So I look at the guy and I say get the fuck outta here. If he's having a problem with his feet, then let him tell me. So the guy says, 'He can't walk. He has a bumble bee stuck in his shoe.' I tell the guy to bring him in the office. Once the guy gets to my office and confirms what his buddy had already told me, I reached in my desk and grabbed my revolver. Startled, Teddy said, 'Hey what's that for?' and I say, 'You've got a problem and here's the solution. Now, give me your foot and I'm going to shoot the fucking bumble bee.' Teddy jumped up as I reached for his foot. He ran back to work and I haven't had a complaint since." Tim laughed until his gut clenched.

"It wasn't that funny," Sol said.

"I'm not laughing at the joke. I'm laughing at the funny joker who told the joke."

Tim was having a good time with Sol. He attributed it to good old fashion friendship. Sol told a few more jokes and Tim criticized a few of them.

"So how's the money business going, Sol?"

"Get the fuck outta here! What are you a schmuck? I stopped that a long time ago. I gave a lump sum to a certain game show and some to charity. How do you guys say it? I spreaded some love."

"Things are definitely looking good for you Sol."

"So what's your story kiddo? Need a job? A place to stay? Some rubbers? What's going on?"

"No I'm doing what I do."

"Which is?"

"Staying low key and running a productive business."

Sol looked at Tim with curious eyes. "Whatever you do, stay away from the pharmaceutical stuff."

Tim smiled. "Okay buddy."

They exchanged a few more laughs and smiles then Tim hinted that it was time to cut the reunion short. "I guess it's time for me to hit the road Jack."

"Okay, but the next time you come over, you better be ready to hit the real road! What cha say we cruise through Bowie, Maryland around December and get some kicks out of the beautiful houses competing for the light show." Tim nodded in agreement, then emerged from the little office chair. They walked outside towards Tim's Camry.

"I need you to deliver the Lexus to my mom's house wrapped in a ribbon," Tim said.

"Sure. Would you like a birthday cake with that?" Sol smiled at his own humor.

They hugged briefly before Tim got in his car. "I'll call you soon." He pulled off.

*****

"Man what the fuck did you do that for? I told you to give me whatever you wanted me to handle in my hand. I cut Jimmy off. He's not reliable," Daryl said to Cliff.

"I wasn't trying to have all of the bullshit on me. I had to get rid of it."

"What did you give him?" Daryl asked.

"I gave him two quarters of blow and ten dime bags of weed."

"Ah shit, you might as well charge that to the game. He's going to shoot up the blow, sell the weed, buy some more blow, and shoot that up too."

"That'll be his ass, too…Those jokers know who to play with."

"Time will tell."

"Yeah, right."

Once Cliff bagged up the goods, his goal was to get them out of his possession as quickly as possible. As he was leaving the dorm, he ran into one of Daryl's runners named Jimmy. He gave Jimmy some heroin and weed. He gave him four quarters of heroin which was worth one hundred and sixty dollars. Each quarter would be broken down to four dime bags. He also gave him ten dime bags of weed which was worth one hundred dollars. Jimmy would have to give him one hundred and forty dollars, which would leave Jimmy with one hundred and twenty dollars. No one else on the compound could afford to give deals up in such a manner.

In the past, Jimmy screwed up a lot of Daryl's money, but Daryl didn't resort to violence. He just gave Jimmy some more and let Jimmy pay him out of the profit that Jimmy made. The money at Lorton was very plentiful, so it was hard to understand why Jimmy couldn't abide by Daryl's guidelines. Then again, he knew why. It was because Jimmy was a stone cold dope fiend.

Daryl, Cliff, and Tony sat on the ball field while Tony was rolling a blunt. Daryl and Cliff were disagreeing about Jimmy.

"Did you talk to Tim?" Daryl asked Cliff.

"Yeah I talked to him about twenty minutes ago."

"What's up with him?"

"Man, slim is just out there enjoying the life. He played a devious trick on Linda, so I guess he's on some get back time."

"Oh, yeah! What did he do?" Cliff told Daryl and Tony about Tim's charade with Linda while they got high.

"Man that's some wild fantasy type shit," Tony said.

"Oh, he told me to break everything down and distribute it to ya'll equally. He said there's no need in me trying to run the show or continue to be organized, because just in case something happens, they can't try to get us as an organization thing. If somebody gets popped, and starts to include all of us, they'll try to jam us as a crew."

"It won't be too much different. We just can't start competing with each other and always have each other backs." They all agreed. They all got higher.

Cliff began to think about how the group came together. Daryl and Tony grew up on 16th Street Southeast, a few blocks down from Tim. Cliff lived four blocks away in a housing project called Potomac Gardens. They all went to Hine Junior High School together, but eventually parted in different directions once they chose to indulge in the unpredictable vengeance of the street life.

Daryl was short and muscular with an ill-temper. Cliff was tall stocky and very laid back but he had a bad side that was uncontrollable once someone triggered it. Tony was a slim tall pretty boy, and he always had Tim, Daryl, or Cliff to intervene in his battles. Therefore, he never really experienced any drama.

"Man I'm about to go to the dorm," Daryl said.

"Yeah, me too. I'm high as hell," Tony agreed.

"Well I'm going to break that thing down tonight and I'll hit ya'll off tomorrow," Cliff said, speaking in reference to the drugs. Cliff paused for a minute. "Tony, don't you have my DMX tape?"

"Yeah you can come with me and get it now."

"Nah, I didn't have to come with you to give it to you. So why should I come with you to get it? Bring my shit with you tomorrow."

"Okay Man." They all hit hands as a sign of brotherly love, then they departed from the ball field.

CHAPTER 10

He looked out the window. Her car was still there waiting patiently. He knew that this would occur and he ridiculed himself for not planning ahead. She was dozing off, but with each nod she would catch herself. *Damn this bitch is crazy,* he told himself. Tim had parked the Camry outback, because he knew that it wouldn't take long for Linda to build her esteem up to post up in front of his mother's house.

He had a plan. He could call Rhonda and meet her someplace else. He could slip out the back door and take her out. But it was 11:40 pm and Rhonda left work at 12:00 am. Where the hell could he take her at this time of night without arousing her suspicion? He would figure something out. He had no choice. How long will she sit out there? *I need to get me an apartment* Tim acknowledged before yelling upstairs to his mother that he'll be back in a few hours.

Tim exited the house from the back door. He went to the Camry, opened the door got in and started the engine. He considered confronting Linda, but he dismissed that notion. He couldn't afford to let brief confrontation turn into a long argument and Rhonda pull up to the house. That would mean that he would have to explain to Rhonda what was going on and he would rather spend his time with her doing other things. Tim called Rhonda on his cell phone and told her to meet him at Johnson Garden Apartments on Suitland Road. He told her that he would be waiting by the front entrance. Rhonda complied.

Before Tim went to his destination, he decided to go sightseeing. He drove through some of the areas that he used to frequent, acknowledging those he knew by beeping his horn and briefly eyeing those who he didn't recognize. He drove through Kentucky Courts, Potomac Gardens, and Author Caper Housing

Projects. He spotted a few females that he had partied with in the past. When he pulled to the corner of L Street Southeast, he noticed an old associate of his talking to a female. He hit his horn twice and rolled down his window.

"Drew, what's up?" The slim figure turned around and walked slowly to the car suspiciously. "Hey Drew ...This is Tim. What's up?"

Drew couldn't believe his eyes. "What's up, Dog? When did you come home?" "I've been home for two and a half weeks."

"Well why haven't you hollered at a nigga? I was just talking about you the other day."

Tim was amazed at how many times he heard that line and how sincere it can sound when you want to believe it. Tim had done a lot of business with Drew before he got arrested and Drew had promised to be there for Tim when he needed him; not because he felt he owed Tim, but because of his own morals and principals. It only lasted for three months. Somehow, Drew managed to lose contact and that was his excuse.

"Man you trying to hang out or what?" Drew asked.

"Nah slim. I have to meet my girl when she gets off work."

Drew was still bent over with his head in the window talking to Tim when he decided to get in the car. Tim knew that he was trying to feel him out and see if there was any animosity between them. There wasn't.

"We have to really get together and discuss some things," Drew said gracefully. "You're not going to tell me that you're a born again Christian or no shit like that are you?"

"Nah man. You know my religion is making money." Tim responded.

"I hear that slim." Drew turned to look at Tim before he fumbled in his pocket to retrieve an ink pen.

"I need a piece of paper so that I can give you my number." Tim reached in the glove compartment and searched until he found a piece of paper.

"Okay, here's my cell phone, pager and home number. Make sure you leave a message if my voicemail picks up. I have a few dollars on me for you. I don't usually carry much with me when I'm out here, but this should hold you until we meet again." Drew reached in his pocket and pulled out a wad of money and handed it to Tim. They both knew that Tim's hand called for much more than whatever the amount that the wad of money contained, but the short notice and willingness was highly considered.

"Thanks Drew. I'll keep in touch with you." They slapped hands, Drew got out of the car, and continued to converse with the female.

Tim pulled off and headed towards Suitland Road, taking the route from Pennsylvania Avenue with the music blasting. He started to sing along with one of his favorite artists. *I'm yours...You're mine...Like paradise...* He loved Sade.

Tim cruised smoothly as he let the fortitude of the city lights keep him in accord with what the future held for him. *Sooner or later, this city is going to be mine*, Tim told himself. *I want it all.*

Tim pulled up to the apartment complex and parked his car where he told Rhonda he would be waiting for her. He sat there for five minutes flicking the buttons on the compact disc player. He was trying to find a song, but he wasn't sure what number it was. Rhonda had been good to him to reveal to her who he really was. He figured that she was probably skeptical about him being able to provide for her as well as she would for him. But, he was certain that he could change her insecurities in the blink of an eye.

Rhonda's teal blue Xterra pulled into the parking lot and Tim smiled. She drove slowly, as if she was trying to find a good parking space, and then she pulled up behind Tim.

Tim got out of the car and got into her truck. She turned to him and they exchanged kisses.

"Damn, I've been missing you young buck," Tim said.

"Nah, you're the young buck." Actually, they both were thirty one years old, but Tim had her by a few months.

"Why are we meeting here?" Rhonda asked.

"Well, let's just say that I have special reservations here," Tim explained.

"But this is not a hotel, this is an apartment building."

"You are a very bright young lady, but this is not your ordinary apartment for rent. There's another world in there just waiting to be discovered by us." He smiled and kissed her again. "Come on."

She paused for a minute. "Do I need to call my son's babysitter and let her know that I will be picking him up late?"

"Yeah…that is a good idea," Tim replied.

Tim's mother had given him a proprietor card which enabled him access to any available apartment in Johnson Gardens. It also allowed him access to the various master keys which would allow him the privilege of inspecting the entire property for business purposes. There were only two people who had proprietor cards for Johnson Garden, and that was Tim and his mother. Rhonda dialed the babysitter's number while Tim occupied his hand between her legs. She gave him a look of annoyance and he gave her an I-just-can't-help-it-look. Afterward the phone call, Tim grabbed her hand, leading her out of her truck and on to the pavement.

When they got to the front door, Tim slid his card across the laser panel that was attached to the lock.

"That's real high tech. Does every tenant have one?"

"No. They use their code...They punch it in on that black box right there," Tim pointed at the side of the door. She wondered what made him so special. But she decided to just go with the flow.

When they walked into the building, Rhonda was amazed at the interior and structure. It was odd seeing so much work put into an apartment complex. She drove pass this apartment building dozens and dozens of times, but she wouldn't have believed what she was seeing unless she had the opportunity to see it for herself. Tim pointed at the desk that was sitting in the middle of the lobby.

"This is where the front desk clerk sits. The person assigned here only works from 8:00 am to 5:30pm on weekdays. He or she is in charge of making appointments and maintenance calls.

"Appointments for what?"

"There's a day care center available for tenants and non-tenants. There's also a swimming pool in the rear of the building."

"Damn, I wouldn't mind living here!" Rhonda said passionately.

"I'm pretty sure that this is nothing compared to the luxury that you go home to every night."

"Shit, I get tired of the work that comes with maintaining a house."

"So if I could get you in one of these would you object?"

"I would have to make proper arrangements, but I wouldn't object at all."

Then it hit her. This is where he works! She told herself. He wants to make sure that I approve of his working quarters before he tells me. I wonder if he's the front desk clerk.

Tim kissed her on the cheek. "Come on. Let's go out to the pool."

"It's kind of cool outside baby."

"We're not going swimming. Besides they have an inside deck overlooking the pool." Tim grabbed her hand, leading her down the hallway until they reached a sign with an arrow pointing that said swimming pool. When they reached the pool, Rhonda was ecstatic. They had to walk on the outdoor pool deck to get to the indoor deck, which was approximately ten feet from the apartment building exit doors that led to the pool.

The pool had sort of a circular motion and the pool's capacity in length was eight feet. They walked to the indoor deck holding hands. Tim pulled one of the beach-like chair recliners out from under a table. Then he laid on it and pulled Rhonda gently to accompany him. She kissed him with aggression, allowing him to taste her passion. Tim unbuttoned her pants. She still had on her work uniform. Her zipper unzipped with ease. Tim gently stroked her pussy while the wetness prompted his motivation. Caught in the moment, she lifted both of Tim's hands above his head while penetrating his mouth with her tongue. Before Tim could object, she had both of his hands cuffed to the leg of the table that sat behind the chair.

"What the ...?"

"Ha Ha. Gotcha." She unbuttoned his pants, then gently pulled them off along with his underwear. She lifted his shirt up to his chest and started sucking on his nipples. He had no control. She took his muscular frame in her mouth as if it were her last meal, pausing only for short intermissions. She nibbled on his abs for a short period of time then took his penis in her mouth. She bobbed up and down in a slow motion while Tim moaned for mercy. She had none. She licked his balls, easing his climax closer and closer to the surface. She sucked and slurped the side of his dick while popping it in and out of her mouth simultaneously. She could feel him tense up. He had no control.

"Shit....I'm cumming," were his only words. She sucked his balls and jerked his dick until she felt his muscles releasing. Then she caught his orgasm in her mouth.

Some of it sprayed on the side of her face. Tim's body went limp as Rhonda used her tongue to climb up his body while massaging his dick with her hand. She kissed and licked his stomach then went to his nipple. He was shaking. Rhonda kissed him on the forehead and said, "I made love to you my way. Did you watch?"

Tim laughed because that statement sounded very familiar to him. Rhonda uncuffed Tim and it was like he was in a trance. She helped him get dressed then they rested in each other's arms.

"So this is where you work baby?" Tim was caught in the moment that he forgot one of reasons that he brought her here.

"Oh... no I don't work here." She looked up at Tim as if she was confused.

"I have something that I need to discuss with you and I just wanted to wait until the right time. So far you have been very forthcoming with me you have taken risks for me and you barely know me. Therefore, I have to let you know who I am and then you decide if you still want to continue this relationship."

Tim's tone made Rhonda uneasy. She wasn't sure what he was about to reveal about himself, but she was sure that it didn't sound too good.

"Who are you?" she asked.

"I'm Tim Johnson" he said.

"I know that," Rhonda quickly responded.

"Well first of all, we both know that I've been down Lorton, therefore, I'm no saint. But, you don't know the extent of my case or my passed livelihood. I was a drug dealer." He paused for a moment to see her reaction. Her expression was motionless. "I also use to move a lot of counterfeit money." Rhonda lifted up from his grasp with a surprised look on her face.

"I didn't move it like that. I knew someone who had it so I would buy it from them and sell it to someone else for a profit."

Rhonda looked in to his eyes and kissed him. "So what happened?"

"One of my runners got caught and snitched on me, but before that happened, I had cleaned most of my money up and made some major investments. My mother was the one who made sure my investments were sound. She even expanded my investments."

"So…what did you invest in? Stocks or something?"

"No…one of my investments is the very garden that you're sitting in."

Since she was lying in his lap, she had to turn around to face him. She said the name slowly, "John-son Gardens. Oh my God!"

Tim smiled and kissed her nose because he missed her forehead.

"That's why you brought me here!" she said.

"Well, that's part of it, but the other reason is because I want to put you in a two bedroom apartment here rent free." She smiled and kissed him again.

"Will you be living here also?"

"Of course I will be."

"I have to make some arrangements first. I don't think that Melvin will squabble any because we're practically divorced."

"Take your time, baby," Tim said cutting her off. "We have a whole lifetime ahead of us. There's one more thing that I forgot to tell you," Tim said.

"I hope that you're not married."

"I wish we were," he said under his breath.

"I heard you," Rhonda said.

"There's a shop also."

She looked at Tim inquisitively.

"What do you mean?" Rhonda asked.

"I own a beauty Salon also."

Rhonda laughed. She was speechless.

"And just where is this beauty Salon located?"

Tim kissed her on the neck and said,"On Florida Ave…It's called Braids R' Us." Rhonda looked up at him.

"Oh my God! That's where my girlfriend has been trying to get me to go. It's yours?"

"Well, my mother and I are partners even though she insists that it's mine. She deserves the glory because she's been promoting, building, and maintaining it since I've been locked up."

Rhonda grabbed his arm anxiously. "Is there anything else you want to tell me?"

"As a matter of fact, since you mentioned it, there's one more thing." He paused for a second. "My ex-girlfriend is stalking me." Tim waited for an expression. There was none, so he continued. "We had a relationship. We were engaged. She did a lot of time with me, but she broke down and left me for someone else. Now that I'm home, she wants me back. I want to be with you, so that's how the ball bounces."

He observed her expression, but he couldn't detect the slightest feeling or emotion through her non-verbal communication. "She was sitting outside my mother's house tonight eyeing the house. I saw her in her red pathfinder," he continued.

"Why didn't you confront her?"

He was guilty. It was written all over his face. He couldn't tell her how he tricked Linda into believing he wanted her back or how he manipulated her into falling back in love with him through several nights of passionate love making.

"I just don't want to be bothered with her period."

Rhonda kissed his shirt where his chest was and said, "I understand, but if this continues, then you're going to have to confront her." Tim nodded to assure her that her point was well taken, however, he knew that it would be best to let her wallow in the reality of what-goes-around-comes-around and all else would heal in due time.

*****

Two weeks ago, there was no question in Cliff's mind whether or not Jimmy would pay him for the dope that he has given on consignment. Cliff thought that his reputation alone was enough to up and down in a slow motion while Tim moaned for mercy. She had none. She licked his balls, easing his climax closer and closer to the surface. She sucked and slurped the side of his dick while popping it in and out of her mouth simultaneously. She could feel him tense up. He had no control.

"Shit....I'm cumming," were his only words. She sucked his balls and jerked his dick until she felt his muscles releasing. Then she caught his orgasm in her mouth.

Some of it sprayed on the side of her face. Tim's body went limp as Rhonda used her tongue to climb up his body while massaging his dick with her hand. She kissed and licked his stomach then went to his nipple. He was shaking. Rhonda kissed him on the forehead and said, "I made love to you my way. Did you watch?"

Tim laughed because that statement sounded very familiar to him. Rhonda uncuffed Tim and it was like he was in a trance. She helped him get dressed then they rested in each other's arms.

"So this is where you work baby?" Tim was caught in the moment that he forgot one of reasons that he brought her here.

"Oh... no I don't work here." She looked up at Tim as if she was confused.

"I have something that I need to discuss with you and I just wanted to wait until the right time. So far you have been very forthcoming with me you have taken risks for me and you barely know me. Therefore, I have to let you know who I am and then you decide if you still want to continue this relationship."

Tim's tone made Rhonda uneasy. She wasn't sure what he was about to reveal about himself, but she was sure that it didn't sound too good.

"Who are you?" she asked.

"I'm Tim Johnson" he said.

"I know that," Rhonda quickly responded.

"Well first of all, we both know that I've been down Lorton, therefore, I'm no saint. But, you don't know the extent of my case or my passed livelihood. I was a drug dealer." He paused for a moment to see her reaction. Her expression was motionless. "I also use to move a lot of counterfeit money." Rhonda lifted up from his grasp with a surprised look on her face.

"I didn't move it like that. I knew someone who had it so I would buy it from them and sell it to someone else for a profit."

Rhonda looked in to his eyes and kissed him. "So what happened?"

"One of my runners got caught and snitched on me, but before that happened, I had cleaned most of my money up and made some major investments. My mother was the one who made sure my investments were sound. She even expanded my investments."

"So…what did you invest in? Stocks or something?"

"No…one of my investments is the very garden that you're sitting in."

Since she was lying in his lap, she had to turn around to face him. She said the name slowly, "John-son Gardens. Oh my God!"

Tim smiled and kissed her nose because he missed her forehead.

"That's why you brought me here!" she said.

"Well, that's part of it, but the other reason is because I want to put you in a two bedroom apartment here rent free." She smiled and kissed him again.

ensure his product, but he was beginning to see that the blow had a far more encouraging effect than his reputation.

Cliff, Daryl, and Tony were coming from the mess hall when Cliff saw Jimmy turn around and walk towards the ball field. Cliff quickly picked up his pace, leaving Daryl and Tony in suspense. Daryl walked over by a tree and reached behind the bushes; Tony watched his back. Even though Daryl didn't alert him, he knew that Daryl probably had some drugs on him and he didn't want to stand where they were with drugs on him.

Tony and Daryl started walking towards Cliff where he had stopped Jimmy.

"What's up with my money slim?" Cliff said aggressively.

"Man I told you I'm going to handle that out of my own pocket because the dope fell."

"What about the weed?"

"The weed …oh…yeah I gave that to my man. He's going to pay me double at the end of the week."

"Man, don't even worry about it. I tried to look out for you. Daryl told me not to give you anything. I'm cutting you off. So when you see me pass, don't even look at me nigga."

Daryl and Tony had already gotten close enough to hear most of the conversation. Before Jimmy could muster any words or assert himself, he felt the force of a 30 pound barbell slam across his face. He stumbled backwards dazed. Cliff had hit him with a right hook. Before Cliff could finish what he started, Daryl intervened.

Daryl's movement was swift, but unrehearsed. He grabbed Jimmy by the shirt and stabbed him in the chest with an ice pick. Blood squirted and sprayed rapidly. It was as if Daryl was possessed. He stabbed and poked Jimmy wildly hitting him in the neck, arm, and chest. Tony walked closer to tell Daryl that he had done enough damage. Before Jimmy fell, blood squirted on Tony's shirt and his face.

Cliff had already started walking towards the entrance of the ball field. He knew that there was no need to stand around watching Daryl. Cliff walked to the same tree that Daryl had reached behind and made sure that the other knife was still there just in case of an emergency. As Jimmy lay there gasping for air, Daryl walked towards the basketball court. He disposed of the ice pick immediately after the assault.

Tony also walked towards the entrance of the ball field, but he was at least forty paces behind Cliff. When he turned the corner, the C.O.'s were en route to the assault. One of the C.O.'s grabbed Tony because he saw the blood on him. Cliff walked in the other direction stunned at how easily Tony allowed himself to get trapped. Correctional officers were swarming the ball field. The officer that had Tony cuffed sat him on the small curb of the entrance and Tony watched in fear as the medical unit and helicopter responded to the scene. Tony knew that this was going to be a long night.

*****

There was no dark room with one light hanging from the ceiling. No electric gadgets to inflict pain. There was no water dripping from a leaky pipe. Yet what seemed like a routine questioning was still an interrogation. Tony felt like they were surrounding him as he sat in the quiet little room in the lieutenant's office. Several officers had walked in the room momentarily either to hand the emergency response team (ERT) lieutenant some paperwork, or to see who the notorious convict was that had brutally and probably fatally stabbed Jimmy Moore.

Lieutenant White looked at the stack of papers that he was holding. It seemed as if he was gathering his thoughts. There were also two other officers in the room.

"Mr. Young," the lieutenant said softly. "My name is Mr. White and I'm the ERT lieutenant assigned to a stabbing that occurred on the ball field. "Is it okay if I call you Tony?" Tony nodded.

"Okay, Tony. You have been advised of your rights and to my understanding...." There was a knock on the door interrupting Mr. White. The officer that was standing by the door opened it. He retrieved a piece of paper and handed it to Mr. White. Mr. White read the contents of it.

"Well Tony, I was about to confirm the fact that you wish to remain silent which I can't understand why if you already told us that the blood you had on you was from playing basketball in which you scratched someone. But, based on some information that I just received, I think that talking to us about something may be in your best interest. I don't care if you talk about the weather or how many times a week you beat your meat, all I know is you need to start talking."

Tony looked up then looked back down at his shoes.

Mr. White figured that he may have to finesse him a little more. "Look, I'm going to give it to you plain and simple. Mr. Moore died at the hospital." Tony looked at him with an expression of terror. "This changes things, Tony. This is no longer an assault and you don't have the benefit of Mr. Moore not identifying you as the assailant. No siree...we have your shirt, and if that's his blood, that's all the evidence that the D.A. needs to get an indictment on you. He won't worry about you slipping through the cracks as you probably would in D.C. Superior Court, because he'll have you in Alexandria's District Court where the conviction rate is ninety-nine percent. Where they find you guilty not based

119

on law or motive, but what you look like. Just the fact that you're an inmate at Lorton is enough to give you the gas mask. Just imagine what a bloody shirt with the victim's blood all over it will do." Tony started to sweat, but he tried to keep his composure and play calm.

"I can't say if you're guilty or not," Mr. White continued, confident that his finessing tactics were slowly breaking Tony down. "But what I can tell you is that I'm giving you one opportunity to help yourself and tell me what happened, because this is not your style. I've reviewed your jacket. But maybe it was self-defense, I don't know. However, if there's someone else you're covering for, then you're going to take the rap because I'm only giving you this one opportunity. Then, I'm calling Alexandria Jail so that you can be officially arrested for murder."

Tony was hysterical. He had heard other inmates talk about Alexandria, Virginia's District Court system and how people often took plea offers because it was so hard to win any kind of federal case there. Tony lifted his head for a moment.

"Take your time, Tony." Mr. White encouraged him.

"Daryl did it," Tony spoke almost in a whisper.

"What did you say, Tony?"

"It was Daryl Jenkins," Tony confessed. Mr. White looked at the other C.O. and told him to get Mr. Jenkins' files. From that point on, Tony revealed everything about the incident, starting from the confrontation with Cliff. He gave horrific details about the relentless stabbing, which left Jimmy gasping and choking on his own blood.

The other staff members envied Mr. White's ability to manipulate, but they attributed it to years of practice, years that they have yet to experience.

*****

The Emergency Response Team raided the dorm that Cliff was assigned to. They entered through the front door and the back door. In the event that the E.R.T. swarms the dorm, inmates automatically assume that the unit is having a shakedown. Lots of yelling, curious eyes, and flushing commodes can be heard in almost every cell. Inmates were anxious to get rid of contraband items.

Cliff was on the phone when one of the officers approached him and advised him to cut his conversation short. He knew what this was about, but he figured that Tony probably used him as a witness or alibi. Cliff was escorted to the lieutenant's office without incident and even though he felt as if he had nothing to fear, he felt uneasy about being summoned to the lieutenant's office. The way he saw it, it was just like being summoned to the police headquarters.

The officers walked Cliff to the opposite side of the hall from where they had Tony. Upon entering the small room, Cliff was subjected to a body search, in which they were looking for cuts or bruises. Cliff turned around revealing his body. He raised his hand and flipped them back and forth. He was a little too quick and sly for them because they missed the bruise on his right hand. The one he got from punching Jimmy.

Cliff started to get nervous, because he knew that they wouldn't have went to this extreme if the reason he was in the lieutenant's office was to corroborate Tony's story.

Once again Lieutenant White felt the desire to exaggerate and profile his expertise. He stepped in the office. This time he had changed from his uniform. He was now wearing a jogging suit. From the moment Mr. White entered the room, he noticed something different about Cliff yet he couldn't put a finger on exactly what it was.

"How are you Mr. Porter? My name is Lieutenant White. Is it alright if I call you Cliff?" Cliff stared him coldly in the eyes and gritted his teeth. "Man you can call me by my DC number if you want, because it's not what you call me it's what I answer to that will determine who I am."

Mr. White was caught off guard. Cliff was out of his league because in all actuality, he was rusty. Tony was easy and that enables Mr. White's rustiness to go unnoticed by himself and others.

"Okay, Mr. Porter. Since you want to be a real live city slicker, I'm going to give it to you raw and uncut. An inmate by the name of Jimmy Moore was stabbed repeatedly on the ball field, and he later died."

Cliff stared at the table and said "Yeah...and."

"I've talked to Mr. Tony Young who had the man's blood splattered all over him and he recanted the whole story. Now, what we have is a federal murder case, which is punishable by death. We also have another inmate's name that actually did the stabbing and we have you and Tony as accomplices. However, Tony's no longer an accomplice, because he did the right thing. So...you have a choice to do what Tony did and verify his story, or deny any knowledge and ride with the other guy in the car full of death."

Cliff laughed at Mr. White as if he was joke. "Man you must be crazy...I haven't seen Tony in two weeks and I sure as hell haven't been on the ball field since the fair. So, if Tony's on your team, then use him. Oh! One more thing, please read me my rights if I'm under arrest, because I wouldn't want your little grand jury indictment or trial to end early because of a little flaw such as the-defendant-wasn't-advised-of-his-Miranda-rights. The tax payer's money is at stake," Cliff laughed a wicked taunting laugh.

Mr. White was annoyed by Cliff's antics. "Cuff him up and put him in the hole. We'll see who gets the last laugh."

After escorting Cliff to the disciplinary unit, a few officers joked and made fun of Lieutenant White's inability to control his temper after Cliff made his disgruntle remark. They immediately went to the dorm where Daryl was housed and escorted him to the lieutenant's office. They went through the same routine as with Cliff. They stripped and searched Daryl for marks and bruises. Surprisingly, they found a fresh scratch on the side of Daryl's neck. Mr. White immediately demanded that one of the officers notify the medical examiner's office and find out if there was any flesh particles found under Mr. Moore's skin. He felt like this, along with Tony's testimony, would be enough to convict Daryl, especially in Alexandria's District Court system.

Mr. White knew that Daryl was a cold blooded convict because he reviewed his institutional jacket. Therefore, he was certain as to what approach he would use, but he knew that he had to come correct.

"Mr. Jenkins. My name is Mr. White and I'm the E.R.T lieutenant." Daryl's expression was gritty. He held this poise for the entire confrontation. "I'm not going to bullshit you. The reason you're in here is because I have a reliable witness who says that you stabbed Jimmy Moore. I'm quite sure that you don't have anything to say. Am I correct?"

Daryl looked at him as if he was speaking a foreign language. "You're absolutely correct," Daryl responded.

Mr. White smiled. He had played this particular portion of the battle rationally. He didn't allow Daryl to make him appear as if his skills were rusted. He cursed himself for not making the same decision with Cliff. He wondered what his fellow officer's thought about his decision to allow Daryl to ponder on the limited information that he gave him. He was the man again, Mr. White assured himself. The officers escorted Daryl to the disciplinary housing unit pending further investigation.

Tony was also placed in the disciplinary housing unit, but he was separated from Cliff and Daryl, and placed in protective custody.

*****

Although a lot of years had been sacrificed to build and rebuild her marriage, Rhonda could honestly say that things with her and Melvin were no longer worth prolonging. It was time for her to move on. They had enjoyed a few good years, but barely endured others. They had conceived a child together, but lost the re-birth of their own romance. Now, her only romantic thoughts were of Tim, but she was a Christian woman, and she knew as long as she remained married to Melvin, she was living in sin. Therefore, Tim and Rhonda agreed that it would be appropriate to handle her divorce before they engaged in sex again.

Rhonda went through the proper divorce procedures. Now, it was all in the courts' hand. She and Melvin had discussed the arrangements for Roland. Melvin would be able to get him every weekend and any other occasions as long as he gave Rhonda ample notice. Rhonda would handle his school transfer and living conditions. She didn't even put the strain of having to pay child support on him. Instead, she trusted him to do his part financially and emotionally as a father should.

*****

There's no way that I could have missed this poem, Tim thought to himself as he browsed through the moonlighting book. Then he quickly considered the fact that he had gotten so engulfed in a few of the other poems that he hadn't had the chance to thoroughly review the book. Tim liked to stay sharp in the game and he felt as if this book would allow him to remember where he came from when he gets lax. He also felt that it would remind him over and over that just because people smile and make you feel good doesn't make them your friends. The *Aftermath* poem helped him see that. But, this particular poem showed him what he's been in the past - a *Gambler*.

Tim sat back on the sofa. He glanced out the window at Linda sitting in her truck. He would have to confront her soon. He never pictured her stalking him as a consequence. For now, he had to regroup his thoughts. He began to read:

Gambler's Theme

Something is wrong…

I'm feeling out of place,

I don't belong…

Without a name or a face.

I feel condemned to my own dangerous thoughts,

I try to blend in but still feel as if I'm lost.

Too many roads to choose, not enough time,

Staying focused on the rules is all in the mind.

Picture perfect aspirations define my disclosure,

I prepare to score within this war cause I'm a full bred soldier

I search for light in lieu of my height, in the darkness

That seems to linger I hold my throat after every note,

Never been much of a singer.

For the songs I've lived ain't nothing nice,

I'll side bet…you roll the dice.

While you're rolling...help me understand

What the game is about cause whenever I play I always crap out.

Tim inhaled the contents of the words that he had just read. He had played the game so many times and crapped out. His guess was it was not his game to win, but only to be a willing participant. Tim knew that if he didn't confront Linda, he would still be playing the game that he had been fiercely beaten at so many times. This time would be different.

He looked through the curtains at Linda sitting anxiously. He gained his composure. He was going to snatch victory from the jaws of defeat.

Tim stepped out of his mother's house nonchalantly and stood on the porch for a minute. As soon as Linda saw him she emerged from the truck.

"Tim!" she yelled. She was parked three cars down from his mother's house on the opposite side of the street.

"Don't worry," Tim said. "I'm coming to you. Can you get back in your truck?"

She was unsure if he was serious or not, but she complied once she saw him walking towards her. Tim walked to the passenger side of the truck and tried to open the door. It was locked. He heard a clicking sound then he tried again. This time the door opened.

Once he got in, they both sat for moment staring at the car that was parked in front of them, but thinking about where to begin.

"Why did you do me like that, Tim?" Linda said.

"I was upset because you left me and I wanted to show you how it feels to be all alone."

"But you ruined what I had with Ronald to prove a point."

Tim turned to face her. "No, not to prove a point, but to show you how it feels when someone you love turns their back. Fortunately, for you there's somebody like me here to help you through this. I had no one, but my cell and a walk man."

"But I told you that I would still be there for you."

"Yeah that's what you said, but I never got another letter from you and I couldn't call you just to listen to the sound of Ronald enjoying the life that was supposed to be ours." Those words lingered in the air. Linda was unsure of where to go from here, but Tim was.

"Linda, I didn't mess up what you and Ronald had by myself. You helped me and you were willing to leave him for the love that never left your heart." Tim paused and gathered his thoughts. "I'm sorry that it happened this way, but I was furious. I can't undo what I've done."

"Yes you can. We can make it work," Linda said.

"No we can't, because I can't trust you. Anything can happen and you'll give up in the long run."

"Well, if you don't want me, then you have to call Ronald and let him know that we were playing a prank on him."

Tim got quiet and looked out of the window. "He knows that it wasn't a prank because we made a bet."

"What the fuck?!" Linda was furious. "Why would he gamble with love?' she asked rhetorically.

"He figured if he lost, then you weren't his anyway."

"That's some cruddy shit to do to someone, Tim. You're going to get yours. Get the fuck out of my truck!"

Tim knew not to provoke the situation. He figured that the best thing to do was to wait until Linda started her healing process. He got out of the truck and walked back to the house. As Linda drove pass, she hurled a bottle that missed him by a few inches.

The mailman approached the house as Tim was walking up the steps. He tried to get the mail, but the mailman informed him that he had to place the mail in the mailbox. Tim waited then, he got the mail.

He noticed that there were a few bills as he shifted through the mail. Then he saw a letter from Cliff. He smiled, and then went in the house to read the letter. Tim noticed that the house was peaceful. He was grateful because of this, as he considered the noise, hustle and bustle that came along with life in Lorton.

He sat on the sofa with the letter and began to read:

What's up Comrade,

I'm writing this letter to inform you that things are not running accordingly. I don't want to go too far in depth because the heat is on.

I'm sending this letter so that you'll know not to proceed with anything concerning us, until further notice and to let you know that Tony is playing foul ball.

Yours truly,

Cliff

Tim understood the letter in its entirety. Playing foul ball was their slang for snitching. Something drastic had happened. Cliff didn't want him to send anyone transporting anything illegal on a visit. Tim decided that he would send two females down to visit Cliff and Daryl. He would have to think about how Tony should be dealt with after he got the full scoop on what's going on. He tore the letter up and threw it in the trash. When he looked up his brother, Calvin was standing in the door way staring at him. Tim stared back as if he was competing to see who would be the first to look away.

"Tim, we need to talk," Calvin said. Tim laughed.

"I've been trying to talk to you for years, but it seemed like you disowned me. No letters, no love, and no understanding. It took a while before I could even try to understand your abandonment. Then it hit me." He paused for a minute, leaving Calvin curious as to what he was about to say. "You were never cut out for the lifestyle that I inflicted upon you. But, you chose to be there enjoying the sunshine. Once it started raining you wanted out. Life is not designed for you to jump in and out of life's experiences at your convenience; especially, at the expense of others."

Calvin digested Tim's words thoroughly, because he knew that Tim was right.

"I know that what I did was wrong, but it was my way of experiencing one of the million mistakes that life has to offer."

"I don't want you to get things confused," Tim said. "What you did was right, but after you did what was right for you, you forgot about the love that existed between you and me before any of this came out." Calvin held his head down for a moment.

"Man, I just want you to forgive me for betraying you."

Tim looked at Calvin with a tear in his eye. He wasn't sure if the tear fell because of the self-pity or because Calvin didn't have a clue.

"It just ain't that easy, Bro. I wish I could turn back the hands of time and help you make a better choice. But the truth is you made your bed and that kind of pain takes time to heal." This time it was Calvin's eye that the tear drop fell from.

"I have to respect that, I'll give the wound time to heal and if it doesn't …I want you to know that I'm sorry and I love you." Tim nodded his head and walked upstairs to his room so that he could gather his thoughts. When Tim got to his room, he laid on the bed with his head faced down in the pillow. He had a lot of things on his mind and how he could get acquainted with his own business. His cell phone rang four times before he answered it. It was his mother; she wanted to have a serious talk with him when she came home. Tim told her that he'll be waiting for her.

*****

Cliff's mind was racing as he recollected the events that had taken place over the last few days. It was amazing how a small confrontation could escalate. It was unpredictable whether or not the dudes you run with would be dependable when shit hit the fan. The more he thought about it, the more it began to fit Tony's character. Tony had vomited at the sight of a stabbing. Tony really had nothing to lose, but his good name, but his name was nothing worth remembering unless it was affiliate with Tim, Cliff, and Daryl.

Cliff had written a letter to Daryl earlier. He told him not to worry about the stabbing, because if push came to shove, it would be their word against Tony's. Cliff was unaware that Daryl had a scratch on his neck that could possibly be related to the incident.

Several investigators had come by to question Cliff. The same information that they had when they came in was the same information that they had when they left. Cliff kept it simple. "It's been two weeks since I've seen Tony, so how could I have been anywhere he was?"

Tony had been questioned again and again. His story had remained the same, but with the results from the forensics lab for the skin under Jimmy's nail being inconclusive, there was not going to be a strong case against Daryl unless Cliff rolled over and corroborated Tony's story. The prosecutor offered Cliff immediate release, but Cliff stood strong to his morals and principals. "Death before dishonor," was the words that he spat at the prosecutor.

After an attempt was made on Tony's life, the institution cut off all visits and monitored the incoming and outgoing mail of Daryl and Cliff. Soon after, Cliff was sent on a federal load with a confidential destination. He was unaware that he wouldn't reach any destination for four months, he was just ecstatic to be leaving Lorton. He wasn't concerned with the drugs he left behind. Daryl was placed in isolation where he was only allowed one religious book and three meals a day.

*****

Tim heard the front door of the house open. He looked at his watch and noticed that only forty-five minutes had passed, but it seemed like he had been asleep for hours.

He heard his mother yell his name so he went to the top of the stairs "I'm coming down in a minute, Ma." He went to brush his teeth and wash his face, and then anxiously walked down the steps.

Tim's mother sat on the sofa with the look of exhaustion on her face. Tim sat down beside her. He smiled at her then grabbed her hand and kissed it.

"What's up Ma?"

"I've been thinking about ways to expand with different projects."

"Ma, I haven't even learned the pros and cons of maintaining what we have."

"You'll learn everything I have to teach you son, but the apartment building and hair Salon is yours. I've made quite an investment from maintaining the two for you and now it's time for me to build a few projects of my own."

Tim smiled at his mother. He understood. She wanted to do her own thing from scratch, just as he had done. He figured that he would probably need Rhonda's help in the beginning and if she wanted to build herself a career in business, they could earn the experience together.

"Okay Ma, I understand. If you need my help, I'm here for you. He kissed his mother on the forehead then went to the kitchen to get some orange juice.

"Would you like some orange juice, Ma?" he yelled from the kitchen.

"No thank you, baby."

When he walked back into the dining room, his mother was dozing off. He grabbed a quilt blanket from the closet and placed it over her. Afterwards, Tim went to his room. He reflected on the conversation that his mother had just had with him. He was having fun with the minimal responsibilities his first couple of months home, but he also realized that it was time to get down to business. After all, it was his business.

Tim picked the phone up and dialed a number. He had been hesitant to make this phone call, but he was a man of his word. Tim listened as the phone rang. As soon as Drew answered the phone, Tim heard a loud sound echo. *Pop...Pop...Pop!* The sound of a window shattering and his mother's scream soon followed.

Tim dropped the phone and rushed down the stairs in a frantic state. When he reached the dining room, his mother was faced down with the quilt over her head. Her body was shivering. Tim held his breath for a minute, and then he looked at the shattered window. He quickly pulled the quilt off of his mother. She looked up at him with eyes that were flooded with tears.

"I have to get away from this crazy city!" she said hysterically.

Tim was speechless. He was unsure whether she had been struck by a bullet or not. But from her statement and from his visual assessment of her, he could see that she was okay physically. He unlocked the front door and opened it slowly. There were people gathering around the sidewalk whispering.

"Did anyone see who shot at my mother's house?" Tim asked aggressively. No one responded. "You mean to tell me all of you just happen to appear *after* the gun fire?!" he continued.

"I heard some shots...I mean I think I saw a truck pass by...it just happened so fast."

Tim looked as the young man who was speaking approached him carefully.

There was a loud sound of tires screeching. Most of the people who were standing around took cover as the black Corvette turned the corner. Tim controlled himself through his excitement; he was cautious and curious as he tried to identify the individual behind the wheel of the corvette. Drew climbed out of the Corvette, with concern and confusion painted all over his face. He walked over to Tim.

"What's up, Slim? I heard the phone drop and you never came back, so I drove over here as fast as I could."

"I don't know what the fuck is going on, but I'm about to holla at this youngin right here who could possibly shed some light on the situation."

Tim's mother came to the front door with a streak of embarrassment on her face. She knew none of this was her fault, but the unsolicited attention to her home made her a bit uneasy. Tim told Drew to make sure his mother was okay while he talked to the youngin.

"What's your name, youngin?" Tim asked.

"Gerald," the young man said without looking at Tim.

"I know that you don't really know a lot but I would appreciate whatever information that you can give me."

Gerald had to get his thoughts together because everything happened so fast.

"I was coming from the store. When I turned the corner, I saw a truck passing by. It slowed up and then I heard a popping sound."

"What color was the truck?" Tim asked.

"Red"

Tim was awe struck. Even though Gerald hadn't given him the make and model, he knew that this situation could be no coincidence. It had to be Linda. Tim knew that this wasn't her style, but he also knew that love had a way of making people do some weird things; and revenge had a way of making people do some even crazier things.

Tim reached in his pocket and fumbled with a few bills. He pulled out a one hundred dollar bill and two fifty dollar bills and handed them to Gerald.

"Thanks youngin. If the police ask any questions, don't repeat anything you told me."

Gerald looked at the money that Tim had given him in disbelief. He ran to his house after thanking Tim. Tim looked around eyeing the spectators. The police had arrived. They were standing on the porch taking measurements and collecting evidence.

Tim walked up the stairs, passing by the police. There were two detectives questioning his mother. Drew was in the kitchen getting Tim's mother a cup of water.

"Mr. Johnson. I need to ask you a couple of questions," the detective said. "My name is Detective Smith and I need to know what happened here today."

Tim told him exactly where he was when he heard the shots. He didn't see who did it and he didn't know if the person or persons involved were aiming at someone else.

For some reason, detective Smith didn't believe him. Tim felt uneasy talking to a detective because he was always on the other side of the law, and even though he owned a legit business (which gave him no reason to feel uneasy), he was stuck in his ways. Tim refused to tell them what he knew. He would handle the bitch himself.

After the detective was convinced that Tim was either stuck on playing it safe or just refused to give up any information because of the street code, he directed a few questions at Drew. Drew couldn't tell him much either. He had been on the other line when Tim dropped the phone. He didn't hear any gun shots. He knew for a fact that Tim wasn't in a gang. He answered questions the way detectives expected someone who was guilty of something would answer them.

After a few police officers came in the house without any additional information to add to the investigation, Detective Smith decided to wrap it up. There wasn't much to go on, so he would have to trust that it was an accident. But he still was annoyed by the fact that whoever did the shooting is still roaming the streets and there were too many killers already roaming the streets of Washington, D.C. for Smith to take it lightly. Once the officers gathered their equipment and forensics bagged the evidence, they left and the same house that was filled with commotion and mystery was back to its quiet self.

Tim's mom had gone upstairs to rest while Drew and Tim lounged in the dining room.

"What is going on Tim?" Drew asked.

"Man...this shit is wild," Tim said as he tried to figure out where to begin. "I played a prank on Linda to get back at her for leaving me and ever since then, she's been parked outside of the house every day. She's been on some stalking shit. I confronted her and we left it at that, but the little dude that saw what happened described her truck."

"This is some serious shit. Do you want me to handle her?" Drew asked.

"I have to think about it. I really think she needs to know who she's fucking with, but I can't let it be fatal. I need to slow her down though."

"We'll get on top of it soon enough. Were you calling me because you had a premonition or what?"

"Nah. I have some things that we need to discuss."

"Like what?" Drew asked.

"Like business ventures."

"Oh…okay. But things are not the same on the streets as they were before you left, so we'll have to have a long talk."

"I want to make some major moves so that I can get out of the game for good. So what's pumping on the streets?" Tim asked with a curious look on his face.

"Everything is pumping, but if you want to make some real scratch, heroin is where it's at." Drew looked at Tim hesitantly, wondering if he should offer any additional information. "I thought that you were pretty well off before you got locked up."

"I'm pretty decent, but as soon as I start living like I want to live, my expenses are going to increase. I need to acquire some of this free wealth that they have to offer in Drama City."

"Some people may think it's free, but other people are paying a hell of a price. You should know. You paid seven years of your life for what you now call free money."

Tim nodded his head. He knew that Drew's statement had some validity to it.

"You don't seem to have a problem with taking risks," Tim said.

"Man, I'm still doing my thing here and there just like you would've continued doing if you hadn't got caught. But you need to know that the game is different now. These youngins out here are not playing. They'll kidnap you and take you to your stash house, then kill you."

Tim smiled at Drew. "I'm not trying to rush into anything. I'm just searching for options. I'm a businessman. But whatever I decide to do, I hope that you'll assist me when I need it, slim."

"I got your back, but I need you on these streets with me, not sitting in a jail cell."

Drew lifted his fist up and Tim connected his fist to Drew's.

"Make sure you call me and let me know what you want to do about that bitch. She could have killed your mama, nigga."

Tim hadn't considered that. Linda had come close to killing his mother all because of a charade that she initiated.

"Hold on for one second," Tim said as he reached into his dresser and got a pen and paper. He jotted down Linda's address and gave it to Drew.

"Look, you have to promise me that you won't kill her. I don't care if you break an arm or a leg, though."

"Okay, slim. I promise I won't kill her." They hugged then Tim walked Drew to the door.

CHAPTER 11

Rhonda was almost finished with gathering Roland's and her own belongings. She had unpacked most of the essential things and she had already conjured up an idea of how she would decorate the plush apartment. Tim had furnished the apartment, but the arrangement was that of a single man with his first apartment. He had good taste, but the structure was all wrong Rhonda thought as she filled a coffee pot with water and placed it on the stove.

She looked at her watch. She had approximately three hours before she had to pick Roland up from school. The phone rang and Rhonda rushed to answer it.

"Hello, Hi baby...I'm getting things in order. What about you? Uh huh...Okay I'll see you later. I love you." Tim called to tell her that he was going to bring some of his clothes over later.

Rhonda heard a loud whistling sound. It was the coffee pot. She walked to the kitchen and turned the stove off and let the temperature of the boiling water simmer before making her a cup of coffee. This was what she needed to get cranking. She moved the small table from the kitchen and placed it in the dining room. She grabbed the ceramic pottery from one of her boxes and placed them in several areas of the dining room. It blended perfectly with the furniture. She had accomplished a small mission of bringing some structure and jazz to the average looking apartment.

Rhonda decided to pick Roland up from school early. She wanted to surprise him, but she was unsure whether she would take him to Chuck E. Cheese or to Jeepers. She knew that it wouldn't have mattered to him one way or the other. She took one last look at her ability to design the apartment with such provocative detail then she left.

*****

This was Drew's field; a little out of his area location wise, but surely his line of work. He had been sitting in the black Caprice classic for nearly two hours and he wondered if he would be able to carry out his mission. He wondered what the end result would be.

Drew hadn't stalked a potential prey in years. His involvement in drug dealing had changed everything. He no longer had to kill people in order to earn a living. In fact, he paid other people to do the killing for him if need be. He could have hired someone to carry out almost any mission, but he sometimes missed the action, the thrill, and the kill. Drew never wanted to get rusty in his line of work so he had to keep his skills polished. He always referred to his prey as the target. This made it easy for him to detach his remorse or feelings from the victim.

"Who could have any remorse for a target?" his teacher would ask while he was training him. He certainly had no remorse for a target, but he did have an aim for one. He adjusted himself in the seat as he noticed his target walking to the automobile.

His hand was adjusted firmly on the glock nine millimeter. He felt a surge of nervousness rush through his fingers as he stepped out of the Caprice and rushed to meet the target at the killing point. He grabbed the target aggressively, pumping two shots in the leg. It felt so right for the predator. He missed the rush.

The target turned around swiftly. Her screams were compatible with his arousal. Her pain was defined by her lack of strength. His face looked so familiar to her. She wondered where all of her neighbors were as she collapsed to the pavement. The wind camouflaged her moans. No one heard the shots. He had a silencer. She recognized his face. He was a black comedian, but his face was so blurry now. She wasn't sure if he was Eddie Murphy or David Chappelle. He was walking away leaving her alone to die. *Please come back Mr. Comedian, I'm dying,* her thoughts said, but her mouth never moved. Linda passed out.

Drew got back into the Caprice classic and stripped the mask from his face. Then he picked up his cell phone and called the police, informing them of an accidental shooting. He smiled as he headed from Clinton, Maryland back to D.C. He put the gun, mask, and gloves in a shopping bag. He would bury them in one of his secret stash spots. He called Tim and informed him of Linda's mishap, and then he drove to his stash spot listening to the sounds of Marvin Gaye.

*****

Tim hadn't been to a club to energize himself since he had been released. He wasn't a frequent party goer, but he enjoyed going to jazz clubs. He skimmed through the Washington Post newspaper he noticed that a few jazz bands were performing, but tonight he wasn't in a jazz mood. He needed something that would alleviate his demeanor or compliment his struggle. He continued to thumb through the weekend section of the Washington Post until he came across something that caught his eye. Terrance Trent D'Arby was performing at the 9:30 Club on V Street Northwest. *This was it*, he thought. He remembered buying D'Arby's cassette when he first started dealing drugs. Just listening to the songs placed him in that time and place. It complimented his struggle.

Tim dialed the club's number on his cell phone to find out what time Terrance Trent D'Arby would be performing. He got an answering service that suggested he press certain numbers on his phone to establish different options. He hung up. The advertisement said that D'Arby was performing tonight, but Tim wanted to make sure because he knew from experience that the ad will say one thing then change without notice. Just like that kitchen menu at Lorton.

Tim turned his television on and decided to take a shower and get dressed. He was treating himself to a night on the town. He deserved it. He had big things coming his way. After his shower, he packed a lot of clothes in his Eddie Bauer luggage kit. He would put them in the trunk so that he could drop them off at the apartment.

Tim packed his clothes, but was unsure of what he wanted to wear to the club. He looked in his walk-in closet and grabbed a pair of trade agreement shoes by Kenneth Cole and a pair of Donna Karen rusted slacks. He looked in his dresser and pulled out a rusted Geoffrey Beene sweater and held it up to himself while eyeing his reflection in the mirror. *Perfect,* Tim said to himself, but one more thing was missing. He needed a jacket, but it had to be explicit. He opened the closet once more and browsed through his jackets. He decided that the leather Kenneth Cole trench coat was perfect. He wasn't sure if the weather had gotten a little cooler than earlier, so he called the weather information center. The forecast was slightly cooler than earlier and there were no signs of rain in the forecast. He splashed on some Fahrenheit cologne. The fragrance made him complete. It was time for Tim to experience the night life.

*****

Rhonda rubbed Roland's head as he slept. The trip to Chuck E. Cheese's really wore him out. He was so hyper and energetic at Chuck E. Cheese that it was hard for her to keep up with him. She smiled to herself as she thought about how excited he was and how quickly he had made new friends. Even though she was driving through the roughest part of D.C. her fear for being robbed or carjacked had subsided years ago. Partly because she had grown up in Southeast and she had become accustomed to the violence that plagued the city, therefore, it was either going to happen to her or it wasn't, but she wouldn't live her life in fear.

She was unsure if her girlfriend Yolanda would be home as she turned off of Alabama Avenue on to Stanton Road. Rhonda decided not to call her because she wanted the visit to be a surprise. Rhonda needed to talk to her friend. Even though it may seem crazy, she needed a stamp of approval on some of the choices that she made. When she pulled up to the house, she noticed that a few guys were standing by Yolanda's house. There was another group of younger guys shooting dice by an alley that was four feet away from Yolanda's house. One of the guys walked towards Rhonda's truck.

"You looking for some trees?" the guy asked. Rhonda waved her hand and shook her head "no" to the gentleman who was trying to sell some marijuana. Roland had awakened and he knew where they were. He got excited at the thought of going to see Aunt Yolanda as he referred to her. When they walked pass the three guys standing by Yolanda's house, Rhonda felt as if she was an exhibit as the stares they gave her seemed as if they were intended to melt her outfit away and reveal to them what was for Tim's eyes only.

Rhonda knocked on the door three times before she heard a shallow voice say, "Who is it?"

"It's Rhonda," she responded.

The door opened. What now stood in the door way was a slim, brown skinned good excuse for a black woman. Yolanda was well kept in the hygiene and personal appearance department. She held her four year old daughter in her arms with grace as she waved Rhonda into her house with a jovial smile.

You could tell by the interior of her house that Yolanda took a lot of pride in making sure her house was not like most of the other people who live in the projects.

She sat her daughter Tionna on the sofa and gave Rhonda a hug. "

"Come here my little soldier and give your Aunt Yolanda some sugar wugar," Yolanda said. She picked Roland up and frowned at how heavy he had gotten since the last time she saw him. Rhonda picked Tionna up and kissed her. They both smiled and hugged again.

"Damn, girl. It's been almost three months since I've seen you. What's been up?" Yolanda asked.

"So much has been up. I don't know where to begin."

"Why don't you start from the beginning and summarize it." Rhonda looked at Yolanda still unsure where to begin.

"First, of all Melvin and I are separated. Our divorce should be final this week."

"What!" Yolanda responded.

"Things weren't working out for us we started neglecting each other and I became complacent and frustrated." Rhonda paused in an attempt to read Yolanda's facial expression. No luck.

"As time went on, I met someone on my job. I was cautious with how I dealt with him, but in time he proved to be everything a woman could want."

"So, let me get this right. Unless you've been messing around with this dude the last time I saw you, it couldn't have been no longer than three months since you met him. Right?" Rhonda nodded in agreement. "Yet you left the man that you've been married to for um-teen years to be with one of your co-workers which you've just met?"

"Not actually."

"What do you mean not actually?"

"Well…..he's not a co-worker he was an inmate."

"Oh, I see. You left Melvin for a hardened criminal."

"No. He's actually a very handsome, intelligent, financially secure man with love in his eyes."

"Yeah, right. They'll have you believe that until they get out. Then they'll start making up lies about the money getting stolen or the car being impounded. Girl, you better get hip."

"He's not locked up. He's out and he just moved me and Roland into one of the apartments that he owns rent free."

"Damn, heffer…you done got your groove back?" Yolanda said sarcastically.

"This is no joke, Yolanda. Everything seems to be legit with him. He's a good man and we've fallen for each other."

"What's his name?"

"His name is Tim. Tim Johnson he owns Braids R' Us beauty Salon and Johnson Garden Apartments."

"What!" Yolanda uttered excitingly. "I don't know why you're so tense everything seems to be working out for you."

"I know, but that's what scares me. I've never had everything work out for me. I'm so use to making things work out; things are beginning to seem so superficial. It's like Tim was my knight in shining armor, but I wasn't ready to be swept away just yet! Tim used to sell drugs, but he says that everything is legit with his business." Rhonda paused for a second, and then continued once she realized that she had Yolanda's full attention. "I feel as if there's a certain lifestyle that comes with the hustle and bustle of the street life. The women, the high priced things, and the glamour. I just don't want to get caught up."

Yolanda looked at Rhonda with sympathy in her eyes.

"If you feel that way about it, give him to me," Yolanda said as she laughed aloud.

"See...I felt like I could come to you for support, but I can see that you're going to be of no help whatsoever."

"Damn, bitch, you can't take a joke?" Yolanda asked amused. "Okay since you've come to the Southeast Ghetto Queen for assistance, I'll help you, but I only accept credit cards."

Rhonda gave her a look that said I'm serious.

"Okay, okay, I'll bill you. First of all, it seems as if you've come too far to have doubts. You're getting divorced and you've agreed to move into the apartment, so evidently the question is not whether or not you should back away, but if you can be open with him and express your fears as they relate to his old lifestyle. Secondly, you have to give him a chance to show you what he's about. Trust is the dominant aspect of a relationship."

"I guess you're right," Rhonda responded. I probably over reacted when he told me that his ex-girlfriend was stalking him after he told her that he didn't have any feelings for her."

"Hold on a minute missy. You never mentioned anything about an ex-girlfriend stalking. Don't make me drag information out of you because I charge extra for that," Yolanda insisted.

"Well, he told me everything involving her," she lied. "But, I haven't asked him to go in depth about his past. Plus, I'm not sure of the details involving their years of romance, but I've come to realize that it must have been something wonderful going on for her to stalk him." Yolanda stared at Rhonda.

"Girl, ain't no use in you wrecking your brain trying to figure it out. When niggas go to jail bitches...some bitches.....hang in there for a minute, then they leave. Then they want to be all on a nigga's nuts when he get out, but what they don't know is nigga's despise them for it because dudes often feel like they can no longer trust the broad if she abandoned him. When Chris went to jail for six years, I was lost. I didn't know what I was going to do. It was hard on me the first few years, until I realized that I didn't have to be tied down to be loyal to a man. So I started dating and getting my thing off with a few dudes. I called them sport coats. But I never left his side neither. I continued to support him. And even though we are not together now, I can call and get anything I want from him because you never lose that kind of respect once you earn it. You can trust me, Tim doesn't have any respect for that bitch, and neither do I."

Rhonda was shocked at Yolanda's aggressive words, but she knew that her friend, the Black Ghetto Queen, was right. Yolanda had spent several years at the University of the District of Columbia (U.D.C.) pursing her Associate's Degree in Computer Science. Although, she never finished her education, her street smarts allowed her to be a Ghetto King's Fantasy.

Rhonda looked at Yolanda and smiled. "That's why I knew I had to bring this issue to you. Everybody doesn't understand the pros and cons of being a certified diva."

"Ha Ha, so you're a diva now?" Yolanda asked.

"Uh huh. You better know it." They both laughed as Rhonda gave her a hug.

Yolanda probed into Rhonda's life as they sat and reminisced. She listened as Rhonda gave her explicit details of how she and Tim met and the events that had taken place thereafter. Yolanda was happy for her friend. Rhonda promised to show Yolanda the apartment and let her meet Tim. A few hours had passed and Rhonda decided to let Yolanda get ready for a date that she was waiting on. They hugged once again, Rhonda kissed Tionna and Yolanda hugged and kissed Roland and they left.

When Rhonda got to the apartment, it was 10:45 pm. She saw some of Tim's clothes lying on the sofa. Therefore, she knew that he had stopped by. She tried to call him, but his voice mail was the only thing that she got.

She opened one of his luggage bags and noticed that he had a good taste in clothes. There was a lot of expensive name brand clothing inside. Some of the names she knew, but some of the others were foreign to her.

She told Roland to undress for a bath. She did the same. After both of them bathed and she tucked Roland in, she listened to Kenny G. on the compact disc.

Just as she was about to doze off, Tim called her. He told her that he was going to see Terrance Trent D'Arby and he asked her if she wanted to join him. She said no and told him to enjoy himself. He told her that he'll be home by 2:00am.

*****

When Tim reached V Street he drove around the block looking for a good place to park. After driving around for ten minutes, he found a parking space. It was one block from the 9:30 Club. Tim was dressed to impress as he waited in the short line to enter the club.

Once inside the club, Tim observed his surroundings discretely. This was a skill that he developed years ago. He needed to know where everything was that may have threatened his life. He noticed that a real live bunch of females were staring at him, but he played it off nonchalantly. He walked over to the bar and ordered a Bacardi straight with lime. He sat at the bar for a minute and nursed the drink.

The music that the disc jockey was playing sounded like it was coming from a live band, Tim thought. It was clear and crisp. He almost couldn't tell the difference when his song came on. He bobbed his head to the sound of Terrance Trent D'Arby's "Wishing Well." Then he realized that it sounded a little livelier than the other songs. When he turned around he was in awe, as D'Arby charismatically handled the microphone, stealing the attention of the audience. Tim moved to the music as the lime

Bacardi drink loosened him up. After D'Arby performed a few songs, he disappeared from the stage, and then the disc jockey took over. He played hits from the mid-eighties to the late nineties.

Tim was really enjoying himself. As he sat at the bar listening to a tune by Al B Sure, he thought about picking up where he had left off in the game. He had a business to elevate and there was no time to be wasted in the drug game. Tim had seen so many good men fall victim to the consequences of the drug trade....even himself....but not this time. This time he was willing to sacrifice everything so that he could score the big lick. He wouldn't take any prisoner's he assured himself. However, he would be careful with who he dealt with because that's the mistake he made last time. He dealt with a weak link and he paid for it dearly.

"You want another drink buddy?"

Tim was brought back to the present by the bartender's suggestion.

"Uh... Yeah. Let me get a corona with a slow gin."

Tim turned around on the barstool and observed the woman. They came in all shapes and sizes. They came from different ethnic background and cultural differences.

As Tim stared off into space, he was stopped in his tracks by the sight of a pretty young lady who threw occasional glances at him. Something about her was familiar. Tim's memory was temporarily incoherent as he searched his mind for a time and place in which he'd met her before. After struggling with his thought, the recollection struck him like a baseball bat he remembered. Tim waited for her to glance at him again then he motioned her over with one of his finger. She looked around then pointed at herself. Tim nodded and she walked towards him.

"Don't I know you?" Tim asked rhetorically. He had to talk over the noise of the music and the clubbers. She started laughing as she sat on the barstool beside him.

"What's so funny?" he continued. She looked at him and smiled.

"You could have at least offered me a seat before you hit me with such a typical corny line." Tim was offended but he didn't show it.

"Oh...I'm sorry. I hope that I haven't discredited my manners by not offering you a seat, but as I can see, you have no problem with taking what you want," he said referring to the barstool. "As far as me shooting you a corny line, I don't practice pickup lines, they're too hard to remember and it's easy to get them confused," Tim explained.

"Well if that wasn't a pick up line then you have to convince me that there's a slight chance that you know me, or guess what? I'll be convinced that it was just another pick up line and I'll be compelled to remove myself from your presence."

Tim noted how feisty she was.

"I may have been a little out of line," Tim said.

"Would the young lady that's accompanying you like a drink sir?" the bartender said, interrupting Tim.

"You'll have to ask her," Tim replied. Before the bartender could ask her she responded, "I'll have whatever he's having."

Tim looked at her inquisitively. There was something about her demeanor that sparked his interest.

"As I was saying, I don't know things about you, but I do believe that we have crossed paths. In fact, I'm so sure of it that I

would bet the rest of my night on it." She sipped her drink, and gazed at him as he continued.

"If my memory serves me correctly, your name is Ms. Johnson." The woman was stunned. He knew her name.

"Are you playing a joke on me?" she asked. She looked around to see if she saw one of her girlfriends standing around laughing. They were known for playing practical jokes and they knew that they couldn't send just anyone to catch her attention because she chose her men carefully.

"No, I'm not playing a joke on you. When we crossed paths, you probably didn't notice me because I was in a jail uniform. But I noticed you."

"Oh. You were locked up at D.C. jail?"

"No. I was down Lorton and the day I was released, I saw you. I realized that I was just another inmate in uniform once you passed me without a second look, but I knew that I would never forget you."

"Are you stalking me or something?"

"No. Us meeting here is coincidental, but what a wonderful coincidence."

"I think that you are at an advantage," she said.

"Why is that?" Tim asked.

"Because you know my name, but I don't know yours."

"Well I don't know your first name," Tim said.

"I don't know your first name or your last name," she replied.

"My name is Tim Johnson" She laughed as if he was joking about his last name.

"Damn, you are a stalker. I guess you married me in your little fantasy."

This broad has a lot of spunk. Tim suggested to himself. "Nah... That's my real name. What's your first name?"

"My name is Traci." Tim looked at her with curious eyes. He didn't know if she was serious, but if she were, that would mean that they had the same initials and that would be a little too coincidental.

"How long have you been home?" Traci asked with the intentions of changing the subject.

"It's been about two months now."

She looked him up and down in a sexual manner and said, "You're probably wore down by now. I know that you probably had the ladies going wild over you."

Tim blushed. He attributed her sudden flirtatiousness to the glass of lime Bacardi that she drank. Tim played his cards well, he didn't bite the bait.

"I'm a business oriented dude, therefore, I didn't waste any of my time trying to catch up on the females that I had in my past because I know that they come a dime a dozen. I also know that when the time comes, I will have the opportunity to explore my options, but I like to have something to bring to the table and not depend on anyone else to take care of this grown-ass man." He paused for body language. Her body language told him that she was all ears, which encouraged him to continue. "I'm not saying that I didn't get my man, but I wasn't running around trying to play catch up for the seven years that I was locked up."

Traci was turned on by his ability to take control of the conversation. "What are you doing at a place like the 9:30 Club?" she asked.

"I usually attend jazz concerts, but I'm a big fan of Terrance Trent D'Arby, so I decided to come and see him perform live."

She was truly taken by his personality. They both got silent for a moment.

"What are you doing at a place like the 9:30 club?" Tim asked.

"Well, this is one of the half-decent places that I can go to without being harassed by one of the ex-inmates from the jail."

Tim laughed aloud.

"What's so funny?" she asked.

"Now it's all beginning to fit. You thought that I was one of them dudes from the jail the whole time. I can't blame anyone for pursing you, but I can imagine that it gets frustrating."

They talked for an hour. She found out things about Tim that she thought was intriguing. Tim listened as she told him how her modeling career plummeted after she refused to sleep with her agent. They shared a lot of personal information. They even indulged in a good night kiss before exchanging numbers. Tim told her about his relationship with Rhonda, while she insisted that there was no one special in her life. Tim offered to walk her to her car, but she decided to stay a little longer. Tim was exhausted.

"I'll call you," he said before disappearing through the crowd.

"Bye Bye," she whispered.

When Tim reached his car he pulled out the paper with Traci's phone number on it. He kissed it for good measure, and then he hit his car alarm switch.

Once inside the car, he sat for a moment and gathered his thoughts. Things were definitely falling in place for him. However, he realized that things could quickly go sour in the game of life.

He called Sol and asked him if he took care of the plan for him. Then he called Rhonda. "Wake up baby, I'm on my way. I have a surprise for you," he stated.

When Tim got to the apartment, he was surprised to find the door open. He pushed the door gently and even more amused to find rose petals on the floor. The voice of Will Downing's "Can I" bounced gently off the walls in surround sound.

The sofa was filled with Rhonda's nakedness as Tim approached her with lust in his eyes. He attempted to take off his jacket, but Rhonda jumped up and stopped him. She started kissing him passionately, while rubbing his pants where she found a print from his erection. She was naked and he was fully clothed.

Rhonda unzipped his pants and took him in her mouth. She gobbled long strokes. Tim was fully aroused by her spontaneous wit. He tried once again to undress, but she stopped him. Rhonda kissed him some more while stroking his dick with her hand. She rubbed his dick on her face while taking short intervals to lick it.

"Damn baby," Tim said. This turned her on even more. She laid on the sofa and pulled Tim to her.

"Fuck me, daddy," she demanded.

Fully clothed with nothing exposed but his dick through his zipper, Tim entered her with ease. After a few strokes, her legs were around his waist compelling him to thrust harder.

"Oh God...Tim, oh Tim...shit...oh!" Rhonda moaned in ecstasy while Tim made long deep thrusts in and out of her pussy.

It was the high that both of them received almost in sync that complimented the next song that spoke gently through the speakers as Tim started to sing along.

"Kissing you, loving you all through the night," he sang along with Keith Washington while Rhonda kissed his neck gently. Tim was exhausted. He undressed and he and Rhonda fell asleep holding each other on the sofa.

CHAPTER 12

The sound of the phone awoke Tim.

"Hello?" he said with a squeaky voice. "What's up? Okay I'll check it out as soon as I get a chance."

Tim hung up and kissed Rhonda on her head.

"Let's get up, baby. I have something I want to show you."

Rhonda was exhausted. She fantasized about her and Tim spending the whole day together in bed, but she knew that they both had other responsibilities to tend to. Tim kissed her. Then he pulled her to the edge of the bed.

"Come on baby, you have to get yourself together. I know that I worked you out last night, but what did you expect?" Tim said sarcastically.

"Don't toot your own horn, stud muffin," Rhonda responded.

Rhonda got out of the bed slowly as if she was bruised. She washed her face, then brushed her teeth. Tim had already done both, so he waited patiently for her.

"What's the surprise?" she asked.

"Are you ready?"

"Yeah I'm ready! Well...not quite. Let me check on Roland first."

When she came back, Tim had a black scarf in his hand

"He's still asleep," she said as she looked at Tim strangely. "What's that for?"

"It's for the surprise," Tim said.

"Well, I hope that we don't have to go far because Roland is in there sleep and I hate to leave him alone for long periods of time."

Tim smiled. "No baby, we don't have to go far. Now let me blind fold you."

Tim placed the scarf over her eyes carefully.

"Is that too tight?" he asked.

"If it were any looser I'll probably be able to see everything," she stated in a sarcastic tone.

Tim pulled the scarf a little tighter. "Okay smart ass."

Tim guided her out of the apartment. She stepped strongly as her trust in Tim allowed her to. He held her hand intimately. She imagined that they were walking down the aisle that led to the altar. All of her friends were there and Tim's friends and family as well. The sounds of wedding bells filled the room. As she stood side by side with Tim, she heard a voice speak. She thought it was the preacher, but she realized that there was no wedding. In fact, she hadn't even realized that Tim had walked her through two doors and down a flight of stairs.

Tim unfastened the scarf, revealing Rhonda's fascinated eyes.

"Oh my God!" she said as she stared at the gold convertible Lexus SC430 that had a red ribbon around it and the words "I Love You, Rhonda" written with erasable marker. Tim had called Sol and arranged for the entire decoration.

"It's yours, baby," Tim said.

"What am I going to do with a convertible?" she said. Tim laughed.

"Drive it. I'll drive your truck. It doesn't matter as long as you know that it's yours to do as you please," Rhonda smiled.

"I love you, baby."

They hugged then walked back towards the apartment from the parking lot. Tim stopped at the news paper machine in front of the building. Drew had called him this morning and told him that the job had been taken care of. He also told him to pick up a Washington Post and check the Metro section. When they reached the apartment Roland was in the kitchen.

"Hey Big Boy. What's up?" Tim said.

"What's up, Big Man?" Roland responded.

Rhonda smiled. "What are you doing Roland?"

"Mama!

"Don't 'mama' me. You need to eat a fortified breakfast."

"What's that mean?" Rhonda looked at Tim and Tim shrugged his shoulders.

"That means a breakfast that will fill you up and give you strength," Rhonda said. Roland stared at his mother unsure of what to say.

"Guess what Roland?" Tim intervened.

"What?"

"I have a surprise for you soon."

"Oooh! What is it?"

"I can't tell you. That's why it's a surprise." Roland stared at Tim with curious eyes. He was anxious to know what the surprise was.

"Can you give me a hint?" Roland insisted.

"I'll give you a hint when we get there," Tim replied.

Rhonda and Tim embraced each other. Tim gave her a long passionate kiss. She was caught off guard because this was Tim's first time kissing her in this manner in front of Roland. Roland covered his eyes. He was embarrassed to see his mother getting kissed. Afterwards, Tim sat on the sofa and began to browse through the metro section of the Washington Post.

As he browsed he noticed the large number of homicides that had gone unsolved in the nation's capital. He then realized that the majority of the murders occurred in Southeast. Tim promised himself that he would get as much money as he could from the drug game in a six month period, then he would get out and relocate moving his family as far away as he could from Drama City.

Tim's heart pounded as he reached the article that concerned him. The article said that Linda had been shot twice; once in each leg. There was not a lot of information given in the article. It stated the hospital that she was sent to and her condition. Tim wasn't concerned with the horrific details. However, he was curious about the statement that she made in the article about seeing a popular comedian after she was shot.

Tim continued to browse through the paper until he reached the style section. He was looking for an appropriate play to take Roland. After searching persistently he came across the perfect play. He circled the address. He was taking Roland to see a play called *You're a Good Man, Charlie Brown,* at the Thomas Jefferson Community Theatre, but first he had to go to the Prince Georges County hospital to visit Linda.

*****

When Tim reached the hospital, he quickly found the location of Linda's room. His charm and wit allowed him to solicit information from vulnerable woman a little quicker than it would have been if he used the plain Jane technique. Tim walked into the room holding Roland's hand. He wanted to show Roland what happens to bad people.

Linda had IV's connected to her arms. She also had a couple of tubes connected elsewhere as well. She had trouble focusing on Tim and the words he spoke as she stared at him. Her vision was blurred and her hearing was inconsistent. Tim hadn't spoken a word yet, but it appeared to her as if he was talking.

"Hey Linda, how are you?" Tim said. He walked towards the side of the bed holding Roland's hand. "Silly of me to ask you such a dumb question."

He paused as she struggled to turn her head to the side to keep him in sight.

"You don't have to move if it's uncomfortable for you, just listen. Something similar to this almost happened to my mother. She was in the dining room and someone fired shots through the window. They could've killer her. Some little boy in the neighborhood said that he saw who did it. In fact, the truck that he described fit the description of your truck."

Linda tried to mumble, but Tim placed his finger on her mouth.

"When I read the newspaper, I immediately had to see if you were okay. You have to be careful in those streets Linda, especially when you start to create enemies. You never know what'll be waiting for you once you leave the security of your own home. Hell, my mother didn't even have to leave her house to be accosted; the predator came to her house." Tim smiled as he tasted the words of immorality that he spat with no remorse.

Linda squirmed in the bed. Her vision was no longer blurry. She could see Tim clearly now.

"Why...?" she asked she could hardly speak. "Me?" She tried to fit her words together, but the drugs that they gave her caused her to be incoherent.

"Shhh," Tim said. "Don't try to talk, you'll just make it worst. I just came by to let you know that I have a family now, so you have to let our experience be a memory." he picked Roland up.

"I want you to meet my step son. Say hi." Roland waved. "You made a choice, Linda, Please leave me and my family alone. If you want drama, I can play that game, but you need to know that when I shoot, I don't miss." Tim put his hand up in the form of a gun and mouthed, *pow*.

Linda started shaking the bed. She pressed the emergency button to alert the nurse.

"Let's go, Roland," Tim said.

Roland looked at Linda and asked, "Is that lady okay?"

"Yeah, she's just bored. She'll try anything to have some fun."

Tim put Roland down and they left the hospital. When Tim got to the Thomas Jefferson Community Center, he called Rhonda. She told him that she had got chosen randomly to work overtime. Therefore, she wouldn't be there when he brought Roland home.

She asked him if he wanted to take Roland over the baby sitter's house, but Tim insisted on letting Roland stay with him. After the play, Tim took Roland to Baskin Robbins for ice cream. Tim was content with Roland, because it was like spending time with the son that he always wanted.

CHAPTER 13

Cliff woke up only to find the bus that he was being transported in was still moving. The temperature was cool on the inside of the bus, but he could tell that the temperature on the outside was humid. He wasn't sure where he was this time. He wasn't even sure how many days that he had been on the road. He had no way of letting anyone know his whereabouts and the more he thought about it, they had no intentions on catering to his wishes.

Cliff had stood strong in the face of adversity. He remained silent when he was questioned about the stabbing, and in return, he was given a federal destination. The executive staff at Lorton no longer wanted him at the facility. The ERT lieutenant had a little clout with the transportation lieutenant. Therefore, he requested that Cliff be given a little diesel therapy.

Whenever an inmate became a disciplinary problem or refused to cooperate, he would be given a disciplinary transfer. Once he was designated, upon request the transportation lieutenant would not allow him to meet his expected destination for at least two weeks. In that case, the inmate wouldn't be able to receive mail or let anyone know his whereabouts. They called this diesel therapy.

Cliff didn't mind. He had been in far worst situations than this. The way he saw it, if this was his consequence for standing on his morals and principals, then so be it. Cliff laid his head back and dozed off. He wasn't sure where he would end up, but one thing was for certain, his time would still be running.

****

Tim was asleep when Rhonda got home. Roland was laying on the sofa also with his head on a pillow that was between Tim's legs. Rhonda was touched by the sight. She immediately went to get her camera. She snapped four pictures of them while they were asleep.

Rhonda quickly took her shoes and went to run her bath water. When she got up off of her knee from checking the water temperature, Tim was standing in the door way.

She jumped. He had surprised her with his sudden appearance.

"Hey baby," Tim said.

"Hi," she responded while giving him a kiss.

"I missed you baby! I wish that you could have gone to the play with me and Roland."

Rhonda smiled as she imagined the sight. "I wish I could have been there also, but we have the rest of our lives to experience special moments," she kissed him again.

"Can I take a bath with you?" he asked.

"Of course you can." They both undressed and got into the bath tub.

Tim told Rhonda about the play and the wonderful time that he shared with Roland. Rhonda informed him of the stabbing that occurred, which resulted in the death of Jimmy, and that Cliff refused to talk, but Tony had already identified Daryl as the assailant. Tim was not surprised, but he was furious. She also told him that Cliff had been transferred, but she wasn't sure where he was going. That would explain the return letters that Tim got back.

He understood exactly what had occurred. Cliff was experiencing a little diesel therapy.

*****

Four months had passed since Tim was released and things were running smoothly. His mother had ventured off into a commercial cleaning business, leaving the responsibility of handling Johnson Gardens and Braids R' us solely to Tim and Rhonda. Tim hired a financial manager to maintain the paperwork of both establishments while he exceeded in the drug game. Somehow his business was not his number one objective. Instead, he allowed his lust for money and the lifestyle of a street hustler barricade the plans that he had to get in and get out of the game. There was no need for Tim to stay in the game because his income was way above average, but for some people it's not as easy as just making a choice when you're powerless over your addictive mind state.

Tim and Rhonda's apartment was fully furnished. Tim had hired an interior decorator for the finishing touch. The divorce was final and Rhonda was completely his. As a matter of fact, Tim hadn't even had any further incidents with Linda.

Tim had an every other day routine. He would call Drew to find out where he wanted to meet. Then he would pick up a large quantity of heroin and marijuana. He would go to several different stash houses so that it could be bagged and packaged, then he would pay several of his lieutenant's to deliver the product to his runners.

Tim got into his truck and turned on the CD player. He fumbled in his pockets for the directions to Drew's new house. He pulled a piece of paper out of his pocket only to see half of the phone number written. When he pulled the paper apart to reveal the full contents of it, he was ecstatic. It was Traci's number. He met her at the 9:30 Club,

but never called her because he lost her number. He wondered if she still had the

same number. He grabbed his cell phone and called her.

After three rings she answered.

"Hey," Tim replied.

"Who is this?" she asked.

"It's Tim. The one you met at the 9:30 Club about two months ago. I had misplaced your phone number and I just found it so I'm calling."

She laughed.

"What's funny?" Tim asked.

"I was just talking about you to one of my girlfriends the other day. I'm about to go to work, but I get off at 10 o'clock tonight. Call me later and maybe we could hook up."

"Okay I'll do that. I'll hit you tonight. Bye Bye." Tim couldn't believe that he had finally found her number. She had something that was different about her and Tim liked it. Tim never planned to cheat on Rhonda but it was something about Traci that had him intrigued.

Tim drove to his mother's house first. He wanted to surprise her so he didn't call her before he left. When he arrived at her house she wasn't home. He wrote a short note then he left.

He decided to drive pass the beauty Solon. He hadn't been there in two weeks and he needed to show his face. Rhonda hadn't taken as much interest as he did. Maybe it was because it was *his* business he thought. Even though he tried to make her feel as if what he had was hers.

As he reached the intersection on Seventeenth Street Southeast, he noticed that a black Nissan Maxima was still in his rearview mirror. He noticed the car when he first arrived at his mother's house, but didn't pay it much attention. Now, it was obvious that he was being followed. Tim dealt with situations such as this before and he had friends who had been followed, kidnapped, and then robbed for large lump sums of money. Some of them were even killed, whether they cooperated or not with the kidnappers.

Tim on the other hand would give the would-be kidnappers the slip whenever he was followed. But this day and time, Tim had a new attitude. He had zero tolerance for anyone who would try to take what was his because they were too lazy to struggle until they got on their feet such as he did.

Regardless of the fact that Tim was still on parole and he was not permitted to carry a firearm, Tim insisted on keeping a .45 caliber pistol with him. The lifestyle that he had lived allowed him no room for error.

He wondered if coincidence could explain this situation, but he knew that coincidence wouldn't be so obvious. Tim watched his rear view mirror closely as he thought about what to do. Then it hit him. He had a plan.

He drove through Potomac Gardens in Southeast. Stopping occasionally to indulge in brief conversation with old friends and acquaintances, this was an opportunity for him to drive around the city. He drove through Arthur Capers with the hopes of seeing Drew, but he didn't. He would glance at the mirror from time to time as he stopped to talk to those who acknowledged his presence. It seemed as if the Maxima would disappear and reappear at its own convenience.

Tim realized that he had to take action. He told one of the dudes that he knew from Lorton that he was being followed. As soon as the Maxima drove down a distant street, he showed his comrade. The dude, whose name was Roscoe, got in his 300Zx. Roscoe informed two of his buddies of the situation and they got into their cars as well.

They circled the block from different directions. Tim pulled off in an attempt to lure the Maxima. It worked, the Maxima followed at a distance, while Roscoe and his buddies followed the Maxima.

When Tim pulled up to the stop light by the Navy Yard, the Maxima stopped at a distance. It was six cars behind Tim. Roscoe stopped two cars behind the Maxima and got out of his car. He tapped the window, but no one rolled it down to see what he wanted. The windows were tinted, so Roscoe couldn't see how many people were in it. One of his buddies went to the other side of the Maxima with his gun drawn and pointed it at the rear passenger side window. As soon as the car in front of the Maxima started moving, so did the Maxima. Roscoe hit the back window with the butt of his gun, but it didn't shatter. Then Roscoe pointed his pistol and shattered the rear window. The other dude fired also, but he missed the mark.

The Maxima skidded then drove pass a few cars including Tim's. It turned on to a small side street and disappeared from the assailants. As soon as the Maxima reached a safe distance, it pulled over by a corner store on Eighth and H Street Northeast.

The occupant got out the car to assess the damage.

"Shit," Linda said as she vented her disgust for the damage to the car.

Blocks away, Tim thanked Roscoe and his buddies for their assistance while they tried to figure out who was following Tim and why.

"Man, I don't have the slightest clue who that was, but my guess is that they were probably following you to learn your routine so that when they ran down on you they could get you along with all of your stash spots," Roscoe said.

Tim agreed because it made since. He had to be careful he thought as he shook each one of the dude's hands. He wanted to clear his mind of the event, so he decided to go down to Georgetown. Maybe he would shop or just sight-see. He wasn't sure, but one thing was for certain - he needed to stop by his Solon before he did anything.

After leaving the Solon he decided to search for an appropriate gift for Traci. He had lost her phone number and he wanted to show her that he was not just blowing her off. He stopped at a gift stand and brought a large white teddy bear with roses attached to it. He had a little time to kill, so he decided to call his brother Calvin and invite him to lunch.

Tim wasn't sure what he would say, but he knew that it was time that he made amends; even if he chose to continue playing his brother at a distance. He picked Calvin up from his girlfriend's house, and took him to Marcel's Piano Room on Pennsylvania Avenue Northwest. During the ride neither of them talked much.

Tim noticed that Calvin had on a second hand sweat suit. Therefore, he made a mental note to give him a few of his outfits. He felt odd in a seven hundred dollar Gucci suit, while his brother sported nothing worth remembering. Tim realized that everyone makes mistakes, but God is forgiving so why couldn't he be? He had learned a lot from reading the *Moonlighting Poetry Book,* which partially explain his new attitude.

When they got to the small eatery, Tim introduced his brother to the exotic dish called Marrakesh De'Paris Lamb Tagine. Calvin had a hard time figuring out what was what on the menu. Therefore, he basically had what Tim had. Tim glanced at Calvin a few times before he spoke.

"I've been home for almost six months now, and I've seen a lot of dudes that we've grown up with. When I see them still hanging in there with their cousins or brothers through thick and thin, I know that they are working together to weather the storm." Tim paused to gather his thoughts. "I can imagine that they have had their ups and downs, but they work through them. There's nothing I can do or say to keep you from being my brother. I don't condone what you did because it is called betrayal. But at least you didn't snitch on me. I could never have forgiven you for that." Calvin remained silent and fully attentive while his brother spoke.

"I hope that you don't think that this whole ordeal was like a walk in the park for me," Calvin said. "It's hard to walk away from such a lifestyle, especially when you don't have to do any work. I felt good going to school with a high rated image. I was Tim Johnson's little brother. I had respect and control. All I had to do is drive your cars and wear the nice things that you bought me. But, I started to get curious; I wanted to work the field instead of playing the background. I never mentioned this to you because I didn't know how to say it," Calvin looked at Tim wearily as a tear fell from his eye.

"I knew that I had either two choices. Take over and walk in your footsteps or walk away. I knew that if I would have taken over, then I would have risked the chance of momma being without either of us. I chose to walk away. I knew that I couldn't straddle the fence. I had to completely walk away." Tim paused before speaking while the waiter delivered the food to their table.

"I think that I can live with that part of it. But, I just don't understand why you didn't keep in contact with me," Tim said.

Calvin picked over his dish collectively before he tasted the lamb.

"Um," he mumbled. "This is good." Calvin placed his attention fully on Tim before he spoke. "I knew that if I was in touch with you, then I would have the desire to live the life that you lived if only to show you that your little brother could handle it."

The tears started to flow more rapidly. "I can settle for the smaller things in life now. Momma was not the same when you left. I couldn't add trauma to her pain. It would have killed her." Calvin paused to wipe his tears.

"Momma will let me have anything I desire, but I've learned to appreciate the simple things that life has to offer. I want to make her happy. And being able to see me every day is what makes her happy."

Tim nodded his head in agreement. He knew that Calvin was right. He knew that he would have urged Calvin to keep his drug empire afloat. The whole time he was holding a grudge against Calvin, he never thought about it this way. He listened and absorbed the message that Calvin was sending: You're either in or you're out. There's no straddling the fence.

This message encouraged him more. He had to get out of the game soon.

He hugged his brother then he kissed him on the fore-head. They both continued to eat while holding minimal conversation. This was a part of the healing process and it was time for both of Shannon's sons to start healing.

CHAPTER 14

Tim put his After 7 CD in the compact disc system, while adjusting the rear view mirror. He smiled to himself while he assessed his plan. He was going to take Calvin back to his girlfriend's house, then take Traci her present. Tim and Calvin talked extensively during the ride. This was the first time that Tim held a grudge with anyone and squashed it.

After Tim dropped Calvin off, he phoned Traci's house and informed her that he was on his way. When Tim arrived, he splashed on some Michael Jordan cologne. Traci lived in a quiet neighborhood on Longfellow Street in Northwest.

Tim rung the door bell and before long, a pretty figure answered the door. He was intrigued by her frame. Tim had forgotten how pretty and sexy Traci was until now.

"Hi," her soft voice spoke.

"Damn...I mean....um...hey!" Tim responded.

"Come in," she said.

As Tim walked in Traci's house, he visually inventoried her neatness. She had a few paintings on the wall that were very intriguing. The interior design of her house was respectfully coordinated. Tim was impressed with her style.

"That's nice," Tim said as he pointed at one of the Indian vases that were being used to stabilize a tall exotic flower.

"My mother gave it to me years ago," Traci said.

Tim couldn't help but notice her sexy shape as her ass bulged out of the side of her jeans.

"Can I get you anything to drink?"

"I'll have some water. Thank you. You have a nice house, Traci."

"Thank you. I inherited it when my mother died."

"I'm sorry to hear that," Tim said.

"She lived a very long time," Traci said almost silently.

Tim figured that the picture he saw on the dining room table was a picture of her mother. Traci handed Tim a tall glass of water.

"Thank you," Tim said.

She smiled then shook her head as she handed Tim the glass.

"What's so funny?" Tim asked.

"I was just thinking about your keen memory; unless you took a lucky guess!"

"A lucky guess at what?"

"Remembering me after seeing me only once."

Tim smiled and took a sip of water. "This may sound like a bamma line, but there's something about you that makes you hard to forget."

Traci stared at him persistently while trying to hide her blushing. It was obvious to Tim that her attention to him was mutual. Traci picked up the remote control and hit one of the buttons which ignited her compact disc player. The sound of Terrance Trent D'Arby's, *Sign Your Name*, whispered provocatively through the speakers.

"Damn...you sure know how to set the mood," Tim said.

"That's what friends are for," Traci said while staring at Tim indiscreetly.

"I'm still trying to figure out why a woman off such prestige doesn't have anyone in her life."

Traci sipped from the cup of water that she gave Tim. "That's what makes me a woman of such prestige. I don't settle for any ole thing that comes my way. And it's very seldom that I meet someone who's worth getting into. But, when I do meet someone who I can consider, their either gay or have a woman."

Tim looked at her surprisingly. He wondered how she probably reacted when she met a guy and found out he was gay.

"What would you say if I told you I was gay?" Traci spit the water out that she had just sipped.

"Damn...you're a cut above the rest. When we were at the club you said that you had a girlfriend. So I guess you have a gay lover also." Traci paused and thought about it for a moment. "Ain't that a bitch?"

Tim smiled and grabbed her hand "Nah, boo I'm just bullshitting with you. I like pussy too much to be gay."

"That's good, because I was about to be too through with you."

"So...if you have someone special in your life what brings you here, so far away from her heart?"

"Who said this was away from her heart? Maybe this is somewhat closer to her heart. Maybe you're a replica of her."

"Ha Ha, that's an insult. That's like saying you can replace us with each other whenever you're tired of one of us or whenever it's convenient for you."

"If that's what you really believe I would have to say that you have a very vivid imagination."

Traci smiled at Tim. She was using one of her manipulative tactics just to see where Tim's head was at. Traci had experienced many things in her life to know that different men dated different woman for different reasons. This is why she chose to remain single. She had found so much pain in meeting men and putting her all into a relationship just to get hurt in the end. That's why one day, she decided to do as they do and play the field. Traci switched C.D. Alexander O'Neal was now the musical momentum to set the mood.

"That's my man. I can see that you have a lot of class, Ms. Traci," Tim said sarcastically.

"According to who's definition of class?" She walked over to Tim and held his hand.

"I'm not the fliest dude in the world, but I have a pretty good idea of what class looks like, and if I had to sum it up in one word, I would say …you."

Traci smiled as Tim tightened his grip. They stared at each other passionately.

Tim stood up then he initiated a kiss. Traci gave him her lips. He tasted the moisture that he observed when he first laid eyes on her.

"Hold on." Traci put her index finger on his lip. "I have to use the bathroom."

"Okay, but don't take forever," Tim said.

Traci smiled as she disappeared into the small hallway. Tim fixed his eyes on the interior of the house. He was trying to get a feel for who Traci was. From what he had seen so far, he was happy that he had found her number. He needed another down ass chic in his life.

When Traci returned from the bathroom her demeanor was totally different. She was more upbeat and alert. Tim noticed the change in her persona and began to wonder what brought about the sudden excitement.

Tim noticed that she had gazed in his eyes several times when he first arrived, but now she was staring in his eyes with persistence and apparent lust.

"What do you do for a living?" Traci asked.

Tim glanced away. "I'm a business man."

Traci stared at him and then she giggled. "That's not telling me anything."

"You're right, I'm sorry. I own a small business." Traci looked at Tim curiously.

"That tells me a whole lot more."

"Have you ever heard of Johnson Gardens?" Tim asked nonchalantly.

Traci searched her memory for the answer. "The name is familiar. I just can't put a location with it."

"It's on Suitland Road."

"Oh okay. I know which complex you're talking about."

Traci was acting strange and Tim sensed it. When she got closer to him that's when he saw it. He wanted to confront her, but didn't want to falsely accuse her. Tim believed that she had a powdery substance under her nostril, but he knew that if he voiced his opinion and was wrong, it could cost him the beginning of a friendship which was barely just getting off the ground.

Traci kneeled down and kissed Tim. He was caught off guard by her sudden boldness.

"I like you a lot, Tim," she said.

Tim continued to stare in her eyes "Nah…you don't like me, you just like my doggy style," he said as he pulled her down on the sofa with him.

"Traci, you have something white under your nose." She wiped her nose, but Tim could see clearly that she had totally missed the spot, so he wiped it off and licked it to see if it was what he suspected. The taste was bitter and Tim knew exactly what it was. He had tasted a lot of heroin before purchasing his product and there was no doubt about it this was what he had tasted when he wiped under Traci's nostril.

"I have a confession to make," Tim said.

"What is it?"

"I haven't revealed to the fullest how I make a living."

Tim hadn't revealed his entire endeavors. Traci wasn't aware of the Salon nor was she sure to what extent Tim invested in the real estate of Johnson Gardens. She had met guys before who claimed to own certain establishments, only to find out that they only own ten percent of it.

"What I've told you so far is true, but I also have a side hustle." Tim looked at her to detect any negative body language.

"What do you do?"

"I'm a drug dealer. I sell what's similar to what I tasted when I licked your nose."

Traci was speechless. Tim had caught her off guard, but she was prepared to go with the flow.

"And how are you so sure that whatever you tasted is the same drug that you sell?" She asked with a curious look in her eye.

Tim realized that she was implying that he must be a user if he knows what it tastes like. "Every time I purchase my product I have to taste it. Therefore, I know what it tastes like."

"Is that right?" Traci said in a very sexy voice as she moved closer to Tim. She touched the front of his pants where she saw his slight erection flourish.

"Don't start anything you can't finish," Tim said.

"I can start it finish it and start it back up again," Traci responded.

She stepped closer to Tim and kissed him. He pulled away when he tasted the bitter substance that she transferred from her mouth to his.

"Damn!" Tim spat. "That shit is nasty. You need to brush your teeth because I can taste it."

"Okay I'll do that for you." Tim could tell by the glossy look in her eyes that the effect of the heroin was beginning to influence her. She was looser than she had been when he first arrived and it was fully evident. When she returned she was wearing nothing but a g string. Tim was awe struck by her sexy figure.

"What you see is what you get," Traci said as she walked closer to Tim.

He noticed that she had something folded in her hand.

They were face to face now violating each other's comfort zone, but they both seemed intrigued by the violation. Traci kissed Tim passionately giving Tim an erection. She felt the bulge throb against her pussy. Traci opened her hand revealing the folded envelope she had. Then she opened her other hand and dipped the straw in the envelope.

Tim could see the white substance on the tip of the straw as she emerged with the straw from the envelope.

The toot that she inhaled was quick. She dipped the straw in the envelope again and held it up to Tim so that he could join her.

"Nah baby, I have too much going for me to start slipping now."

"Just try it," Traci insisted. "I want some dope dick."

Tim knew exactly what she was talking about. The chemical in heroin affects the male in such a way that it prolongs ejaculation causing him to be able to have sex for hours without ejaculating. Traci caressed and fondled Tim persistently. She had put him completely in the mood and he was ready for action.

She took his clothes off for him and she was impressed by his muscular figure, but she knew that she wouldn't be able to receive his full potential unless she persuaded him to take a toot of heroin. She teased Tim continuously, not allowing him to get but so far sexually. Tim was so aroused that he finally gave in. He wanted a piece of this woman so bad, that all rational thought went out the window. When he sniffed the heroin the affect didn't immediately hit him. But seconds later, he felt as if he was going to be sick.

He grabbed his mouth suddenly and Traci guided him to the bathroom. After vomiting twice he was feeling the euphoria effect of the heroin. Tim felt free and easy as he kissed Traci.

They were all over each other like animals. There was no fore-play needed. In fact, the heroin in their systems demanded vigorous sex. Tim penetrated her with malice. She was lying on the sofa with her legs on his shoulder, taking all of him inside of her. They sexed for hours nonstop. Tim gave her what she demanded....some dope dick.

Tim still had a few more rounds of fun left in him, but Traci was worn out. They had started in the living room and ended up in the bedroom after spending at least thirty minutes experimenting with different positions in the kitchen.

Tim rubbed her breast gently trying to initiate a response of pleasure, but Traci was so sore that she only responded by patting his hand. As Tim laid there, the feeling from the heroin was mellowing out, leaving his mind more room to wander. There was no doubt about it; this feeling was what he was missing in his hustle. But, he wondered how people became so hooked on heroin. Although this was a beautiful feeling to him, it was not a feeling that he would want to feel all day long.

He would rather be in total control. He wondered why people went back and forth for more all day long, when the high lasted long enough for a person to be satisfied all day long. He knew nothing about a tolerance level. He never considered the fact that most junkies probably felt the same way in the beginning, but as their addiction progressed, so did their tolerance level.

"How long have you been getting high?" Tim asked.

"Two years," Traci responded. She turned over to face Tim and continued. "I had a male friend who was into it. He introduced me to it. As time went on, he developed a very bad habit, which eventually got him killed."

Tim looked into her eyes curiously, wondering whether or not he should continue.

"I've seen a lot of junkies in my lifetime, so I know how severe it can get. I guess it affects everyone differently because you seem to have your life in order."

"Well everybody can't be like Ms. Traci, because Traci is a bad bitch; you have to know when to hold and when to fold."

Tim kissed her on the neck "I hear you talking, Ms. Traci." He paused for a minute. "But don't they give random urinalysis where you work at?"

"Well, they only test people who are either under investigation or have tested positive in the past. They send the ones who test positive to drug treatment the first time, and then they give you a suspension the second time and termination if the person tests positive a third time."

"You've been doing this for two years so I guess you have it under control," Tim stated assertively. Tim decided that he would only snort a little heroin occasionally before sex. He was not the type that would allow him to be engulfed in getting high. He had a mission to fulfill. He was determined to make as much money as he could and get out of the game as quickly as he could without a scratch or a bruise.

He had a good time with Traci, now it was time for him to go home to his family, to his priorities, and to his livelihood.

CHAPTER 15

The mirror looked ugly. Maybe it wasn't the mirror, maybe it was the figure in the mirror. She rubbed the scar on the side of her face. Her mission had gone awry and she had nothing to show for it but her own facial scar.

When the window of the rented car that she was driving shattered, a piece of glass splashed on her face, leaving a flesh wound. She knew that Tim had a lot of friends and wasn't hesitant to use their assistance.

He had warned her. *You never know what'll be waiting for you once you leave the security of your own home.* Those words were sickening to her, but she became a stronger person after being shot. Tim had started this war, now it was time for her to continue the battle until she won. She wondered what exactly would be a victory because she didn't wish to win him back; instead she preferred to equate his misery to hers.

She picked the telephone up and dialed 911 . She explained to the officer that someone had been shot several times. She gave the officer the address and the name of the victim then she hung up.

When Tim got home, he was greeted by the savory smell of steaks. He approached Rhonda from behind as she stirred the contents in the pot. He kissed her on the neck.

"Hey Baby," Tim greeted.

Rhonda turned around and smiled. "You are something else."

"What?" he responded, wondering what she was referring to?

"I can't get Roland to talk about anything else but you and the wonderful time you showed him."

"Don't be jealous. I think that it would be nice if the three of us could go when you decide to take me." Tim pulled his hand from behind his back and handed her the teddy bear with the roses attached to it's hand. He forgot to give it to Traci, but he figured that Rhonda was well worth it. She kissed and thanked him continuously. Then she sat the bear on the dining room table.

Roland was in his room sleep when Tim peeped in to check on him. Tim went to the bathroom and washed his hands, then joined Rhonda for a candle light dinner. Afterwards, Tim explained to Rhonda that he had to review some pertinent paperwork pertaining to Braids R' us. Tim felt uncomfortable with the thought of making love to her after his ordeal with Traci. This was a life he would have to get used to all over again. Tim and Rhonda's room was very plush. Rhonda had decorated it. There was a Persian rug at the entrance of the room that complimented the flavorful coordination of the walls, pillows, and matching sheets. They were white with black and beige under tones. Tim's small office desk sat in the corner of the room along with a small cabinet in which he kept his files. Their room was very spacious. Tim sat on the bed eyeing the paperwork that was evidently in need of his supervision.

Tim thought about the *Moonlighting* book and how much time that passed since he last read it. Tim looked in his closet and shuffled through a stack of books until he reached the book. He flipped through the pages reviewing some of the poems and philosophies that he had previously read until he found something that caught his attention. It was a philosophy. The more he read it, the more it made sense to him:

Here I lay in the wake of confusion, struggling with uncertainties, trying my best not to try enough.

This was him. Even though he had plenty of options, his current demise lies in the wake of confusion and he struggled with the uncertainty of what life would bring his way next. He wasn't focused on running his business. Therefore, he wasn't trying enough. Tim decided that he needed to take Rhonda out to dinner or something. He needed to ease his mind and he also needed to refocus on his priorities.

It was hard for Tim to run a successful business and continue his hustle because he always had his mother in control of his business. Tim needed no assistance in the area of drug dealing. This was what he did best. He closed the *Moonlighting* book and put it in his drawer.

The bedroom door opened slowly, revealing Rhonda and a plate that she was holding with a New York strip steak and a baked potato on it.

"Damn, that looks good," Tim said as he walked towards her and grabbed the plate as she handed it to him.

"It's for a good looking man!" Rhonda said as she kissed him.

"It's coming from an even better looking woman," Tim responded.

Rhonda gave him a slight shove then kissed him again for good measure.

"We're going out tomorrow," Tim said out of the blue.

"We're going where tomorrow?"

"I'm taking you out. Not Roland, just you."

"Oh let me guess, it's a surprise."

"You are smart. What high school did you graduate from? Oh let me guess! Spingarn...Dick Street Academy...or was it H.D. Woodson?" He was being sarcastic.

"For your information, I graduated from Dunbar," Rhonda said as she grabbed his fork that had a chunky piece of steak hanging at the tip of it.

"Um...this is good!" Rhonda said admiring her own expertise.

"I have something that's even better," Tim said humorously.

"I'll try it if you try it first," Rhonda responded.

"I don't think you understand. This meat was made for woman only. It has the fortified vitamins and minerals to balance a healthy eating habit. It may be strong enough for a man, but it's made for a woman."

Rhonda looked at him curiously, and then laughed. Tim was happy with her. He wanted to make this relationship last until the greatness of it expired. As the months passed, Tim became more intimate with his past lifestyle. He began to get larger shipments of heroin once he found out that Sol was using his car business to transport drugs. Tim was bringing in fifty thousand dollars a week through his distribution of drugs.

Rhonda had resigned from her job as a correctional officer so that she could uphold the financial responsibility of Braids R' Us and Johnson Gardens Apartments.

Tim had plenty of drugs circulating in Southeast and Northwest. This was where heroin sold rapidly. He also had a high priced gambling habit that he was developing for snorting heroin thanks to Traci's influence.

This didn't stop his flamboyant attention towards Rhonda. He constantly took her to places like the Arena Stage, the Improv Comedy Club, and Blues Alley. They moved out of the apartment into a townhouse in Charles County, Maryland but Tim continued to frequent his ties in D.C.

Tim parked on the narrow street. He got out of his new pearl colored Cadillac Escalade. The small device that emerged from his pocket with the help of his right hand beeped twice as he punched a button to activate his alarm system. Tim was wearing a jogging suit that he had brought from a local store called Identity Sports and a pair of 498 New Balance running shoes. He smelled the scent of fried chicken coming from a distance as he approached Traci's house. She was expecting him so she was already looking out of the window when he approached the door. Before he could knock on the door, it opened revealing a very sexy nude body.

"Damn," Tim said in an ecstatic tone. "Expecting someone special?"

"As a matter of fact I am," Traci said.

"He must be a lucky dude," Tim said as he walked in Traci's house. He grabbed the side of her hips and squeezed softly while admiring the softness that complimented his touch.

"I won't say that he's lucky, but I will say that he's blessed...really blessed," Traci responded in a sexy tone. Tim noticed that she had rearranged her house since the last time he was there. He also noticed that she wasn't high. Therefore, he decided to enhance the moment. Tim reached in his pocket and pulled out a large zip lock bag. He flashed it at Traci. Tim wasn't surprised to see the look of enchantment on her face as she focused on the beige substance that filled a quarter of the bag.

"This is for you baby, so that you don't have to go out in the streets and risk your life or your freedom in an attempt to cop you some blow." Tim handed her the bag then he pulled a straw from his pocket and waved it, letting her know that he wanted to treat his nose to a snort, so that he could give her a dose of dope dick. She opened the bag and Tim dipped the straw in it. When he pulled the straw out, he had a sufficient amount of heroin in it. He held it up to his nose and snorted it. He repeated this in both nostrils several times. There was no vomiting or sickness though. He had developed a tolerance level. Tim had frequently visited Traci. Most of their encounters were sexual.

Every encounter always included heroin use, except for a few occasions when Tim chose to smoke a joint of marijuana.

In the beginning, Tim was hesitant when offered heroin by Traci. Eventually, it became routine. He snorted heroin mostly when he was with her, but lately he had been dipping in his stash whenever he had to travel long distances to retrieve or distribute his narcotics. The effect from the drug kept him alert and on point. He was also able to use his persuasive techniques more adequately while under the influence of the drug.

Whenever someone would snort the drug the slang term that they used to describe it would be a "one on one." Normally, Traci would have treated herself to a "one on one," but today she wanted to be in her right mind while Tim sexed her. She was curious to see what it was like to be fucked without the stimulation of the heroin. Traci decided that if it was less intense then she would go back to the usual.

Tim undressed himself as the euphoric effect plagued his bodily function. He was becoming extremely aroused as Traci caressed and kissed his chest. He was certain that he had identified what was missing from his life and lately he had been successful at fulfilling the void. The heroin allowed him the freedom that he had desired.

Traci took all of his manhood into her mouth. Her ass was soft and firm, causing Tim to be helpless at restraining himself from gripping it firmly. Not that he would hesitate. She gave his dick her full attention, leaving his balls hanging freely and begging for the same arousal.

Tim pulled the back of her hair gently letting her know that he was ready to apply the same pleasure that she had given him thus far. Traci sat on the top of the sofa allowing Tim free access to the glory of her wet pussy.

With his knees bent and the seating of the sofa comforting him, Tim sucked and licked her pussy swiftly while fingering her in the ass.

"Oh! Tim. This is your pussy," Traci moaned. Tim could never indulge in foreplay with Traci for long because her moans were always too much for him to handle, in addition to the intense feeling that the heroin gave him.

The initial penetration came quicker than Traci thought it would, but the deep thrust that Tim gave blended perfectly with Traci's need to be dope dicked.

"Oh! Shit" Tim screamed as Traci's pussy walls smothered his erection. They sexed for hours. Tim discovered positions that he vowed to himself to try on Rhonda. But for now, Traci was the center of his attention, leaving him no room for thoughts of Rhonda. When they were finished, Tim recollected his thoughts. He wondered how long it would be before Traci demanded more of his time. He wondered if she was really as content as she claimed to be each time he left her knowing that he was going home to Rhonda. His thoughts continued to elaborate as his newfound tolerance for heroin set in.

"What are you thinking about?" Traci asked. They were lying on the sofa cuddling.

"There's so much to think about. I couldn't possibly break it down to you in such a limited time."

Traci squeezed his hand. "Who says that our time together has to be limited?"

"My life and my responsibilities," Traci knew why, she just wanted to hear him say it.

Tim was hiding behind his craving for another one on one, so to camouflage his desire, he misled Traci.

"Whenever you decide that I have the ears that you want to listen to your problems or your thoughts, then I'm right there," Traci said.

"I know baby," Tim rested his head on her breast gently. He wondered where Daryl and Cliff were and if they were still doing their time as if every day counted. Of course they were; he had instilled it in them.

"I have to go and take care of some business. Are you going to be okay?" Tim asked.

"I don't know. It all depends on how long you're leaving me this time."

"I won't be gone forever that's for sure."

Tim kissed Traci. Then he gathered his clothes and quickly dressed. He needed to get high, but he didn't want her to know. He had given her enough heroin for herself and he knew that it would last her because she didn't use very often. When Tim left, he went to 16th Street Northeast near the Trinidad area of Washington, D.C. The drug strip was crowded as usual. He saw a few dudes that he knew and they acknowledged each other's presence by waving. He watched the eyes of curious bystanders as they eyed his escalade. When Tim saw who he was looking for he honked his horn.

"What's up slim?" The short bow-legged dude said. He was dressed in a gray and white Hobo sweat suit. Hobo was a local clothing store brand name. It stood for Helping Our Brother's Out.

"Hop in," Tim said while unlocking the door.

"Pull around this corner," the short dude told Tim. His name was Corey and he was in charge of distributing the heroin and keeping track of who had how many bundles of heroin and ten dime bags of heroin was a bundle. Tim was never concerned with who had what. His sole concern was making sure that his lieutenant gave him the amount of money that they had agreed upon. The lieutenant was in charge of overseeing the whole operation. For each section of the city that Tim supplied with blow, he had a lieutenant.

When they turned the corner onto a small quiet street, Corey pulled out a small bag. He reached inside of it and handed Tim ten thousand dollars. They were hundred dollar bills separated in bundles of twenty which equaled two thousand a bundle.

Tim didn't like small bills. Therefore, his lieutenant would have to go to the bank or find other means of transferring small bills into larger bills. Although Corey wasn't the lieutenant, he was assigned to the responsibility because Mike had gotten arrested.

"What the hell did Mike do?" Tim asked.

"He's at the jail" Corey responded.

"I know that. But what did he do to get there?"

"He got into it with Brenda."

"What?" Tim said in disbelief.

"I told him to leave that bitch alone. He's on parole and he knows that we're getting too much money for this bullshit. Don't worry slim, I'll hold everything down on this end until he get his situation sorted out."

Tim didn't speak. He glanced out of the window at two birds fighting over a piece of bread that an old lady had tossed out of her window.

"I'm not worried. He's the one that should be worried. As a matter of fact, I'm promoting you to lieutenant. I want you to assign one of your runners to your former job as the distributor. Give him the whole run down on his responsibilities and page me next week so that I could meet him."

Corey smiled. "Okay." As he opened the door to step out, Corey turned around and said, "Oh I almost forgot, Brenda is pressing charges against Mike."

"Thanks I'll pay her a visit." As Tim exited from the small street, he saw bystanders staring at his escalade in awe. He'd been home for almost a year and a half and there was no doubt about it, the streets of D.C. belonged to him.

CHAPTER 16

"Get out of the street!" a thin old lady yelled at her granddaughter as Tim drove up. The housing dwelling of East Gate was once a breeding ground for drugs and violence. Now stood a respectable pennacle of townhouses filled with law abiding citizens who vowed to never let East Gate revert to the days that havoc and chaos was an everyday venture. Those days lasted from the late 70's until the early 90's. Tim sat for a moment outside of a yellow house on F Street Southeast.

He wondered what approach he would use. He wondered what effect, if any, would he have on Brenda. He already knew the answer. Tim got out of his truck and stretched. He looked around in amazement at how well East Gate had been rehabilitated. Before Tim went to prison he had a few comrades in East Gate who he supplied with P.C.P. The money that they hustled up was seventy percent of his income.

Tim knocked on the door softly. After getting no response, he knocked harder.

A little boy opened the door. Before Tim could speak, a taller figure appeared in the doorway.

"Can I help you?" Brenda said unsure of who he was.

"My name is Mr. Tim Johnson and I need to talk to you about an important matter concerning Mike." Tim was trying to sound professional and his professional demeanor was appearing to have an effect on Brenda. She was curious to know what his visit was about so she invited him in.

Brenda was five foot six, light skinned with short red hair. She weighed a hundred and forty pounds. Tim complimented Mike's taste mentally and he wondered why any man would even consider putting their hands on someone so pretty.

"Would you like something to drink?" Brenda asked.

"Uh…Nah…No thanks, but I would like to use your bathroom if that's okay?"

"Yeah, sure. It's right up the stairs, you can't miss it." She pointed her finger to show him the direction.

As he walked towards the stairs, he noticed several pictures with Brenda and Mike in them. They seemed to be inseparable. Tim needed a one on one to enhance his manipulation skills if need be. Once he came out the bathroom, he was ready for the world. He had taken a heavier snort than usual and the effect was unbelievable.

"I see that you and Mike have had a lot of memorable moments?"

"What do you mean?" Brenda asked.

"The pictures. You two look very happy."

"Oh…yeah. That was very many years ago. Things are not as romantic as they were then." Brenda paused for a second and glanced at one of the pictures.

"If you don't mind me asking, who are you? And why are you here?"

"Oh I'm sorry!" He was ecstatic. The heroin was really kicking in. "Again, my name is Mr. Tim Johnson." Tim handed her his business card. "I own Johnson Gardens apartments and Braids R' Us hair Solon. Michael Morris is one of my employees. Even though he hasn't been employed for long, I have found an interest in his style and performance. I wanted to possibly promote him to a position that would make him a wealthy young man in the years to come. However, I was informed that he was arrested a few days ago."

Brenda was stunned by Tim's approach and the information that he gave her.

"Are you okay?"

"Yes…yes …This is a shock to me. I mean Mike had told me that he had some good news for me. I didn't even know he was working."

"I understand. We were aware of his criminal past and we gave him a shot. But I can't use him if he has another conviction. It would hinder the integrity of my business."

Brenda listened with a concerned look on his face. She thought about their future together and wondered if their relationship was insane.

"How long have you two been together?"

"It's been eleven years now."

"Do you have any kids?"

"Yeah…we have a son, he's five years old. He's staying with Mike's mother."

Tim knew the answer to most of the questions that he asked Brenda. His motive was to get her to open up to him so that he could comfort her emotionally. This was one of his manipulative tactics.

"If you don't mind me asking, what happened between you two?"

Brenda stared at Tim for a moment. "My lawyer advised me not to discuss the incident between us with anyone but him."

Tim looked away from her and stroked his fingers with his hand. "I understand."

He probed his mind for a method of getting Brenda to confide in him.

"I went to visit him once I became aware of the charge that was filed against him. He assured me that it wasn't what it seemed to be. I explained to him that I had a problem with spouse abuse in which I had to get treated for. It's an ugly thing if you allow it to go untreated," Tim was using his tactics to the fullest extent.

Brenda had a look of admiration in her eyes as she began to open up to Tim.

"Mike is a good man. He just has a very jealous streak. He reacts to the smallest hint of someone else trying to impede on his turf."

"Does he consider you his turf?"

"Yes. But I've told him again and again , He didn't have to worry about me cheating because I'm happy with him. We argue from time to time, but whenever he feels that he no longer has control of the argument, he gets physical. I used to think that it was my fault, but I finally realized that no one deserves that kind of abuse. He never hits me with his fist closed, but that doesn't make it right either."

Tim decided to reverse his intentions just to see her reaction.

"I'm beginning to understand. I guess I don't need anyone working for me who displays that kind of aggression. It shows that he lacks good communication skills. I guess that he'll get found guilty then the parole board will probably make him do back time. Um…he won't be home for at least five years."

Brenda was mesmerized by this assumption. She never considered the fact that he would be gone for such a long period of time. She just wanted him to get some help.

"Do you really think he'll be gone that long?"

"Of course I do, I've seen it happen before. I have a history of hiring ex-offenders because I believe that some of them can change, but every now and then I'm wrong. I've attended parole hearings as a representative for a few of my ex-employers who were violated by the parole board and I can tell you that it ain't nothing nice."

Brenda pondered her thoughts for a second. "I don't want him to go to jail, but I don't want him to feel as though he can abuse me at will."

"I understand. The ball is in your court. I'll consider letting him remain employed with my establishment, but he'll have to remain in treatment for at least six months. I guess you'll have to consider all of the people who'll be negatively affected if he goes to prison."

Tim was sort of surprised by his own ability to control the confrontation. He normally used money, sex, or violence to persuade those who were not easily persuaded.

"Okay, I'll drop the charges. I'll notify my lawyer and make him aware of my decision."

Tim knew that he had to play this to the fullest he couldn't let his guard down.

He grabbed her hand gently. "Are you sure that this is what's right for both you and your family?"

Brenda nodded her head slowly.

"Don't be afraid. I'll give him only one chance and if he chooses to abuse you then he'll throw away a future worth having."

Brenda walked Tim to the door. "I'll keep in touch with you, Mrs. Morris. And if you like, I will arrange it so that you can sit in on a few of his sessions."

"Okay, but only if Mike will allow it."

Tim wondered where Mike had found such a beautiful soul and why Mike hadn't put a ring on her finger. He had called her Mrs. Morris only to make her feel a little more obligated to his best interest. He reached in his pocket and pulled out one of the rolls of money that he had gotten from Corey and handed it to Brenda.

She looked at it strangely. "What is this for?" she asked.

"I told you I was in the same predicament before and I know that my wife had to spend unnecessary money traveling back and forth to court and to furnish a lawyer. I understand, Brenda."

She was taken by his demeanor and willingness to provide in areas that anyone else could care less about.

"Thank you very much Mr. Johnson, I don't know what to say."

"You've said enough. I have to be on my way, my employees seem to fall apart whenever I'm gone too long." They both laughed, then Brenda waved him off as he headed to his truck.

When Tim got home, he was still feeling a buzz from the one on one that he snorted while at Brenda's house, but the high was quickly fading. He never got high in the apartment before, but he couldn't stand the fact that his high was decreasing and his craving was soaring. He looked at his watch and wondered if Rhonda would be home early today. It was 2:35pm and Rhonda would often come home before going to get Roland. He knew that Rhonda was capable of detecting the slightest mood change.

Shit he said to himself as he walked into the bedroom looking for some scissors to cut a straw with. He was satisfied when he found a razor instead. Tim dipped the razor into his small zip-lock bag, filling the tip with a beige colored substance. His product was always good, but lately he found himself having to use more and more just to get his desired effect.

Tim snorted two over-sized dosages in each nostril. His goal was to get high enough to finish some paperwork, Then doze off for a few hours. Instead, he ended up listening to some of his old compact discs.

He listened to Teddy Pendergrass, Al Green, and Lionel Richie before nodding off.

He was brought back to life by the sound of a key turning in the look. Rhonda walked into the house and quickly set her brief case down. She jetted pass Tim who had risen from the sofa to greet her.

"Hey baby," she said as she rushed to the bathroom.

Tim was caught off guard by her sudden arrival. He quickly reached into his pocket and grabbed his zip lock bag and his straw. He snorted a one on one in each nostril in an attempt to revive the feeling that had become a requirement for him. By the time Rhonda came out of the bathroom he was on cloud nine. He grabbed her and gave her a hug and a passionate kiss.

"You better be careful, you might get yourself into something you can't get out of," Rhonda said while Tim held her in his arms.

"Don't make promises that you can't keep," Tim responded. He stuck his hand down her skirt and rubbed her pubic hairs gently. He fondled her for a moment until he found what he was looking for. Her clitoris seemed to be standing at attention as his finger rubbed it attentively. Tim was overly aroused as his erection rubbed against Rhonda's leg.

Rhonda unzipped the back of her skirt allowing it to drop to her feet. But Tim returned her skirt to her waist; he had other plans. She looked at him curiously, but her trust in him enabled her not to question his motives. Tim unzipped his pants and rubbed his dick on her legs. He raised her skirt pass her waist, allowing access to her pussy. After pulling her underwear off, Tim slid his dick back and forth across her pussy, making the interaction more and more intense.

They kissed violently as they both fell to the sofa at a slanted angle. Tim lifted one of her legs up to his shoulder and entered her gracefully.

The sweetness of her pussy was the apple of his desire. The euphoria from the heroin that he snorted proclaimed a feeling of its own, that was totally separate from the sexual feeling. For a moment, he wished that he could persuade Rhonda to take a one on one so that she could enjoy this feeling that he couldn't put into words.

Tim took deep thrusts in and out of her wetness. They made love for hours. Tim's erection wouldn't decrease. Rhonda was experiencing Tim's dope dick, but she wasn't aware of it. After the gestures, the moans, and the screams of passion, there was silence between two lovers who had been engulfed in each other's intimacy for hours. Tim was lying on the floor while, Rhonda remained on the sofa.

"Damn, baby. What have you been taking, Viagra?" Rhonda asked rhetorically.

Tim smiled. "Nah, I've learned a new trick. It's called prolonging ejaculation."

"Where did you learn it from?"

"I've been reading a few books; I want to satisfy my baby in every way. Next, I'm going to read a book on captivating the human mind."

Rhonda laughed. "You won't have to read much, because you already have my mind captivated."

*****

Tim's headache was much worse than any of the previous ones. In fact, he had been encountering intense headaches most of the week. Maybe it was the extreme pressure that he had been under lately, he told himself. What extreme pressure? Rhonda was in full control of the business ventures and his drug pushers did all of the rough work. They bagged and distributed his drugs for him.

It must be the heroin, he thought to himself. If this was so, then he would have to find something to minimize the headaches because he couldn't see himself excluding his new found escape. He turned over to look at the clock. It was 9:15am. Rhonda had left earlier than usual this morning. She was dedicated and Tim acknowledged and respected her drive.

Tim was startled when he heard the buzzing sound that came from his pager. It was laying on the small dresser that was beside the bed. He kept the pager on vibrator most of the time to prevent the loud beeping sound that goes off when someone pages him. He looked at the familiar number then picked up the phone and dialed it.

"Hey what's up?" Tim asked over the phone. "Is he with you? No, you are in charge. I'll holler at him when I get there. I'll be there in two hours."

Corey had called Tim to inform him that Mike had been released and the charges were dropped. Tim knew how the parole board operated and he knew that they would probably still want to have a hearing to see if Mike had violated the terms of his parole.

Normally, Mike would have had to sit in jail until the parole board decided whether or not to revoke his parole, but Tim provided him with a high priced lawyer who specialized in freedom. Tim not only did this because of his loyalty, but to protect his empire. He figured if Mike felt threaten with doing a lot of time, then he would consider bringing other people down in exchange for his freedom.

Even though Tim didn't believe that Mike would fold, he knew that you could never be too sure. Tim told Corey that he was still assigned as the lieutenant and he wanted Mike to lay low until he arrived. Tim got out of bed feeling nauseous. He opened his dresser drawer and fumbled under his under wear until he found what he was looking for. He pulled the zip-lock bag out and plucked it with his finger, causing its contents to fall from the creases in the bag onto the pile that consumed most of the bag. He reached behind the large picture frame on the wall and pulled out a straw that he had hidden.

Tim was hopeful that if he took a one on one that his headache would go away and he would be in full blast. He decided that he would meet Corey and Mike as a professional, so that he could let Mike know his next steps as one of his employees.

CHAPTER 17

A few years had passed, but Cliff was still focused on his mission. He had stood strong in the face of adversity and even though the consequences seemed as if they would never end, he could finally breathe a lot easier. No one could tell him anything after what he had experienced. He had been to several institutions over the past two years. "The people," as he referred to them, didn't allow him enough time to get comfortable. He was paying dearly because of his loyalty. When he was indicted, the statement read the United States versus him. Therefore, he referred to them as "The people."

As the bus rode on he thought about the different places that he traveled at the expense of the government. He was transferred to Manchester, Kentucky then Beckley, West Virginia, then to Memphis, Tennessee. He never stayed long, which positioned him to lose contact with a lot of his friends and family members.

Cliff thought about his struggle to adjust to each environment. No one seemed to understand him. In fact, he often wondered if he understood himself. The Grey Hound bus was a lot more comfortable than the other buses he rode. There were no handcuffs or shackles. There was none of these disgusting lunch sandwiches that consisted of old cheese and stale bread. It was just him, a few strange faces and a long ride home. The Grey Hound drove through Atlanta, South Carolina and North Carolina so far. There was a layover in Richmond, Virginia for one hour.

Now there was nothing standing between him and the civilization that he had left but a few hours. At first it was extremely uncomfortable for him to see so many beautiful woman, kids, and landmarks. Everything looked so foreign to him. But, as he approached a place that he knew so well, things started becoming all so familiar to him. As he sat, staring at a pretty young lady sitting across from him, he couldn't help but smile at her attractiveness.

Once she smiled back that was his signal to approach her. They conversed for at least thirty minutes. He took control of the conversation as if his nine years in jail never existed. When the conversation was over he knew enough about her to write a short story and she knew enough about him to say that they crossed paths.

Afterwards, he decided to take a nap. When he awoke at the hand of a man in a suit he was startled.

"This is your stop partner," the voice said.

He adjusted his eyes briefly, and then he became anxious at the familiar site of home. Cliff Porter was finally home in Drama City.

CHAPTER 18

16th Street Northeast was full of drug dealers and high priced cars as Tim drove up looking for Corey and Mike. He noticed a few heads turn curiously as he drove slowly in his Escalade. Tim smiled at the sight of a couple of dudes shooting dice in the open as if they had a license. At first he didn't see Corey gathered in the mist of the crap game. But then he spotted Mike and found that Corey wasn't too far away.

Tim pulled around the corner and got out of his truck and stretched. He had on a satin Versace chambray shirt and a pair of Hugo Boss slacks. It was slightly breezy in D.C. in the month of May, but Tim was used to the unpredictable sway of the forecast. Tim's dress code was always dapper. He looked down at his Steve Madden shoes complimenting his own attire.

As Tim walked towards the crap game, Mike noticed him and rushed to greet him. Corey was so engulfed in the gamble that he never noticed Tim and rushed pass Mike. He never even noticed the rage in Tim until he felt the grip of a strong arm grab him.

"What the...?" were the only words that Corey's mouth could conjure.

"Man, what the fuck are you doing out here gambling?" Tim asked aggressively.

Before he could answer, Tim pushed him to the side of a vacant house. Tim didn't want to embarrass him and cause Corey to react stupidly out of self-pride. Corey was no match for Tim and they both knew it. Mike never moved from the spot that Tim had left him standing because he knew that they would work it out and if he intervened it would intensify the altercation.

"I put you in charge of things. That means that business comes first and anything else that you decide to do is done on your own time," Tim said while Corey eyed him dumbly. "If these niggas see you out here slipping they're not going to respect you. In fact, your workers are going to think that you're just one of the boys. But you stopped being one of the boys when I gave you this position." Corey nodded in agreement.

"Do you see me out here gambling and shooting the shit? No, of course not, because I know that if I'm slipping like that then one of these suckers will get in my mix and lay me down, leaving me with nothing but a prayer." Tim was fuming with hostility towards Corey, but Corey remained nonchalant.

Tim turned around to glance at Mike, then he turned back to face Corey.

"If I didn't intend to teach Mike a lesson for being so stupid, I would put him back in charge and have your ass bagging up dime bags." Corey was silent. All he could do is stare in disbelief.

"Man, I can't believe this shit," Tim said. He looked himself up and down and noticed that his outfit had gotten wrinkled. "I should make you buy me a new outfit," Tim continued.

Corey knew that Tim was about taking care of business. He also realized that if he leaves this confrontation without a scratch or bruise that it was a blessing.

"My truck is parked around the corner. I want you to drive it around here while me and Mike discuss a few things."

Corey nodded and walked away quickly.

"Hey!" Tim said loudly. "I'd like to see you get it around here without the keys," Tim said while tossing the keys to Corey.

"Don't sleep on me. I've been known to pop a few key ignitions back in my juvenile days," Corey responded.

"If you keep bullshitting you might just have to resort back to stealing cars for financial security," Tim stated sarcastically.

Tim waved at Mike, gesturing him to come over where he was standing.

"What's up?" Tim said while adjusting his slacks and shirt.

"Man, I know that it was dumb of me to react the way I did with Brenda, but I've been going through a lot of trials and tribulations with her."

"That's no excuse, slim," Tim cut him off.

Mike was trapped. He didn't know what to say because he only wanted to say what he thought Tim wanted to hear. After all, Tim was the one who took care of things for him, and he knew that Tim would help him when it was time for him to see the parole board. Mike knew that he had to get a job or make it appear as if he had a job and Tim had provided him with a reference thus far. He was grateful for Tim intervening. If it wasn't for Tim's intervention, he would be stuck in D.C. jail awaiting a parole revocation hearing even though his charges were dropped.

The parole board would have had the option of violating Mike and making him do jail time or reinstating his parole. Mike was no saint and he had a lengthy criminal history. Therefore, if it wasn't for Tim, he would definitely be doing at least twenty four months. Tim and Mike walked towards the truck as it pulled up. The dudes who were shooting dice stopped and stared.

Tim got in the passenger seat while Mike got in the rear seat. The loud sound of a local D.C. Go-Go band cranked from the Escalade. The familiar groove of the band named Rare Essence now flooded the block. One of the dudes from the crap game walked towards the Escalade.

When Corey was about to pull off, a dude stepped in front of the truck. When Corey poked his head out of the window to acknowledge him he said, "Slim, you can't just leave the crap game after you've won some major scratch."

Tim rolled the window on the passenger side. "Check this out main man, you can handle your business with him some other time, but right now we have some business of our own to handle."

Jeff was short, muscular, and stocky but Tim wasn't impressed. "This ain't your business so don't make it yours," Jeff said aggressively.

Tim stepped out of the truck and walked towards Jeff. Jeff reached in his pants and pulled out a gun while Tim reached in his pocket and pulled out a wad of money.

Jeff cocked his .45 caliber slowly.

"There's no need for that. I'm just trying to pay you what Corey owes you."

Jeff eyes bulged as Tim flipped through the bills. "He owes me a thousand dollars."

Tim was wondering how he figured Corey owed him money that Corey had won in a crap game. When Tim got within arm's reach of Jeff, he extended his hand to give Jeff the money. When Jeff reached for the money, Tim pulled his hand back and swung a over hand right hook, then a upper cut.

Jeff dropped to the pavement while the gun flew out of his hand. Tim picked the gun up, *pow, pow, pow.* The loud sound disturbed the block intensively. Tim shot Jeff in the leg, then spit on him.

Tim turned around to the crowd of bystanders who were gambling at first.

"Somebody call this bitch nigga an ambulance," Tim said as he walked to his truck and tossed the gun in it. Then he got in.

"We're going to the McDonald's on Nannie Helen Burroughs Avenue," Tim said.

When they reached the Robert F. Kennedy Stadium, Tim told Corey to pull over. Tim got out of the truck and tossed the gun that he got from Jeff. He wiped the gun off prior to tossing it. When they arrived at the Mc Donald's, Tim instructed Corey to park instead of going to the drive thru window.

In spite of a few wrinkles from the scuffle, Tim was dressed well enough to have walked off of a page in a G.Q. magazine, while Corey and Mike were dressed in sweat suits. Once inside the restaurant, Tim ordered a double cheeseburger, french fries and a large cup of water. Mike and Corey followed suit and ordered the same.

Corey noticed that the female who was taking their order was staring at Tim. He noticed the name tag on her shirt and addressed her by her name. She was tall and light skinned with attractive dimples and pretty brown eyes. Corey wanted to impose on her obvious attraction to Tim, but decided against it. Tim noticed her staring, but he had no intentions on initiating any conversation with her because his hands were full. Traci and Rhonda was enough for him.

The cashier eyed him all the way to the table in which they chose to sit. Tim only glanced in her direction occasionally. During one of his glances, he noticed one of the other female cashiers nudged her as if she was telling her to snap out of it.

"The reason I chose this spot is because there's not a lot of traffic," Tim said as he bit into his double cheeseburger.

"Before we get started on whatever it is that you want to get started on, I want to let you know that I really appreciate everything that you've done for me," Mike said.

"Well, it's not over with yet and as a matter of fact that's part of the reason why we're here. There are a couple of other reasons also." Tim spoke assertively. He was the boss and he wanted to make sure that none of his comrades got it twisted.

"First, I want to deal with the matter at hand. I don't know the dude that I just punished and I don't give a fuck about him because he violated. I also don't know if anyone will try to identify me or turn me in. Whatever happens, it's my fault. I acted on impulse, which was driven by the fact that I caught your clown ass slipping," he said as he looked at Corey in an angry manner.

"Things like that happen when you're supposed to be on the streets making money, but instead you're gambling with your money." Corey put his head down as a result of Tim's statement. He knew that Tim was right.

"They have places for dudes like us to gamble and it's not on the corner that we make our money. The places are called Las Vegas and Atlantic City. There you don't have to worry about knocking a nigga out or shooting him because he thinks that you owe him something." Mike nodded in agreement, but Corey remained nonchalant. Tim ate a few of his French fries and glanced at the cashier. He noticed that her eyes were constantly staring in his direction.

"I'm going to send a few of my soldiers from Potomac Gardens around 16th Street with ya'll just in case something jumps off," Tim said.

"Man, I can handle it," Corey responded.

"I don't trust your judgment. I trust my own," Tim demanded.

"I'm not going to go on and on about your situation, Mike, but I will say that if you're not happy in your relationship with Brenda, then you have to move on because you don't need to put yourself in any situation to go to jail. I've decided to split the lieutenant position between you two and that means that you have to share the Salary until I think that the consequences have set it. Then I'll figure out what to do from there," Tim said.

They indulged in frivolous conversation while finishing their burgers and fries. Tim sent Corey to get him a milk shake before they left. When Corey got back to the table he handed Tim a small piece of paper. Tim opened it up and read, *Give me a call 202-889-4124. My Name is Tiffany.* Tim glanced at her and smiled. Tiffany blushed heavily.

The three grabbed their trash and disposed of it before leaving. The muffled sound of a Go-Go band blasted out of a nearby Caprice Classic. Tim nodded his head with the sound as he turned to see where it was coming from. The windows of the Caprice were tinted as the car seemed to rock to the beat of its own drum. Corey focused his attention on the car, but his focus was more suspicion than curiosity. Corey noticed that no one had gotten out of the parked car to enter the McDonalds, but he considered the fact that someone may have been using the parking lot as a get high spot or to make a drug transaction.

The driver side window lowered slowly revealing a midsized nozzle. The loud spray of gun fire was rapid as its bullets bounced off of metal and into flesh. Corey fell first. Two bullets hit him in the neck and upper body.

Tim dived behind his truck, but a sharp pain in his leg was enough for him to realize that he had been hit. When he turned around, he saw Mike and Corey both stretched out on the pavement. He sat on the side of his truck, uncertain of the assailant's next move. If only he hadn't tossed the gun away that he had taken from that dude who tried to violate him. He thought to himself. If only he had brought his own gun with him, but he was a convicted felon so he knew that he couldn't just ride around with his gun on him. It was too risky.

Tim looked at the tires on his truck. Each tire had been flattened. Somebody went out of their way to make sure he wouldn't escape death. Tim was beginning to feel fatigued when the shadowy figured peeped from behind his truck. He blinked his eyes in fear as he heard a loud *pow*. The gun man was precise in his movements. The final shot that was fired was surely the blast that ended Tim's life, the assailant thought as each step brought the Caprice Classic closer to escaping this mission.

Loud sirens could be heard in the vicinity of the assault. Suddenly, the door of the Caprice Classic opened and the anonymous figure fled towards a small park behind the McDonalds. There was a small path that led to a small street behind the park. The assailant traveled that path until he reached the street, dipped into an alley and stripped the all black outfit which now revealed a sweat suit.

The Minnesota Avenue subway station was right around the corner. The assailant walked with medial speed, cautious not to arouse any suspicion. The assailant rode the train to the Stadium Armory subway station. The walk to the assailant's destination was within blocks of the subway station.

The assailant trusted that everything fell into place by the time the destination was reached. There was little time to be killed for everything to fall in place, so the assailant walked slowly making the three block walk seem like eight blocks.

By the time the assailant reached 16th and D Street Southeast, thirty five minutes had passed since the assault. The assailant paused at the bottom of the steps and admired the house.

"Here goes nothing." The assailant mumbled as each step was taken.

After knocking on the door several times the door opened revealing the hostile and grief stricken demeanor of Shannon Johnson.

"Oh my God. Are you okay, Mrs. Johnson?" Linda asked.

Shannon was obviously in a state of hysteria as Linda tried to comfort her. Linda walked in the house instinctively. Calvin was sitting on the sofa with his head down.

"Where is Tim?" Linda asked. She was looking at Shannon, but the question was for Calvin to answer.

"They shot him…Oh God! They tried to kill my baby," Shannon was in a rage.

Calvin started crying also. He couldn't stand to see his mother go through such pain.

"What's going on Calvin?"

"I…don't know. We got a phone call from the emergency room informing us that Tim had been admitted for some gunshot wounds."

"Did they say what the motive was?" Calvin paused at the insincerity of the question.

"It was an apparent robbery," Calvin assumed.

Shannon was distraught. She needed to know that her son was okay, but neither Calvin nor Linda could offer such consolation.

"We have to go to the hospital!" Shannon demanded. Linda eyed them both hoping one of them would solicit her company. Her patience grew thin after several minutes of silence.

"Can I come along?" Linda asked.

Even though Shannon was slightly oblivious, she remembered Tim telling her that he had cut off all ties with Linda. In spite of this, Shannon could not refuse anyone who was trying to help; especially at a time like this.

Shannon looked at Calvin for any sign of disapproval and said, "Of course you can come. You can follow me and Calvin. We're going to the Greater Southeast Community Hospital," Linda's eyes opened wide as if she was startled by Shannon's statement.

"I...Uh...I didn't drive here. I caught the subway."

Calvin was confused. He wondered why Linda would take a chance by coming over unannounced, not knowing if Tim would be there or not. How would she get home? Did she plan to wait on him if he wasn't there?

"I went to see a friend of mine at the jail. As I was leaving, I decided to stop by to see Tim." Linda forced a tear from her eye. "We had a misunderstanding and I wanted to make amends with him."

Calvin wondered exactly what kind of friend she went to visit. He soon realized that he was letting his personal feelings cloud his perception of Linda. He still wanted to dislike her, but this was not the time or place. Calvin had become a pawn stuck between the desire to spend time with Tim and the inability to do so because of Tim's relationship with Linda. Before Tim met Linda, Tim and Calvin traveled a lot and spent most of their time together. Once Tim became trapped in Linda's web of love, most of his time was spent with her. Calvin developed a strong hatred towards Linda because of the feeling of being alone.

Linda was a quick thinker. She developed this skill as a result of being in the mist of Tim's lifestyle. She even enrolled in a super trooper course once. It was an eight week hands on class that taught the participants how to elude a potential kidnapping. The class also specialized in ambush techniques. This is where Linda learned how to ambush the enemy and get away from the scene. She never imagined that the class would come in handy. She never imagined that the person who recommended the class would be the one who ended up on the other end of the learned skill. Neither did Tim.

CHAPTER 19

The clinical smell of the hospital lingered through the administrative department of the Greater Southeast Community Hospital. Shannon approached the front desk with Calvin and Linda tailing behind. She waited for the clerk to get off the phone.

"Hi my name is Shannon Johnson. I got a phone call informing me that my son Tim Johnson had been admitted for gunshot wounds." While she waited for the clerk to give her more information, a female walked over to Shannon.

"Hello, Ms. Johnson. I'm Rhonda."

It took a minute before it registered in Shannon's mind.

"Oh! Hi, baby. Are you okay?"

"Yes, I guess. They wouldn't let me see him. They said immediate family only."

Tim hadn't properly introduced Rhonda to his mother because Shannon had told him that she didn't want to meet any of his female friends. She said that until he was ready to introduce her to his fiancé, he could save the introduction.

The clerk hung the phone up.

"Ms. Johnson, if you could wait right here, the doctor in charge of your son's surgery will be down in a minute."

Linda looked at Rhonda strangely. She finally got a chance to see who Tim had abandoned her for. Linda wondered if Tim had survived her ambush. As strange as it may have felt, she found herself not wanting him to die. She wondered if it was because he hadn't suffered enough or if it was because there may be a chance of her winning him over. Rhonda and Shannon began to get acquainted when the doctor arrived.

"Ms. Johnson? Hello, I'm Dr. Beckum. Can I have a word with you?" The doctor gritted his teeth and looked at the floor tile. Shannon and Dr. Beckum stepped away from the others. "Your son is a very strong young man. From my understanding, his truck took most of the bullets that were fired at him. The other two guys who were with him took most of the rest. One is paralyzed and the other one is on a respirator. He's not going to make it. We're trying to contact his immediate family to confirm their wishes on terminating his life support system."

Shannon was sad for whomever Tim's friends were, but she was happy that Tim's situation wasn't as bad.

"Your son was shot in the arm and a bullet grazed his ear. The event was obviously too much for him."

"What makes you say that?" Shannon asked.

"He went into shock. He's stable now. The detectives are speaking with him at this time, but if you want to wait then you can."

Shannon thanked him then she turned to tell Rhonda, Calvin, and Linda the good news. The doctor waved to get her attention.

"Ms. Johnson. He's only allowed three adult visitors at a time."

Linda almost immediately eliminated herself. She felt odd being there with Rhonda and she realized that she hadn't the slightest idea of what she would say to him.

"Ms. Johnson," Linda said while pulling her away from anyone who could hear what she was saying. "I want you to give Tim my best wishes."

"The best thing would be for you to put them in your own words," Shannon responded.

"I know, but since he can only have three visitors, I feel that the right thing for me to do is to allow his closest loved ones the opportunity."

"Okay I understand. But how will you get home?"

"I'll call a friend of mine. She lives right down the street," she lied.

Shannon hugged Linda as Calvin and Rhonda waved good bye to Linda.

"Come on. Let's go and see my baby," Shannon demanded.

When they got on the elevator, Rhonda asked, "Who was the woman?"

Calvin rolled his eyes. "That was nobody important."

Shannon intervened quickly. "Linda is an old acquaintance of Tim's. She came by my house after visiting a friend at the jail. After she heard the news, she decided to tag along."

Shannon was purposely being evasive. She didn't feel that Rhonda needed to know that Tim hadn't broken his relationship with Linda. In fact, the more she thought about it, if Rhonda didn't know who Linda was then evidently Tim hadn't revealed the contents of their relationship.

The more Rhonda thought about it, the more familiar Linda's name started to sound. She wasn't sure, so she dismissed her thoughts. When they reached Tim's room Shannon paused.

"What's wrong, Ma?" Calvin asked.

"I didn't bring my baby any flowers!" Shannon said.

"That's okay. We didn't know his condition until now, and I would've never thought that he would be in any shape to enjoy them. Besides, Tim's not a flower type of dude. He'd rather get some tough love like only you know how to give," Calvin said.

"I'm going to go easy on him now, but when he gets better, you can bet that I'm going to dog his ass," Shannon said as she pushed the room door open. Calvin was shocked by the language she used, because she had strayed so far away from using profanity that he thought it would never exist in her vocabulary again.

When they walked in the room, Shannon saw two other patients. She wondered if these were the other two guys that were with Tim. She soon realized that the doctor had told her that one of Tim's friends would not make it. One of the patients was in a full body cast. While the other one had tubes running through his nose and attached to his veins. Tim was resting on the hospital bed watching television when they walked in.

"Hey good looking," Tim said when he saw his mother, trying to make humor even in a time of pain. His smile made Shannon think about what she would have missed the most had she lost him.

"Don't 'good looking' me! Whenever there's gunfire then there's most likely something crooked behind it!" Shannon said aggressively. "Why were the police here?"

Shannon was obviously distraught. She had many confrontations with law enforcement officials because of Tim's past lifestyle. She often lied, cheated, and fended for Tim's freedom. She wasn't trying to venture down that road again.

"Nah, Ma. You got it wrong. I was the victim of an assault. I think somebody tried to rob me. The only problem is they never asked for any money."

Shannon had an entourage of questions. How many were there? Did he see any of them? Why would they want to rob him? Who were his friends? But, Tim lived by the code of the streets. Even if he would have seen who it was, he would have never given the police a description.

He didn't know what happened to Corey or Mike, so he decided that he would inquire about them whenever he was alone with the doctor. He also had no idea that Linda came to the hospital with Calvin and his mother.

"How do you feel soldier?" Calvin said as he stepped pass his mother to get closer to Tim.

"Come here, I can show you better than I can tell you." When Calvin came closer, Tim gave him a hug so tight that it nearly cut his oxygen supply short.

"Now, ya'll get to give my baby some room to show me some love." Rhonda grinned selfishly. She was blushing and she was embarrassed because Tim put her on the spot. This didn't stop her from rushing to Tim's bed side to embrace him. Rhonda held Tim tight as tears rolled down her eyes.

"Baby I didn't know what I was going to do. She was distraught and she was rambling on to the point that Tim became confused.

"What were you going to do about what?" Tim asked.

Rhonda pulled back from his embrace. She turned around. Shannon and Calvin were wondering what she was talking about also. She stared at Tim with frustration and discontentment in her eyes.

"Uh you know...whoever they were, they might try to rob you again or maybe they were after your friends."

Tim was stunned by the comment. It wasn't the fact that her assumption was ludicrous, but simply because she had thought so far ahead.

"Speaking of your friends," Shannon said, "The doctor told me that one of your friends is critically hurt and the other one is on a respirator fighting for his life."

Tim was shocked by her statement. He hadn't considered Corey's or Mike's fate to be no more serious than his. Dr. Beckum walked in the room with an uneasy look on his face.

"Excuse me. If you don't mind, I need to speak with Mr. Johnson alone. I understand that you all just arrived, but something urgent just came up." Shannon looked at Calvin, and Calvin looked at Rhonda.

"Oh…Okay! I'll just give my baby a hug and come back tomorrow. I'll sleep better knowing that he's in good hands," Shannon said.

"No, Ma. You don't have to leave" Tim said. He tried to lift up, but was stricken by a pain in his shoulder.

Oh shit!" he said painfully.

"Don't worry, I'll be back tomorrow," Shannon said. She gave him a kiss on his head for good measure.

Calvin gave him a hug. "Stay strong soldier."

Tim looked at Rhonda "Are you leaving too?"

"No, I'll be outside of the door until the doctor finishes."

Rhonda began to walk out then she turned around. "Oh I almost forgot I brought you a change of clothes." She sat a full set of clothing on the chair including underclothes. When they left, Dr. Beckum walked to the door and pushed it shut.

"You're a very lucky man, Mr. Johnson. I was talking to one of the officers who described the crime scene as horrific and disastrous." Tim wondered where this conversation was headed to.

"I'm glad to see that you are doing well," Dr. Beckum paused before he continued. "Unfortunately, one of your friends didn't make it."

Tim put his head down. He felt guilty. His mind was scrambling. It must have been a retaliation hit for the dude that he shot on 16th Street, he thought to himself.

But that was too quick. Maybe Corey owed someone or had beef with someone. Tim continued in thought.

"Mr. Morris is paralyzed. I guess it won't take much to figure out the rest. We had Mr. Jackson on a respirator after his heart failed, but his parents couldn't afford to hold out any longer."

"What…is that it?" Tim was furious. "I have money. You could have kept him on it for months as far as I'm concerned." The tears started to roll down his eyes heavily.

Corey was dead and Mike was paralyzed. This was his closet brush with death and there was nothing he could do to change the event.

"I'm sorry, Mr. Johnson, but we never considered the fact that you would be willing to spend that kind of money. It would have cost you no less than two hundred and fifty dollars a day."

Tim wasn't concerned with the doctor's assumption at this point. He realized that there was nothing that he could do to bring Corey back. However, he could lend his financial and emotional support to Corey's family.

Tim needed a break from the lifestyle that he was living. He needed to get back into running his business himself and not put that burden on Rhonda. She never complained, but he knew that she wanted him to share the duties and gratification of being in the midst of a business as it develops. Without a doubt Tim needed to redefine his mission, but most of all he needed a one on one to sooth his soul. Tim hadn't even noticed that the doctor had left as he gazed out of the hospital window.

"We have to talk baby," Rhonda's voice startled him.

"Hey...I was day dreaming. She left huh?" He was referring to his mother.

"Yeah...she told me to tell you that she loves you," Rhonda said.

"Thank you for the clothes baby."

"That's what having a strong black woman is about right?" The sarcasm in Rhonda's tone made Tim sense that this was not going to be a pleasant conversation.

Tim turned to face Rhonda. "Something wrong? Speak your mind."

"I don't want to assume anything, but when I was searching for something decent for you to wear, I found this," she held up a large zip lock bag that was half full of heroin.

"I thought that you had put the drug dealing behind you."

Tim was caught completely off guard. He knew that she had been searching his belongings because everything in his dresser was decent. Therefore, why would she have to search for something decent? He thought.

"I'm not mad because it was in there, but I'm mad because we are supposed to be partners. But it seems as if you don't trust me. Plus, whenever your life is in jeopardy because of this," she held the bag up again "then me and my son's lives are in jeopardy also."

Tim was awe struck that she hadn't spoken a false word.

"So I guess this is what the robbery attempt was about," Rhonda continued.

"No, this was no robbery. I'm not a street hustler and niggas know me out there. There's other ways of getting the top dog. This was something else."

Rhonda gritted her teeth as Tim spoke. "Oh, I see you're the top dog. So I guess I'm the top dog's bitch. Well give me something to smuggle since I'm your down ass bitch. We'll go down together. In fact, I'll take the beef for you." Rhonda threw the zip lock bag on his bed and left.

Tim knew that he had to let her cool off. In no time flat his mind drifted to finding a straw so that he could take a one on one. He fumbled in his pocket with his left hand. It was difficult for him to retrieve anything from his pocket because of the cast and sling that banded his right arm.

Tim grabbed a few of the contents in his pocket. There was a pack of Wrigley's double mint gum, a straw and a piece of paper folded up. Tim quickly sat the zip lock bag between his legs and dipped the straw inside of it. It took him a couple of tries before he actually got a sufficient amount of heroin in the straw. Tim was anxious as he lifted the straw to his nose quickly. He didn't want anyone walking in on him while he was in the midst of taking a one on one.

As the euphoria engulfed him he realized that this was the stronger batch that he had put aside for Traci. The pain in his arm was subsiding and he felt like jumping out of his hospital bed. Tim opened the folded piece of paper that he got out of his pocket and examined it. He had forgotten the chic at the McDonald's, as well as the decision he had made not to call her. He looked at the paper a few times. Then he noticed that the first three digits of her phone number were eight, eight, and nine. *A southeast hoodrat,* Tim said out loud to himself.

He picked up the phone and called her. The phone rang several times before she answered. Tiffany was surprised, but happy to hear from him. She told Tim that she had saw the whole thing and she could provide him with the proper information to help him find his enemy. Tim asked her if she told the police what she knew; she said no. That was a point in her favor Tim thought to himself.

They talked for a few minutes more before Tim asked her to come to the hospital.

He also told her that she would have to act as if she had the wrong room if there was a female present. Tiffany told him that she would be there later on in the evening.

When Tim hung up the phone he realized that his bodily functions were alerting him. His dick was hard and he needed to relieve some tension. He called Traci and acted as if it was urgent that she come and see him. Her response was just as he expected it to be. She was on her way. By the time Traci arrived, Tim had snorted another one on one.

The heroin had diluted most of the pain that Tim was feeling as a result of the gunshot wound. Tim was ready for the world. About an hour later, Tim smiled delightfully at the sight of Traci's appearance.

She was wearing a long trench coat and a pair of satin slippers by Helmut Lang that Tim had given her as a present.

"Damn…you look good," Tim shouted startling the other patient who was in the body cast.

Traci smiled. "You think that's something! Check this out." Traci opened the trench coat revealing her half naked body. She had on a black laced thong with a matching open tip bra.

"You keep on, you're going to make me stash you in here over night."

"You got a good talk game, but you and I both know that your boo ain't having that."

"Shit I run this," Tim said while turning his attention to her slippers. "Let me see those pretty ass feet of yours." Traci slipped her feet out of her slippers and wiggled her toes. Tim looked at her and smiled.

"Damn, ain't you gonna ask me how I'm doing?"

"Well from the looks of things you seem to be fully recovered."

"Don't let the great taste fool you." The room was filled with silence. Traci stared at Tim provocatively until he broke the silence.

"I have something for you." Tim revealed the zip lock bag and handed it to her.

"Thank you, boo!" Traci said.

"Don't worry about leaving me the leftovers. I'll be okay until I get out of here," Tim said. He was acting as if it was a small thing to him because he had already taken a small amount of heroin out of the package for himself. Traci went into the bathroom for at least five minutes and when she emerged she was ready for action. She walked to Tim's bed with an intriguing look in her eyes. She grabbed the rolling partition and pulled it around Tim's bed so that they could have privacy. As her coat dropped to the floor, Tim noticed how perky her nipples were. He was fully erect as she clinched on him. Tim penetrated her with full force while she straddled him.

"Oh shit!" Tim moaned. He was in love with the feeling that he got from the mixture of the sex and heroin. He could go for hours, he thought.

"Bust me open daddy!" Traci screamed.

Tim loved the fact that Traci was a talker in bed. Rhonda moaned and talked occasionally, but Traci was another case all together. Tim's eyes rolled to the back of his head with satisfaction. When he opened his eyes, his vision was blurred at first. He saw his lonely days in jail...he saw Mike and Corey getting shot.... and then....he saw Linda.

"Uh um!" Tim heard a voice say.

"Shit! Don't you see the partition is around my bed! That meant knock or make your presence known," Tim said.

Traci was startled. She didn't know who Linda was so she jumped up quickly.

"Who the fuck are you?" Traci stated.

"I'm his long lost ex-girlfriend." Linda stared as if she had walked in on a conversation instead of them having sex. "Who the fuck are you?"

"I'm his wife and I don't appreciate you coming in here invading our privacy."

Linda was offended. "Well, I didn't know that he was married, but the only reason I looked behind the partition is because I heard moans and I thought that Tim was in pain," she lied.

"Well, as you can see, he's in good pain now you can see yourself off."

Tim was enjoying the feud over him, but he knew that enough was enough.

"Hold on a minute, I'll say who goes around here. Baby, I have to take care of some business with Linda, so you may want to take care of what we talked about."

Traci was confused at first, but once Tim winked his eye she understood.

"Okay, but are you going to be alright?"

Tim looked at Linda, and then he turned to Traci and said, "Yeah baby, we just have to take care of some small talk."

Traci was offended at the thought of Tim ending such an intense moment to satisfy Linda with some "small talk" as he called it. But, her thought quickly swayed to the small package of heroin that Tim gave her. Therefore, she no longer felt neglected. Traci gathered her belongings and kissed Tim as if she was really his wife. Then she left.

Linda rolled her eyes at the sight of this. She was actually feeling herself become jealous. Not because of this, but because Tim was comfortable and laid back in spite of his demise.

"Hi Tim," Linda said hesitantly. Tim laughed.

"What's so funny?"

"You are. The way you stroll in here unannounced, ruin a perfectly good rendezvous then speak to me as if we just reunited from an overseas trip." Tim glanced at his arm then back at Linda.

"I don't know how you found out what happened, but I know for sure that you knew that I was in jail but you didn't break your neck to visit then."

"Yes I did. I'm only human and I'm woman enough to admit my faults, but are you man enough to admit yours?"

"What are you talking about?"

"You really did some dog shit to me Tim. I realized that I made a mistake and I wanted to make it right, but in return you manipulated me."

Tim's face went blank.

"Let me tell you something...the only reason you wanted to make things right is because I made you feel complete again. I was in your life to give you the dick that you longed for. But you didn't expect me to be here, so you abandoned me at first."

"That's why your ass is in here now" Linda blurted out spontaneously.

"What?" Tim was furious. "Is that what you think? I deserve this because of what I did to you?"

"No, that's not what I meant."

"Well enlighten me."

"What I meant was this is what you'll get if you continue to do the same things."

Linda was a thinker, but she realized that she had to think fast because she was giving him indications that she had been watching him.

"And just what some- things are you talking about?" Tim asked.

"Lying, manipulation, and deception," she replied and took a deep breath. "Look Tim, I didn't come here to argue I was just concerned about you."

"I'm glad to see that you..." His words were killed by a certain thrust of pain in his leg or was it his shoulder? He wasn't sure. What he did know for sure is that Linda revealed a large needle when she drew back her arm from reaching toward him.

"What the..."

"Shh, don't try to talk you'll just make it worst," Tim was speechless as the effect of whatever it was that she injected in him seem to take precedence over the heroin that he snorted.

"Can't you just let things be?" Tim asked.

"I tried, but you did some dirty shit, nigga, and you're going to pay for it."

Tim was dozing off, but he was trying to fight it. Linda looked at him and laughed. She was standing over top of him breathing fiercely.

"You have to be careful in those streets Tim, especially when you start to create enemies. You never know what'll be waiting for you once you leave the security of your own home." Linda had complete focus on the helpless figure that laid before her. She slapped his face.

"Wake up. I'm not finished talking." She grabbed his face and squeezed it with the tips of her hand. "You made the fucking choice to trick the wrong bitch."

Tim saw the gun, and heard the trigger cock. He heard Linda's voice, *gotcha*, then everything went blank. Linda exited Tim's room with swift precision. She didn't want to be noticed. She threw the needle in the trash can as she bent the corner that led to the emergency steps. Everything that Tim taught her was paying off. She thought about how easy it was for her to slip into the paternity ward and steal a needle and some anesthesia. She wondered if she had a child, if it would be this easy for someone to kidnap her baby. When she got outside, she flagged a cab driver down and disappeared from the hospital as quickly as when she arrived.

CHAPTER 20

It was the winter of 2002 and things were in full swing with Cliff. Getting himself established was hard for him at first. When he got out of prison, his parole officer was very strict because of Cliff's long rap sheet and criminal history. But unlike the past, Cliff was humble and patient. He had no intentions of going back to jail. Cliff's stomach turned as he thought about how he had scrubbed and cleaned toilets at the Super Eight motel before he found a job working as a parking lot attendant. The pay was minimal, but seven dollars an hour was better than working for eighteen cents an hour in jail.

"Sir, we're not selling the McRib sandwich at this time. It's a promotional item," the McDonalds cashier said bringing Cliff back from his short daydream.

"Okay, I'll take a fish sandwich instead."

The cashier read his order back to him. "Will that be all Sir?"

Cliff paused for a minute. "You wouldn't happen to have a number that I can reach you at would you?"

The cashier was caught off guard by Cliff's spontaneous question. She looked no older than twenty-two, but her light skinned complexion and her long hair couldn't be ignored by Cliff.

"You can call me here. My name is Michelle."

Cliff was insulted. "Why can't I call you at home?"

"Because I don't know you".

Cliff smiled. "Okay, here's my cell phone number, call me." Cliff pulled off after he paid for his meal. The loud sound of Anita Baker blasted through his Suburban truck as he drove across the Sousa Bridge on Pennsylvania Avenue. There was no mistake about it; Cliff had paid his dues. He was en route to deliver some drugs to one of his runners in Southeast.

When he reached the Barry Farm public housing projects, he felt a ton of weight being lifted off of his shoulders. He was traveling with two kilograms of crack cocaine and four pounds of marijuana. When he saw who he was looking for, he beeped his horn twice, he then pulled into a narrow alley. The transaction was already preset. Cliff would pull into the alley and dump the drugs into the empty trash can and his pick up would wait for three minutes then he would ride his bicycle into the alley and retrieve the drugs, tucking them away in his back pack. When his runner rolled away on his bike, he looked totally innocent of any wrong doings.

Cliff drove through the alley pulling on to a street that led to the freeway. He had one more stop to make and this was the worst part of transporting drugs for him; driving from Southeast to Northwest with a full truck of narcotics. This was the risk that he was willing to take.

Cliff could have hired someone to transport the drugs, but he figured the less people he had in his business, the less his chances were of someone snitching on him.

Not only did Cliff have runners who distributed his drugs in Northwest and Southeast, he also had dudes that sold a large quantity of drugs in District Heights and Suitland, Maryland, bringing his drug Soles to at least thirty thousand dollars biweekly.

When he arrived at Clifton Terrace apartments in Northwest, he parked his truck across the street, watching as a crack head attempted to buy some crack with short money.

"Come on man. All I have is eight dollars. I always spend my money with you," The crack head said completely ignoring his entire surroundings.

"Nah man, I can't keep taking no shorts," the dealer replied. He looked in Cliff's direction and noticed that Cliff was nodding his head, giving him the go ahead to serve the crack head with short money.

Bink didn't need Cliff's permission, but he knew that he had to get the crack head away from him so that he could tend to his business with Cliff. Bink was one of Cliff's most respected associates because even though Bink had runners to sell his drugs, he would take a large portion of what Cliff sold him, bag it up and sell it himself, tripling the street value. He was very low-key and drama free and these were the type of dudes that Cliff liked to deal with.

Bink walked over to Cliff's truck "What's up slim?" Bink said.

Cliff started laughing.

"What's so funny?" Bink asked.

"Nothing man, I was just wondering when you're going to stop selling those dimes and twenties and move up to moving some weight?"

"Well for your information, I do move weight. Ice Cube said he push rhymes like weight, but I'm Bink and I push dimes like weight, nigga."

Cliff got out of his truck and hugged Bink. "I know slim, you do what you do when you can do it."

"Nah slim, I do what I wanna do and I do what other dudes are afraid to do."

Cliff looked around to absorb the surroundings. Then he reached in to the back seat of his truck and handed Bink the large teddy bear.

"Do you have a minute to kick the Willy Bo-Bo?" Bink asked.

"Yeah what's up?" Kicking the Willy Bo-Bo was a termed that was use to describe having a conversation.

"Hold on, let me run this beautiful gift to my car," the teddy bear was stuffed with heroin and crack. Bink walked swiftly to his Nissan Maxima and threw the bear in the back seat. Then he returned to join Cliff.

"Let's walk for a minute before speaking," Cliff said.

After a few moments, Bink shared some news about Tim.

"Man, there's a bamma that just came home from jail trying to intimidate and extort my youngins."

Cliff held his breath as he absorbed Bink's words. He knew that he had to make sure that this issue was taken care of, because whatever affected Bink's runners, affected Bink, and whatever affected Bink, affected him. As they stepped inside the corner store Bink stopped in his tracks

"What's up slim?" Cliff asked.

"That's that bitch nigga right there," Bink said.

He was referring to a tall slim dude who was standing at the cash register buying a box of Philly blunt cigars and a forty ounce of beer. He was wearing a black sweat hoody and a pair of black jogging pants. Cliff knew that so called gangstas enjoyed wearing black because it allows them not to be seen in the midst of doing dirt.

Bink wanted Cliff to handle the situation in any way possible, because Bink had a very uncontrollable temper when it came to negative confrontation. He had been boxing as a professional for five years and he had no problem with using his hands out of the ring. However,

Bink was trying to stay altercation free ever since he knocked a dude unconscious with one blow for mistreating his sister. He was jailed and fined as a result of this and Cliff was not happy. Cliff told him that they didn't need any unnecessary heat on them. Cliff also gave him the instructions of letting him know whenever he has a problem so that Cliff could make sure that it gets taken care of.

Cliff stared at the tall figure for a second. Bink thought that Cliff was sizing him up, but Cliff was trying to remember where he knew that dude from. Cliff never forget a face, but he had a hard time putting this dude's face with a time and place. When the dude walked away from the cash register and walked towards the door where Bink and Cliff were standing, it hit him.

The tall figure walked passé them, giving Cliff a double take. Bink gritted his teeth and frowned up as he glanced in his direction. Cliff turned to Bink.

"It looks like he's going to enjoy his forty ounce. Where does he hang out?"

"He hangs on fourteenth and Upshur Streets whenever he's not around here. He has a female that he comes to see him around here."

Cliff knew that there was only a matter of time before one of Bink's youngins get fed up and put a stop to this bully spree.

"I know him," Cliff said. "Look, grab me a apple juice and catch up with me. I'm going to holler at him." Cliff jetted out of the store. He watched for a minute as the dude stopped to take a sip of his beer. Cliff walked towards him and spoke.

"What's up slim? Ain't your name Rabbit?"

"Depends on who's asking" Rabbit said.

237

"You've seen my face before, you should know who's asking," Cliff replied.

Rabbit immediately became paranoid; he had done so much dirt that it was hard to remember who he had done dirt to.

"Look slim, I'm not the enemy, but I do need to talk to you. My truck is right there; get in so that I can holler at you."

Rabbit looked at Cliff, then he looked at Cliff's truck.

"How do I know that you're not a hit man fulfilling a contact on my hands?"

"Because if I was a hit man I would have killed you were you stand."

Rabbit smiled, "Okay, but time is valuable."

Cliff reached in his pocket and gave Rabbit a fifty dollar bill. "This should cover your time."

As they sat in the truck, Cliff could see Bink talking to a couple of raunchy dudes across the street. Cliff turned towards Rabbit momentarily, then he turned the radio on low before speaking.

"I have a small problem, Rabbit," Cliff began, "I like to sell narcotics." Cliff smiled while Rabbit looked at him confused. "That's not the problem though, because I have succeeded thus far at eluding the police and I haven't had to create any violent scenes because somebody owed me money. But lately there's been someone threatening and extorting my runners and that is a real big problem."

"Why are you telling me about this? Do you need the problem taken care of?"

"Good question. As a matter of fact I do need the problem taken care of."

Rabbit bit his lip. He didn't want to be a hit man, he just wanted to chill and smoke his weed and drink at the expense of petty hustler's who he felt should pay him his dues in return for selling drugs in his neighborhood.

"If you need to make money, you need to holler at me right now and stop strong arming my runners," Cliff said brief and to the point.

Rabbit was shocked by the sudden change in direction of the conversation. But he knew that the streets talked, so there was no need to play games with Cliff.

"Okay slim, I respect where you're coming from. I've been doing what I do for so long, that I've become accustomed to it. But if you have something lined up for me so that I can get some bacon, then I'm all for it. But I'm not trying to stand on no corner and sell dime bags. That's why I do what I do, because in order for anyone to get put on, they have to start nickeling and diming and I'm not with that."

Cliff nodded his head in agreement "I feel you. I'm not going to put you out on no corner, but the job I have for you is risky and it requires a lot of trust."

Rabbit smiled slightly and said, "Just give me the word and I'm ready."

Cliff glanced at Bink and his comrades as they stood front and center as if they were waiting for Cliff to give them the word to snatch Rabbit out of the truck and beat him down.

"I need a trusty transporter to deliver some packages to several different locations on a weekly basis. The pay is a thousand dollars a week and I'll provide you with two cars. One of the cars is for you to make drop offs. The other one is strictly for your personal use. You are not to use the drop off car for personal business."

Rabbit nodded to show Cliff that he understood the details of his job.

"I'll make sure that you have a pager and cell phone also."

Rabbit was awe struck he had finally caught a break.

*****

Months passed since Tim had been assaulted. He had lost Corey, and Mike was confined to a wheelchair. The doctors told Tim that Mike would probably walk again if he worked diligently with the physical trainer that had been assigned to him. As Tim sat in Mike's living room, he thought about the events that led up to his current demise. After Linda had drugged him up and scared the daylights out of him, his life seemed to take a turn for the worst.

Tim started seeing Traci more and that led to getting high much more. Because of this, he let Rhonda take full responsibility for the management of Braids R' Us and Johnson Garden apartments. Over time, Tim was able to conceal his drug use, at least, until he met Kay Kay.

Kay Kay was Traci's cousin. He used to visit Traci from time to time while Tim was there. Tim had sold him heroin occasionally and Tim had also given Kay Kay free testers so that he could tell him if he had too much cut on the heroin or not. Tim had started complaining that he was no longer feeling the effects of the dope and decided to quit altogether. Kay Kay feared that Tim's demeanor would change if he quit. Therefore, Kay Kay influenced him to shoot the heroin intravenously. Tim was totally against it, but his hesitant comply wasn't strong enough to withstand the peer pressure of Traci and Kay Kay combined. After trying it, he was dissuaded by the sickness and vomiting that came as a result of the heroin.

Somehow, Tim's cravings grew stronger after he experimented with shooting the heroin, so he started shooting up every day. After his drug connection learned about his drug use, he started digging into his personal and business savings and investments just to buy dope because

they no longer trusted him. He brought three ten packs of heroin a day for two hundred and sixty dollars. Sometimes he spent more, whenever the heroin wasn't as potent as he anticipated.

As Tim's addiction advanced he started caring less about anything else that didn't involve him getting high. He caused Rhonda to distance herself from him and his mother was always worried about him. Tim never realized how severely he was victimizing his family. His commitment to heroin blinded his morale and distorted his principals. He had sold most of his expensive clothes and his jewelry for a third of what he had originally paid for them.

He no longer drove an escalade. Instead, he was driving s nineteen ninety Nissan Sentra. Tim hadn't seen Linda in a while and he was glad. He knew that she would have been more than thrilled to see him at his all-time low.

"Tim!" Mike shouted. "Snap out of it."

"Huh! Oh! I was just day dreaming."

"I see, but there's another world outside of that fantasy one you're in, and it's called the real world. Welcome back."

Tim stared at Mike. He didn't want to look at Mike's legs so he looked him in the eyes.

"Man, it's my fault that you're in that chair."

Mike smiled. "Come on, dog, I have enemies too."

Tim walked over to the window and glanced through the curtains.

"Yeah I know, but on that day, your enemies weren't after you."

Mike lifted his arm in an attempt to find a comfortable position.

"Don't beat yourself up about it. They say that there are only two ways out of the drug game and that's death or jail. I consider myself lucky because I came close to death but I'm still alive," Mike said, pausing only for a second. "I may not be up and running, but I have enough feeling in me to please my wife."

Tim turned around and frowned.

"That's easy for you to say. I'm not in a wheelchair and I still can't please anyone. I've lost most of my possessions; I'm embarrassed to go around my family members because I don't want to mistreat their eyes by the sight of me wallowing in my own death, and to top it off, I have to get money in small sums from Rhonda because she's afraid that she may someday lose everything to my dope habit."

Mike rolled his wheelchair towards Tim and stopped when he was planted right in front of him.

"If this is what makes things so miserable for you then why don't you just stop getting high?"

Tim looked down at Mike. "I've tried but it's not that simple. I've also done some research on addiction and I found out that once you're an addict there's no cure; you'll always be an addict."

"So basically what you're telling me is that you'll always have to get high no matter what?"

"No, that's not what I'm saying. There's treatment centers designed to help recovering addicts cope with fighting their addiction, but I can't see myself sitting in a room full of strangers listening to horrific stories that I probably can't identify with. That's not my cup of tea."

Mike nodded slowly to acknowledge that he understood. "Well I have to be blunt. You have to do something because this dope fiend shit is not your cup of tea either."

"Yeah slim I know, but I have yet to devise a plan to straighten this mess out."

As Tim ended his sentence, Brenda walked in the living room. She didn't really notice Tim's appearance as being that of a dope head doing bad. She figured that he was probably dressed to do some maintenance work at his store, but little did she know that Rhonda was hanging on with all of her might to Braids R' Us, and Johnson Gardens was basically running itself.

Tim had paid for a personal trainer for Mike, but that was before he totally gave in to heroin.

"I'm sorry did I interrupt something?"

"Uh nah," Tim said.

"No baby. Come here and give me some sugar," Mike said filled with excitement.

As they embraced, Tim was forced to remember the wonderful times that he had shared with Rhonda.

"We have to get ready for your training session baby," Brenda said to Mike. "Would you like to join us Mr. Johnson?"

"Oh no… I have some business to tend to. I was just leaving."

Once Tim left Mike's house, he jetted to his car. He sat aimlessly as he gathered his thoughts. It occurred to Tim that he was no longer in control of his life. He no longer had to wonder how people became so hooked on heroin. It became a sickness that progressed from a desire to a must-have.

Tim wondered what his next move would be. He needed a quick fix, but he had to make it happen without bothering his mother or Rhonda. He still had a little pride left.

The thought came to him swiftly. Tim had been watching some street corner hustler's every move whenever he was uptown copping dope, and he noticed a lot of loopholes in the way that they stash their drugs. Tim's mouth got watery as the plot he had in mind slowly developed.

But first he had to go home. Rhonda was probably worried about him and he knew that she didn't deserve the worst of him. She was a queen, so he knew that if he didn't get it together she would have no problem finding a king to replace him. When Tim got home Rhonda was sitting on the sofa in the living room watching television.

Tim walked pass her and said hello. He heard no response. Tim turned around and walked towards Rhonda.

"What's wrong baby?" Tim asked empathetically.

Rhonda couldn't keep the tears from falling as she turned around to answer Tim's question.

"I had to make an investment decision today."

Tim was confused. He didn't know what she meant by that, but her body language told him that whatever it was, it was negative.

"An investment decision concerning what?" Tim asked.

Rhonda put her head down then she grabbed the T.V. remote control and flicked through a few channels on the television. She was trying to find something to take her mind off the conversation she knew was necessary. Frustrated with the programming, she put the remote back on the table and prepared for the one thing she had been avoiding.

"I've been talking to some business managers and financial advisors about becoming partners."

It took a moment for Tim to process what Rhonda was saying.

"What do you mean? Partners for what?" Rhonda stared at Tim with a cold look in her eyes.

"This is the real world Tim, no fantasy shit. As a matter of fact, you can live in a fantasy, but you better bet that reality will bite you in the ass." Tim hadn't seen Rhonda react this way often, but he admired her for being in control.

"I've been telling you for weeks that your businesses have been taking a fierce beating because I can't manage them by myself, but for some reason you've chosen to keep me in charge."

"Listen baby," Tim cut in.

"No you listen. This is your shit, but I've been gullible enough to fulfill every task for you. At this point, I will sell Braids R' Us and Johnson Gardens, take a small percentage for my time and effort, and let you blow your money on that shit that has you so in love."

Tim was shocked to hear those words come out of Rhonda's mouth. He knew that his dope habit affected her tremendously, but to hear her words of anger was enough to make him feel less of a man.

"Rhonda," Tim said in a low tone. "I'm sorry I…I don't know what to say."

Rhonda smiled at Tim. It was the kind of smile that said, '*You've messed up a good thing*'.

"Since you don't know what to say, let me help you." Rhonda got up and stood face to face with Tim. She put her hand under his chin.

"Say you'll help me help you find the Tim Johnson that I fell in love with. Say you'll get some help."

Tim couldn't look her in the eyes. He was embarrassed. He had a strong woman who loved him while he was down and out. Tim smiled slightly. He knew he had to get himself together, but Rhonda was right, he was in love with another woman and her name was Lady Heroin.

CHAPTER 21

Things were going just as Cliff had promised for Rabbit. He had a 2000 Hyundai Elantra that Cliff had furnished him for his personal use, and a 1999 Toyota Camry that Cliff also provided him with to transport drugs. Rabbit had saved more money in six weeks then he saved in a three year period. Most of his runs consisted of delivering four or more ounces of crack cocaine. For each ounce delivered, Cliff gave Rabbit two hundred dollars. Therefore, most of the time, Rabbit made no less than eight hundred dollars for one delivery.

Every other weekend, Rabbit would make a delivery that he called, "The Big Score." This was when he had to deliver a kilo of cocaine. Cliff gave him five thousand dollars for each kilo delivery. The money didn't faze Cliff, because he was getting each kilo for ten thousand dollars and selling them for twenty five thousand. He made a ten thousand dollar profit with each delivery after he paid Rabbit.

"So you wanna play rough, you cocka roach?" Rabbit said. He was amused by the reflection of himself in the rear view mirror as he imitated Scarface. "I got it not you. So you can pretend that you're the big fish in the pond, but when the water dries up and you can no longer swim, you'll realize that I have the big score."

It was the weekend and Rabbit had two kilos in the trunk of his Camry. This meant that he would have ten thousand dollars to spend as he pleased. He had already decided that he would stash seven thousand dollars of it with the thirty thousand dollars that he had already saved. Cliff was good to him, but Rabbit had plans of his own. He figured that in due time, he would have someone transporting for him if he saved his money and met the right people. Rabbit turned up the radio and blasted his favorite go-go song by Rare Essence entitled, "Overnight Scenario."

When Rabbit finally arrived at the drop off point, he turned the radio down and focused his attention on the black Chevy Blazer that was parked in the alley.

He was in a low income housing area in Southeast called Condon Terrace, and he wanted to handle his business and leave as quickly as he had arrived. All of the deliveries had gone smooth thus far, but this was a new customer as far as Rabbit was concerned.

Rabbit pulled into the alley slowly. He drove beside the blazer and stopped. The window of the Blazer rolled down, revealing the upper body of a stocky dude with a pair of Kenneth Cole spectacles on.

"What's up slim?" Rabbit uttered.

"Pull in front of me," the dude in the Blazer replied.

Rabbit did as he was instructed. They both got out of their vehicles at the same time. The dude in the Blazer was taller than he looked while he was sitting in the truck, Rabbit thought to himself. Rabbit introduced himself as usual and Daryl did the same.

"Here's my business card. I'm about to start selling weed soon and if you know someone interested, give me a call," Rabbit said.

Daryl was amused by Rabbit's attempt to politic and generate side line clientele for his own product.

"Okay, that's cool, but let's deal with the business at hand."

Daryl put the piece of paper that Rabbit handed him in his pocket and stared at Rabbit. It was like Rabbit was on some type of emotional high. He was often nervous at the initial contact with the person who he was delivering drugs to, but once the monotony was broken, he was in control.

"I hope it's that hard shit, instead of that white shit," Daryl said as he looked around to make sure that the alley was secure enough to continue the transaction.

"To be honest with you, Slim, I haven't looked at it because it's wrapped up tight, but Cliff always gets the best," Rabbit said as he walked to his car and reached inside to pop the trunk. As he turned around to speak, he heard a loud sound that he never heard before. *Pow*! Rabbit's body fell back between the driver's seat of the Camry and the driver's door. Daryl turned around to make sure that the loud sound didn't arouse anyone's suspicion. The alley was that of an abandoned park and chosen specifically for the reason of getting away with murder.

Daryl quickly reached in the trunk and grabbed the medium sized package that Rabbit had hid in a panel inside the trunk. Daryl was not nervous at all. In, fact he moved with persistence and ease. He drove off just as quickly as he drove in the alley.

Daryl picked his cell phone up and dialed Cliff's number.

"What's up slim?" I took care of that phone bill for you," Daryl said.

He was talking in codes to inform Cliff that he had killed Rabbit. Daryl had been home for a few months when he called the phone number that Cliff had given him years ago while they were doing time. When Cliff told him that Rabbit was making drop offs for him, Daryl went haywire. Tim had instilled in Daryl the importance of having morals and principals and standing on them. Daryl explained to Cliff that certain beefs don't get squashed verbally. Someone has to die before the beef is squashed. Cliff felt as if the beef was in the past, but after Daryl drilled him constantly, he agreed to set the hit up.

Cliff wrapped a fake package up and sent Rabbit to the hands of death. Daryl was so upset about Cliff going soft in the beginning that he insisted that he did the hit himself, and he handled it like a true soldier.

When Daryl reached a small street off of Southern Avenue Southeast, he tossed the fake package out of the window.

Afterwards, Daryl slowly took off the black gloves that he was wearing.

"Ha Ha you bitch niggas. I'm that nigga that you fake gangster's get paid for making songs about," he said to himself while turning his radio up."

Cliff and Daryl arranged to meet up on Shipley Terrace Southeast. Shipley Terrace was approximately nine blocks from Condon Terrance. Cliff had a few runners who hustled heroin around Shipley Terrace and wanted to introduce them to Daryl. In fact, he wanted to show Daryl the power that he earned since he's been home.

*****

Tim sat in his car impatient and angry. He was unsuccessful with his attempt to get any more money from Rhonda. She had given him twenty five dollars, but he knew that he needed at least twenty more dollars just in case he brought some heroin that was a five on a scale from one to ten. He used every trick he could to persuade her, but she wouldn't succumb to his wishes. Tim started his car and drove off. As he drove up Southern Avenue Southeast, he spotted a liquor store with a drive thru window. There was no line. Therefore, Tim drove his car directly to the window.

The window cashier was fairly pretty Tim noticed. He felt uneasy as she stared at him. Even though the clothes he had on was rough looking. Tim was still handsome and athletic looking.

"Hello sir, may I help you?" the cashier said.

"Uh yeah, let me have a bottle of Wild Irish Rose."

"What size would you like sir?"

"Huh? Oh, let me have the smallest size."

The cashier smiled. She was amused by Tim's hesitant gestures.

"Would you like anything else sir?"

"Um I would like a pack of cigarettes."

"What kind of cigarettes would you prefer?" Tim smiled.

"Were on a roll, huh? Let me have the cheapest pack you have."

The cashier hesitated and looked at Tim strangely.

"Oh, there not for me they're for a friend," he lied.

"Okay, sir. That'll be five dollars and ninety cents."

"Damn," Tim uttered.

That would leave him with nineteen dollars and ten cents. He needed twenty dollars to buy two dime bags of heroin. He would have to holler at someone who was willing to give him a deal, he thought to himself. Tim had never brought heroin from anyone on this side of town, but as soon as he drove from the liquor store, he spotted someone he knew standing on Central Avenue which intersected with Southern Avenue.

Tim beeped his horn and called the skinny tall dude to his car.

"What's up, slim?" the tall dude said.

"I need to get a couple of bags so that I can holler at this broad," Tim lied. "What's out here?"

The skinny dude, whose name was Scott, looked at Tim and smiled. He could tell by Tim's appearance that he was probably using the dope himself.

"I got some matrix. It's the best thing out here," Scott said.

Heroin was given a name once it hit the street market. This allows the potential heroin user to identify a preference and this helps the dealers to separate the best from the worst.

"Can I get two bags for eighteen dollars?"

"Yeah man, just hurry up. I'm not trying to go to jail."

Tim exchanged his money for the heroin and pulled off. He began to feel jittery as he anticipated his first hit of heroin. He turned his radio up and sung along. He drove in the parking lot of Shade Elementary School on East Capitol Street Southeast. There were plenty of cars in the parking lot. Therefore, his parked car would blend right in.

Tim looked around to make sure the coast was clear. He then took one of the dime bags of heroin out of his pocket and plucked the bag with his finger. The smell of wine filled his car as he poured the wine out of the bottle. Tim reached into the glove compartment and grabbed his hypodermic needles. Afterwards, he reached behind the car seat and grabbed a bottle of water. He sat the water between his legs then he reached in his pocket and retrieved the cigarettes. Tim didn't smoke, but he needed the cotton from the cigarettes to fulfill his mission.

Tim's blood was rushing as he took his belt off and wrapped it around his arm.

He poured some water into the top a few drops at a time. Afterwards, he heated the bottom of the top with a lighter until it turned into yellow looking liquid. Tim was aroused by the process. He put the cigarette cotton into the top then drew the liquid into the needle from the cotton. This was it. This was the beginning of a beautiful day, Tim thought, as he tapped his arm searching for a vein.

As he injected the heroin into his vein, his view of the world began to change. Everything was beautiful once again. There wasn't a worry in the world to Tim. As soon as the feeling subsided, Tim repeated the same process again until he had shot the two bags of dope into his veins.

Tim got out of his car and stretched. He needed to get some more dope so that he could take the high home with him and sleep on it. He thought about different ways to get some money then it hit him. He thought about how vulnerable the dudes around Shipley Terrace were when he used to deliver drugs to one of his runners. Tim drove as the euphoria from the heroin turned into a desire for more.

When he finally reached the intersection of Alabama Avenue and Shipley Terrace, his stomach was filled with butterflies. Tim slowly pulled to the side of an abandoned house that sat across the street from an apartment complex called Shipley Gardens. He watched patiently as the eager hustler's walked back and forth to their stash spot. When the time was right Tim made his move.

While watching, he noticed the exchange of the chip bag and thought that it may contain what he was looking for. So once he had made his play, he looked inside of the potato chip bag that he saw one of the dudes get some dope from. He grabbed a bundle of heroin from that batch then he waited and hit another batch that was hidden under the steps of the abandoned house. Before long, Tim had four ten packs of heroin. Not following his gut instinct, Tim decided to make one more hit, but only after he decided to go to his car and shoot some dope.

CHAPTER 22

Cliff watched his runners move back and forth from the street to an abandoned house to an apartment complex. They were transacting heroin Soles to their everyday customers. Cliff smiled as Daryl drove up blasting Anita Baker through the speakers.

Daryl rolled his window down and spoke to Cliff.

"What's up, bamma? Long time no see slim."

Cliff had the power and he was willing to share a percentage of it with his long time comrade.

"Pull your truck over here dog," Cliff said pointing to a parking space a few feet away from where Cliff had parked his new BMW M3 convertible. As soon as Daryl got out of his truck, he embraced Cliff intensely. They had been through a very trying ordeal in which could have separated them forever. But, here they were together and nothing could come between their bond; not even Tony.

Daryl knew that he didn't have to kill Rabbit himself, but he had to stay abreast of his principals or they could become lost.

"Man what's up? You looking good," Daryl said admiring Cliff's attire.

"Nah, nigga. You look a little jazzier than me."

"Don't even try it, slim. You're the one with the fresh BMW and the fly Gucci shit on. Me, I'm just a plain ole thorough bred killer," Daryl said while laughing wickedly.

Cliff was about to respond when he looked down by the abandoned house and saw what appeared to be a scuffle.

"What the ..." Cliff said before running down the hill. The abandoned house was about fourteen feet from where they were standing. Daryl ran closely behind Cliff.

"Get him. Get that chump," one of the dudes yelled. They were all surrounding the perpetrator. Someone had swung a wooden stick and barely struck the perpetrator. But a lot of punches landed right on target. Cliff stepped into the circle in which they had the dude surrounded.

"What's going on?"

"This bamma got caught stealing our stashes."

Cliff turned the perpetrator over. He had his face covered. There was blood on his clothes and a gash in his head. Cliff pulled his hands down and almost fainted.

Tim opened his eyes. He was in awe. It was Cliff. He cut his eyes at the many faces that were staring at him. He started coughing and choking when he saw Daryl.

"Man what the fuck happened to you?" Daryl said.

Cliff turned around and said, "It don't matter what happened. We have to undo it." Cliff hugged Tim and held him tight. This was the man who was responsible for Cliff having the attitude that he had to get this far in the first place.

Neither one of the dudes knew what this was about except for Daryl, Cliff, and Tim, who was obviously incoherent.

"Man, this nigga ain't nothing but a dope fiend," someone yelled.

"Who said that?' Cliff looked at Daryl and Daryl walked over to the dude who had uttered the words. The slap was cold and vicious as Daryl lifted his hand and swung with no hesitation. Cliff stared at Tim for a moment.

"Man what happened to you? You were always against that get high shit. You are one of the main influences in my life that helped me stay above water."

Tim couldn't respond. He was too high and he was extremely happy to see Daryl and Cliff.

"I need some help," Cliff said.

"Let's pick him up and put him in your truck, Daryl, so we can take him to a detox center."

As promised, Tim was taken to a detox center at D.C. General Hospital.

Cliff got Tim admitted under his name and paid a few extra dollars to make sure that he was kept informed of Tim's recovery and to make sure that Tim was given special care.

The nights were not very pleasant for Tim. He awoke most nights shaking and sleepless. He vomited for three nights and had diarrhea as a result of withdrawing from the use of heroin. Tim knew that he was lucky because heroin users have been known to die when their body couldn't handle the withdrawal symptoms of heroin.

Two weeks had passed since Tim was admitted into detox. Even though he was confined to a detox room, his primary care provider paid close attention to his adjustment to the detoxification process. The nurse that was assigned to Tim checked on him every fifteen minutes and tapped on the door window to give a hand wave letting Tim know that he was not alone.

There was a psychologist assigned to Tim also. He stood at the door from time to time, watching as Tim curled up into the fetal position. Dr.

Smith took his job very seriously and because he had an extensive education in addiction, he could immediately attach himself to the addict's behavior and empathize with the suffering.

He had heard many stories told by recovering heroin addicts. One addict told him that detoxing from heroin is like being dead, but being alive to feel the agony of death.

Dr. Smith had been in this field for thirteen years, which brought him plenty of unforgettable stories that were linked to unforgettable people.

Minus the experience, minus the degree, and minus overcoming the hardships of growing up in poverty Dr. Smith knew that he could have easily ended up in the same position as any one of the addicts who he's worked with thus far.

The very first stages of recovery were always fascinating to Dr. Smith, because there was the disbelief of seeing a person at their lowest state, but at the same time seeing someone who had the power to allow you never to see them like this again. Dr. Smith had a few success stories in his career, but for the most part, the majority of his patients reverted back to the use of heroin or crack. This did not make Dr. Smith any less persistent in his efforts to aid and assist recovering addicts.

Tim turned over to see who had entered his room. There was always someone looking in on him. He remembered most of the faces vividly, but this was a new face.

"How are you doing in spite of your condition Mr. Johnson?"

Tim didn't speak at first. He was still tired and miserable, but the pain was not as intense as before.

"My name is Dr. Smith and I will be assisting you in your recovery. Your family is aware that you are here and they plan to visit you this weekend."

"Man I don't need to be here. I'm not one of those dope fiend niggas on the streets with nowhere to go. I have a business to run." Tim was frustrated and in denial about his addiction.

"I understand Mr. Johnson, but what you don't understand is that you're an addict and if we let you go right now, you'll pick up right where you left off. Not because of the habit, but because you will feel as if you're going to die without. Trust me Mr. Johnson, if you don't run off somewhere thinking you're superman and stay here for a few months, you'll thank me later."

For some strange reason, Tim saw the sincerity in Dr. Smith's eyes.

Tim turned over and laid down.

"Fuck it. You win."

Dr. Smith smiled.

"Nah, you win, my brother. Life is about choices and you just submitted to a positive choice."

Dr. Smith turned around to exit the room.

"Oh Doc!"

"Yeah."

"Send me one of those pretty nurses in here. I'll prefer the one with the blond hair. She seems to have a special interest in me," Tim said.

Dr. Smith smiled. He was impressed by Tim's optimism. He realized that he probably had a one in a million patient in Tim.

CHAPTER 23

Tim awoke to an entourage of onlookers. As his eyes inventoried the visitors, he hadn't felt this much love and support since his release from jail. Rhonda, Calvin, Cliff, and Tim's mother stood at attention. Their eyes seemed to have been in disbelief as Tim adjusted his own vision.

"Baby, are you okay?" Shannon asked.

"Uh yeah. It seems as if I've managed to screw up everybody's life including my own," Tim said.

Rhonda walked over to Tim's bed and kneeled down. She spoke soft and gently.

"You're a strong man baby, and I'm here for you. We're all here for you, so don't stay stuck on your mistakes from yesterday. Instead, focus on what the future holds. Roland misses you."

Cliff was astounded by the support of Tim's family and he admired Tim's ability to hold the fort down even in his vulnerable state. Cliff remembered Rhonda from Lorton, but he didn't think that Tim would still be in contact with her. The sight of Rhonda reminded Cliff of why he respected Tim so much. Tim was chosen by Rhonda out of hundreds of other inmates and she's still by his side even though he's a dope fiend.

Calvin was amazed by the roughness in Tim's appearance. He had always known for his brother to look, smell, and act as smooth as silk. One thing that Calvin couldn't dispute was the fact that Tim's attitude stayed stable during the entire visit.

Shannon walked over to Tim's bed.

"This is such a small room. Are you going to be alright baby?" Tim nodded. "Do you need anything?"

Tim shook his head. "Nah I'm alright."

Tim paused as a tear fell from his eye.

"You see that man right there, ma?" Tim pointed at Cliff. "We go way back. He saved my life when most of these dudes would have left me for dead."

Shannon started crying she held her son with a fierce passion. Then she turned around and hugged Cliff. Calvin stood there silently. Somehow he felt guilty for Tim's ordeal. If he would have been there to go places and do things with Tim, none of this would have occurred Calvin told himself. He wouldn't have let it occur.

Hesitantly, Calvin walked towards Tim's bed. Tim looked as if he was in slight pain. Calvin felt empathy for him. In fact, the whole ordeal reinforced Calvin's beliefs about the lifestyle of drug dealing. The end result is either jail or death and he was watching his brother slowly fall to the mercy of death. The visits were not usually like this. After a patient is admitted into detox, there's a six month drug rehabilitation program to follow. Once the patient has successfully completed sixty days of the program, he's allowed a thirty minute visit. This was designed so that the patient wouldn't become too detached from treatment and so that the patient would be affected by the consequences of victimizing others.

"Okay folks, I've done the best that I could. I gave you twenty minutes. Now, me and Mr. Johnson have some important business to attend to," Dr. Smith said.

"Thank you very much, doctor," Cliff said. The rest of Tim's family joined in unison. Everyone hugged Tim before they left and Rhonda asked for a few minutes alone with him. When the door was closed and everyone left, Rhonda smiled at Tim.

"Hey baby, I have some good news and some bad news. Which one do you want first?"

Tim smiled. "Nothing could be worse than this, so give me both of them in a nutshell."

Rhonda paused for a minute.

"Do you remember those investors that I was supposed to have a meeting with?" Tim nodded but he didn't remember. "Well I decided not to sell your businesses. I chose to stick it out. But it's killing me. It's too much work involved."

Tim processed what she had just said. *He didn't even know she think about selling something that was theirs.* Tim thought to himself.

"Come here, baby." Tim said in a low voice. They embraced intensely.

"I have a few comrades who are willing to help us out. Just hold on okay!"

Rhonda smiled. "Okay baby." Tim closed his eyes and when he opened them he hoped that somehow Rhonda would be gone so that he wouldn't have to endure the pain of watching her leave. But, that was not the case. Instead he opened his eyes only to see her eyes flooded with tears.

He remembered a poem that he had read in the *Moonlighting* book that spoke about tears of misery and pain. Tim wondered if there could ever be enough misery to cover up the pain.

"I have to go, baby. But you can bet your bottom dollar that I will be one of the first to return," Rhonda said.

Tim laughed.

"What's so funny?" Rhonda asked.

"You said one of the first. You're either the first or the second or the third and so on. How could you be one of the first?"

Rhonda shoved Tim. "You know what I mean." They hugged once more. Then Tim watched his partner in love head for the door.

"Hold on," Tim said suddenly. "I almost forgot." Tim told her about Cliff and Daryl. He explained how important loyalty was to them and how they would be willing to keep his business in order until he was in order enough to manage them. They both decided that it would be a good idea to sell the apartment complex so that Rhonda could focus on managing the beauty Solon.

*****

Two weeks had passed since Tim had completed the detoxification phase of the drug rehabilitation program. His assigned doctor had transferred him from the isolation room to an adjustment room. The name of the program was, "Just to Get By." It had been up and running for eighteen months and the success rate of an addict not reverting back to the use of drugs was thirty percent, which meant that there were not many success stories.

The adjustment room was designed so that the patient could properly adjust to life after withdrawing from drugs. The average addict was moody, angry, and sometime annoyed after detoxing. Therefore, it was not a good idea to mix them with addicts who were working through the phases of the rehabilitation program.

As each patient on the adjustment unit waited for their name to be called, you could sense the high level of anticipation in the air. Addicts shared stories with other addicts. Promises of sticking together were made. But Tim remained silent. For some strange reason, he felt as if he could walk out of the door and never use again. Little did he know that each and every other addict in the room felt the same way.

There were twenty patients assigned to the adjustment unit waiting to be transferred to the program unit which held three phases: beginners, the survivors, and advanced. Each phase lasted two months long.

As participants and addicts they were each responsible for each other's behavior. This was called group accountability. This was the sole foundation of the programs concept. The program had fifty three participants, but the numbers were growing monthly. The beginners phase was a whole new change in lifestyle and information for the participants. By the time they reached the survivors phase, the addict would have absorbed enough information to survive the initial shock of living clean and sober.

However, some survivors struggled more than others, which sometimes resulted in them being set back to the beginners phase. Once the survivor reaches the advance phase, they would have willingly adapted to a new way of living free.

The advanced addict was expected to assist new comers as much as possible until he or she had transferred to the independent living program. The independent living program consisted of helping recovering addicts regain a responsible role in society. They were assigned to living quarters within a ten mile radius of the rehabilitation program. The living quarters was a one bedroom apartment which was used as a tax write off for the owner of the apartment complex for allowing the program to contract it's independent living participants to reside in the quarters.

Tim inhaled a breath of fresh air as his name was called by one of the treatment coordinators. Most of the addicts were in a hurry to begin treatment, but once they got there, a lot of them were disappointed because of the expectations and responsibilities that were placed upon them.

Even though it was very clear to the staff members that Tim was willing to participate in the program, he had to be formerly interviewed by several of the staff members before he could begin treatment. The interview consisted of an array of questions about the participant's abuse history, future goals, and the competency of the individual if accepted into the program. Tim's interview wasn't as long as the average interviews usually were, because unlike many of the other addicts Tim didn't have a long history of drug abuse. Ms. Thorne was impressed by Tim's honesty and willingness to be open as she interviewed him.

Although the participants weren't always assigned to the coordinator that interviewed them, Ms. Thorne decided to do everything in her power to make sure that Tim would be assigned to her case load. She identified a potential leader in him and she knew that Tim would be capable of persuading other participants to be open, because of his willingness to be.

"Okay, Mr. Johnson, here's the deal," Ms. Thorne said as she eyed him intrusively. She handed him a name tag that had Johnson printed on it.

"You'll have to wear this during the hours of eight a.m. to four p.m." Tim nodded.

"Here's a list of rules and regulations that you will be expected to abide by while in recovery." She handed Tim a two paged regulation memorandum.

As he glanced at the many different rules, his eyes bulged in disbelief. There was no sharing items of any sort, and no wearing your shoes in your room, (you have to leave them at the front door). There were daily inspections in which participants were scored. No profanity, no horse play, and the list went on and on.

"There are a lot of rules in here," Tim said.

"Yes, there are, and you better do your best to follow them because they are an integral part in you becoming a new man," Ms. Thorne responded.

Tim smiled, "I never thought that I would end up in a place like this."

Ms. Thorne stared at Tim and said, "I didn't either."

Tim was confused at first, because he assumed that she was talking about him. Then it dawned on him that she meant herself.

*****

"Man, I would have never guessed that my man had so much going for him," Cliff said as he went over the financial prospects of Braids R' Us with Rhonda.

"Well, Tim started out of the gate so fast when he came home." Rhonda put her head down as if she was ashamed. "I kind of feel that it's my fault because I didn't pressure him into helping me manage any of his investments and he just ventured off into those streets."

Cliff smiled at Rhonda. "You're a strong woman. You deserve a good man like Tim. He's a soldier. He's just a fallen soldier and he needs your strength."

Rhonda suddenly felt a surge of reinforcement within herself emotionally. She needed a good pep talk and that's what Cliff gave her.

"I'll help you with the management aspects. I'll run errands or whatever until my man is back in action. Money is no problem and if you need labor done I'll handle that also," Cliff continued.

"That's nice of you but…"

"Shhh," Cliff placed his hands over Rhonda's lips. "No ifs, ands or buts. Maybe one day Tim will sit down and explain to you the true meaning of death before dishonor, just like he explained it to me." Cliff smiled and shook his head. "As long as I'm alive, I will treat my comrade with honor."

Just when Rhonda had lost a small sense of respect for Tim, Cliff helped her regain it.

****

Two months had passed since Tim had started the rehabilitation program. He had successfully completed the beginner's phase of the program, now he was a survivor. Tim had taken the role of a leader from the start. He was open about his drug use and was diligent with helping other addicts become open about theirs. The participants were assigned to GGI groups (Guided Group Interaction) based on their treatment coordinator. There were participants from every phase assigned to the groups. Therefore, if you were a beginner and you were reluctant to speak about your addiction, then a survivor or a participant in the advance phase would offer intense encouragement.

"I don't want anyone in here to think that I was a saint, because I'm not. I was a grimy dope fiend who would do whatever it took to get high," Earl said. He was in the advanced phase but he prided himself on Tim's guidance. "I stole money from my wife, kids, and even myself at times, just to make love to Lady Heroin" Earl put his head down while his tears rolled down his face.

Even though this wasn't Earl's first time in GGI, he was able to relive the horror of his past each time he opened up in group. What most of the addicts had in common was that in spite of their horrible past, they still had loved ones willing to support them. The same loved ones who were victimized time and time again by them. Tim stared at the participants in the beginners phase to see their reaction to Earl's outwardly expression.

"Well Earl," Tim said, "If this was the case, then why didn't you try to find some help? Or better yet, why didn't you just stop?"

Earl looked around the room while the others stared at him with anticipation. "I couldn't stop even when I wanted to."

The treatment coordinator intervened at this point. Even though Tim and Earl were role playing, they were serious. The point that they wanted the group to see was that when you're an addict, you can't get clean by yourself.

The program didn't just consist of recovery support groups. The participants had extreme informative classes on criminology, lifestyle changing, living drug free and coping skills, which helped them, develop some survival skills while they fought a daily battle with their addiction. This was what Tim needed to regain his morality. The more groups he went to, the more he wanted to be a part of positive change.

Tim didn't want to look back on his past too often; he wanted to move forward.

Rhonda had brought him a lot of new clothes. Tim had told her untrue stories about how his clothes and jewelry had gotten stolen, but with the programs help, he was able to face her and tell her that he had sold a lot of his jewelry in exchange for drugs and money.

The visits were okay, but they were too short for Tim likes. However, they made the most of them. Rhonda was content with every passing minute, while Tim was anxious to return home.

Cliff was very consistent with making sure that Rhonda had the support that she needed to keep Tim's business ventures afloat. He had set up the deal with safe guard realtors to sell Johnson Gardens Apartment for 1.7 million dollars at Tim's request. Tim had explained the reason for this sudden desire to sell the complex. He had a few other ideas in mind. Tim wanted to lease a lot and buy fifty used cars. Sol had promised to show Tim the ropes of the used car business.

Tim had been advised in one of his independent living classes to find something that he liked to do and stick with it. Tim realized that he enjoyed selling things, so he decided that instead of selling drugs, he could sell cars. This would allow him to work at the car lot and oversee the production of his company without having to wear Rhonda down. Rhonda was fond of the idea, but Tim's mother was hesitant because she had put a lot of work into the apartment project.

"Thank you very much," Rhonda said to Cliff, as she grabbed his hand. "You are a good friend." Cliff smiled. "I don't know if I would have handled the business transaction as you did. I'm more passive and light hearted. But you took control."

Cliff was attracted to Rhonda from the start, but he fought the feeling as much as he could because he knew that she belonged to Tim.

"Are you always so in control?" Rhonda asked.

"You know I…" before he could finish, Rhonda had reached over the seat and kissed him. They were sitting in the car right in front of the rehabilitation program where Cliff waited while Rhonda visited Tim.

"Oh. I'm sorry, Cliff. But that was well deserved." They both were silent

"How's Tim doing?"

Rhonda laughed.

"What's funny?" Cliff asked.

"Oh nothing; he's okay. He likes to play between my legs when I visit him and that shit gets me hot and dammit I can't have any because he's in there."

Cliff thought about what she said then it hit him. She's horny as hell. He didn't know what to do or what to say.

"Look, Cliff, I'm going to get to the point. I'm not going to run around sneaking to get some sex. Instead, I would rather get it from you. No feelings or anything involved, just something to tide me over until Tim gets out."

Cliff was turned on, but he knew that Rhonda was just caught up in the moment.

"That wouldn't be right."

"It's just between me and you. No one has to know."

Cliff knew that if it started here, then it wouldn't end here, especially if the sex was good. The consequences were far more severe than Rhonda could imagine. Neither one of them would feel comfortable about this whenever Tim was present, but in spite of this factor, Cliff's flesh was just as weak as Rhonda's and she knew it.

"Okay...I'll do it as long as you realize that this will changes things between us."

Rhonda ran her fingers through her hair, and then she turned towards Cliff.

"I don't feel good about this, but I've had a hard time dealing with all of this by myself, so come with me."

Rhonda and Cliff went to a motel. Cliff was amazed at how wild and explorative Rhonda was in bed. He realized that he had violated his friendship with Tim, but while he was in Rhonda, delusion kicked in and he began to feel like Tim was the one violating the friendship. Cliff imagined that Rhonda was his. With every stroke came a need for more entry.

Whenever it was time for Tim to get a visit, Cliff was there to take Rhonda to the rehabilitation center. Afterwards, Rhonda practically ran into his arms so that they could make their escape to the motel. Tim didn't have long before he transitioned from the advanced phase into the independent living phase of the program. The six months had passed so quickly and it seemed as if Tim was a whole different person to Rhonda.

This was Rhonda's last visit with Tim. Tim had a month left in the program and he wanted to keep his mind free from distractions. Tim's craving for heroin had subsided a few months ago. He still remembered the torturing feelings and withdrawal that he felt and he had no problem sharing his entire experience as an addict with the group.

Tim was required to attend narcotics anonymous meetings during and after his stint in the independent living program. This wasn't a problem for him. He acknowledged his fears, relapse triggers, and the people, places, and things that he must stay away from in order to sustain his recovery.

CHAPTER 24

Cliff and Rhonda sat in the car waiting for Tim. The rehabilitation program didn't have a graduation for the participants in the advanced phase. It was said that treatment would last a lifetime; therefore there was no need for a graduation. However, the participants were encouraged to reward themselves in a positive way for their achievement and they were given a certificate acknowledging their completion of the program.

"Do you think that it's going to be easy to just ignore you as if none of this never happened?" Cliff asked Rhonda.

Rhonda gritted her teeth. She didn't blink nor did she turn to look at Cliff.

"I told you the rules of the game before we started" Rhonda replied.

"Yeah…you're right, but I wouldn't leave imagined that my feelings would get so involved." Rhonda rolled her eyes as she turned to Cliff.

"It was just a fuck. Something to hold me down until my man, who is your main man, returned." Rhonda paused as she watched Tim walk out of the center. "You did say that you would do anything for your main man didn't you?"

Tim knocked on the window, then opened up the passenger side rear door.

"Hey baby!" Tim said in an ecstatic voice.

"What's up, slim?" he said to Cliff.

They both spoke almost in sync.

"Here's my new apartment address. I have to stay there for three months, then I can go back home with my baby."

Cliff looked at the paper that Tim handed him with the address on it.

"Man, this is right around the corner."

"Yeah I know. They try to keep us close to the center. But hey I'm out of there."

Rhonda was beginning to feel guilty and she didn't want her guilt to be recognized by Tim.

"I hope you're ready back there, because here I come," Rhonda said as she climbed over the seat into Tim's lap. "Drive Mr. Driver. I have some unfinished business to tend to," Rhonda said as she unzipped Tim's pants.

Cliff was jealous as he glanced in the rear view mirror at Tim.

Cliff noticed Rhonda's head moving up and down. This drove him insane.

Cliff taunted himself for getting involved with her. Now he would have to stay as far away as he could from her in order to protect his feelings.

"Can't ya'll wait until you're in the privacy of your home?" Cliff asked rhetorically. Even though he was ignored, he thought about how crazy the suggestion sounded. Cliff couldn't let jealousy go detected. Cliff glanced in the mirror from time to time during the ride, but each time he did his eyes became his worst enemy.

Once they reached the apartment building, Tim was surprised at the different structure of landscape of what was once called Johnson Gardens. Even though so far Tim didn't have any objections, his arrival didn't feel as comfortable as when he was the owner. Cliff arranged to set up a contract whereas he negotiated the transaction of Johnson Gardens with the agreement of leasing ten apartments to the independent living program in addition to the purchase amount that was immediately wired to Tim's business account.

"I've been in your apartment. I added a little spice to that dull place they gave you," Cliff said to Tim.

"I appreciate that, Joe. Now I get to see if you're really a suave dude or if I have to school you all over again."

They sat for a minute in silence "Well, this is it," Rhonda said.

Tim patted her on the thigh. "Why didn't you bring Roland with you baby, I want to see my, dog?"

Rhonda grabbed his hand. "You'll see him soon enough. Right now we have to get you squared away."

Cliff turned the radio down. "Do you need me to come up with you, dog?" Cliff asked Tim.

Tim looked at Rhonda then said, "Nah slim, you've done enough. I'm going to spend a little time alone."

Rhonda slapped his leg. "No you're not. I'm coming up with you. I'll just catch a cab home later," Rhonda uttered.

Cliff felt a surge of jealousy and envy, but why should he be angry at Tim? Tim had done nothing but caught a bad break in life. Rhonda belonged to Tim and Cliff's carelessness allowed him to become entrapped in his emotions for Rhonda.

"We better get going," Tim said as he opened the door. He stood there while Rhonda got out of the car and he let her lead the way.

"I'll call you main man," Tim said to Cliff before he walked towards Rhonda, who had already reached the front entrance of the apartment building. Cliff's mind wandered off as he looked towards the beautiful landmark of the sky. He was suddenly interrupted by a knock on his car door window.

He rolled his window down as instructed by Tim.

"What's up slim?" Cliff asked.

"Look dog, I wanted to let you know how much I appreciate everything. We'll get together soon and reunite in a more proper fashion," Tim said.

"It ain't nothing, man. You're the reason for me staying above water. I understand that you have to get things in order, just don't let me down and go back to messing with that shit."

"All I needed was a break from it. You don't have to worry about that. It's death before dishonor with me comrade."

Tim and Cliff shook hands, then Tim disappeared into the building. Once inside, Tim didn't notice a significant change in the building's interior structure, but he laughed at the sign that said Welcome to City Line Towers.

"So this was the only name that they could come up with?" Tim asked as they got on the elevator.

"Everybody doesn't have your unique style baby."

"I guess not, huh."

Tim was amazed at how Cliff had decorated his apartment. The whole apartment was black and white. The black carpet blended perfectly with the white sofa. The two white tables they sat on each end of the long sofa had two black hearts; one on each table. The hearts were ceramic moldings. One of them had Tim's name on it in white lettering and the other one had Rhonda's name on it. Rhonda was as impressed as Tim was by the style of the small one bedroom apartment.

"Hold on for a minute baby," Tim said as he picked up the telephone and dialed a number.

"Hello," he said, after letting the phone ring. "Mr. Smith? Yeah this is Mr. Johnson. You told me if I didn't run away, that I would thank you later. Well I'm calling to thank you. Okay I'll keep in touch. Bye, bye."

Tim's phone call to Dr. Smith was brief and to the point. Tim had adjusted to using the direct approach while he was in the program. This was said to have an effect on the listener's ability to absorb the message effectively. After calling Dr. Smith, Tim called Roland. Roland was excited to hear Tim's voice. He wanted Tim to come and get him, but Tim could only promise him that he would see him soon.

Afterwards, Tim sat on the sofa and gathered his thoughts. He realized that his ties with Cliff and Daryl immediately connected him back to his old lifestyle, and to maintain his effective recovery, that was something he'd have to deal with. But, how could he explain this to them without contradicting himself? Tim wondered.

The program had emphasized the importance of detaching oneself from any old acquaintances that are involved in the criminal lifestyle or any narcotic behavior.

In group, Tim said that he wouldn't have any problem cutting those ties off, but as he sat and thought about it, his situation was different. This kind of thinking was what his peers had warned him about, but Tim ignored his responsibility of cutting those ties off while he was in treatment.

Tim also thought about the many tense emotions that he felt during the victim impact class. The class was designed to hopefully deter the addict from further victimizing of their family, friends, and community. Through role plays and essays, they acknowledged what their victims must have went through as a result of their negative choices. Tim realized that anything could have happened to Rhonda or his mother whenever they had to be in contact with Tim, because of his association with Cliff. Someone could have had a dispute with Cliff over drug money and shot whoever was with him. This is how he was an indirect victimizer of his family and this was what he had learned through intense sessions at the rehabilitation program.

"What am I thinking?" Tim said aloud to himself. "I'm dealing with some soldiers who know how to handle themselves accordingly." Tim assured himself that his association with Cliff and Daryl would not be his down fall. Instead, this would be the very thing that helped him survive.

CHAPTER 25

She sat at her small desk clicking away at the screen with her computer mouse. The pictures were vivid and full of potential to please her appetite. She focused on every detail, every proportion, and every story that each picture told. Some of the pictures were old, yet some of the pictures were very up to date and full of life. Linda noticed a smile when she was happily engaged to Tim. She noticed his smile as well. She had pictures on her computer of their most romantic moments and she had recent pictures of Tim as he was out and about proceeding with his life without her. She even had pictures of Tim before he went into the rehabilitation program and his first day out.

Linda had a separate set of pictures that could change the course of Tim's whole life; she called those pictures her Drama City files. Her plan was to put Tim's back up against the wall so that he would have no other choice but to come back to her. *I'll erase everyone's existence from your life and you'll come running back to me!*, Linda thought to herself.

Linda was responsible for placing her cousin in the program to watch Tim from the inside. At times she lost sight of her plans because she was planning it from scratch, but now she was in full control of her motives. Linda picked the phone up and dialed a number. After a few rings the person on the other end answered.

"Hello...yes I need to speak to an agent by the name off Mr. Anthony Scales. Oh, I see...uh no I'll try back in due time." Linda couldn't reach the person she wanted at the F.B.I building, and as she thought about it, now wasn't a good time anyway. She needed to take care of a few more loose ends.

Linda taunted herself for almost reacting irrationally at the hospital. She was so full of rage that she wanted to overdose Tim with anesthesia, but she quickly regained control of her mission. Her plan slowly came together when she observed the characteristics of those who frequented Tim's life. It wasn't easy for Linda to watch Tim and his associates. She had to hire a few private investigators to help. Linda knew that she had to be patient because the smallest mistake could turn the tables against her.

*****

Tim felt more in control of his life than ever before. He had taken full control of the management paperwork that was required for him to keep Braids R' Us afloat. Instead of urging Rhonda to handle the inventory, stock, and small errands, Tim handled it himself. In fact, Rhonda had become bored because she hadn't realized that she hadn't really done anything else besides put a lot of her time and effort into running Tim's business. Two months had passed and Tim had only thirty days left until the independent living phase of his treatment would expire. He had a few urges to get high from time to time, but he never gave in. Instead, he called one of the other program participants and expressed the fact that he had a craving to use. He was given a pep talk and was quickly reminded of the consequences of going backwards. The thought of using subsided and Tim moved on. Tim vowed to himself that he would let nothing stand in his way this time. He was focused.

Tim decided to reward himself with a steak. As soon as he headed towards the refrigerator, he was sidetracked by a knock on the door. He had no idea of who would have the audacity to knock on the door so loud, but he was irritated by the gesture. Tim looked through the peephole while inhaling his anger.

"Surprise! What's up slim?" Daryl and Cliff's voice blended in unison. Tim smiled as they both walked passed him lugging gifts that they had brought him.

"What's up Joe?" Tim said. Daryl turned around and smiled as he put the shopping bag on Tim's sofa.

"Man we know you're probably out of fashion, so we decided to hook you up," Daryl said in a ecstatic tone of voice. Tim looked at Daryl then at Cliff.

"Man, you two fools are full of it."

"Yeah! You're right. We're full of the latest fashion." Cliff tossed one of the bags to Tim.

"Check it out, slim!"

Tim opened the bag and reached into it. He pulled out a pair of Gucci slacks and a Banana Republic silk shirt. They were both a matching beige color. Then Daryl pulled the beige alligator shoes out of the bag that he had for Tim. Tim was awe struck by the uniqueness of the entire outfit.

"Damn ya'll soldiers got a little style with yourselves, huh!" Tim replied.

"Yeah, I mean…when you got style and class it shows in more ways than one," Cliff responded. Tim smiled.

"Hold on a minute! If ya'll brought me this kind of attire I know ya'll don't want me to sit around here in it. If I didn't know any better, I would think that you two were planning on partying with the stars," Tim said in an ecstatic tone.

"Well, I must say you are definitely on to something, but I can't disclose the details, slim," Daryl responded.

Tim's mind was racing. Not for the anticipation of where they may be going, but because he was instructed not to involve himself with old acquaintances who may be involved in any illegal activity. This was a sure trigger for relapse. Tim had heard far too many stories of relapse from fellow peers while he was in the rehabilitation program. He remembered Mr. Snypes telling the group that he had been clean and sober for seven years. Then he started hanging with some of his coworkers who loved to drink and party. After occasionally drinking with them he started having strong cravings for his drug of choice; crack cocaine. One thing led to another and Mr. Snypes was back on crack harder than ever. He victimized his family and friends by lying and stealing from them.

Eventually, Mr. Snypes built up enough courage to rob a bank, which landed him in jail. Because this was his first criminal offense, the judge suspended his seven to twenty one year sentence with the stipulation of him successfully completing an inpatient drug program. Tim knew that this could happen to any addict; even himself. But he felt as though his loyalty to Cliff and Daryl was worth the risk. In fact, he entertained an even stronger thought. Daryl and Cliff's expectations of him would not allow him to let them see him down and out and strung out on heroin.

"Well, since I see that you're not going to let me know where we're supposed to be going, I'm going to call Rhonda and let her know that we're going out," Tim said sarcastically.

"Speaking of Rhonda….Man, I didn't know that you were working your hand when we were locked up," Daryl said.

'That's the key. You never let your right hand know what your left hand is doing," Tim replied.

"Fuck that! I want to know how you pulled her," Cliff stated in a demanding voice.

Tim smiled, then he laughed. He sat down and told his comrades everything that occurred in detail. Daryl and Cliff were mesmerized as Tim explained how he and Rhonda had sexed while he was in the hole. They talked for hours exchanging stories. They told Tim how Rabbit was working for Cliff until they tricked him out of his life. Tim was proud of his boys for sticking to the gangsta code.

"Damn. Rabbit didn't have any idea that he was about to meet his maker, huh?" Tim said.

"Nah. He thought that he was making a routine drop off for Cliff," Daryl said.

Neither one of them mentioned to Tim that Rabbit was a loyal runner for Cliff until Daryl intervened. They both made it appear as if they had set Rabbit up from the beginning. Tim walked to the refrigerator and grabbed some orange juice. He put the juice on the table and grabbed a few drinking cups. The phone rang and he hesitated for a moment before answering. It was Rhonda and Tim's mother calling him on a three way phone connection.

Tim talked to them for a minute. Then, he listened to them as they both tried to squeeze words in at the same time.

Tim told them that he was going out with Cliff and Daryl, but he wasn't sure where they were taking him. They laughed and joked a few minutes more, then Tim sent his love and hung up the phone.

"Okay slim! We're set," Tim said as he poured each one of them a cup of orange juice. When Tim handed Daryl his cup Daryl looked at it and laughed.

"Hey, where's the real deal? I need something strong to go with this. Like some Vodka or something."

Tim paused he was caught off guard. Cliff nudged Daryl as a warning.

"Oh! Man my fault" Daryl apologized. But the damage was done. Tim realized that Daryl didn't understand addiction. He probably didn't even truly believe that Tim was capable of being hooked on any drug. Even though Tim never really drank, he knew that just one drink could lead him back to his drug of choice. Tim quickly changed the subject.

"Has anyone heard from Tony?"

Daryl spit his juice out. "I'll kill that sucker if I ever see him!" Daryl said angrily.

Tim looked at Cliff and Cliff put his head down because he knew that Tim would feel guilty once he told him how Tony had betrayed them.

"Man, Daryl gave a dope fiend down Lorton some work and he messed up the package. So Daryl had to put some work in. The shit got messy and Tony snitched on us."

Tim was speechless.

"Luckily, we worked our way out of it. But if we hadn't, we would probably be doing life in the feds," Daryl added.

"You can never tell who's who," Tim replied.

"Come on man, get dressed. We're going out on the town," Cliff said.

"Okay, give me a minute and I'll be ready."

It had been awhile since Tim had been out for the sole purpose of socializing. He was so into working and maintaining his sobriety that he had programmed himself. He vowed never to revert back to dealing drugs or getting high, but little did he know, the lifestyle that he used to live was easier to get into then it would be to get out of. Not to mention that hanging out with Cliff and Daryl would hurt his sobriety more than it would help it.

"Damn, that broad is phat," Cliff said as they passed a female who was walking along Southern Avenue Southeast. Cliff was referring to the female's nice sized butt.

Tim didn't respond. He was so occupied with thoughts of the surprise that his mind wouldn't allow him to lust.

Cliff and Daryl were dressed to impress. Cliff was wearing an Armani suit with matching alligator shoes, and Daryl was dressed in a silk suit by Helmut Lang with a pair of Stacy Adams casual shoes. As they pulled up to an apartment complex in Benning Heights Tim was puzzled.

"Hold on a minute, I have to take care of some business," Cliff said as he pulled his truck into the parking lot of the complex. There were three guys standing outside and one of them walked towards Cliff's truck. Cliff rolled the window down and gave the dude a large bag in exchange for what appeared to be a couple of rolls of money.

"Man, hold up. I know you're not riding around with dope in your car!" Tim demanded. Cliff was caught off guard by Tim's confrontation. Cliff was used to a programmed system of dealing. He hadn't even considered Tim's situation.

"Damn slim, my fault. I had to take care of that for my man."

Tim knew that being with Cliff and Daryl would be a test. He knew that they wouldn't change their whole system, but he thought that they would be overly discrete.

"Man, you need to get yourself a few stores because that dope dealing shit is going to get you late."

"Look who's talking," Daryl intervened.

"Well I wasn't talking to you, but as a matter of fact, I am living proof that anything centered around dope will get you caught up," Tim said.

Tim looked at Cliff then he glanced at Daryl.

"I hope that you two niggas are on some gangsta shit because if you're in this game then you have to be all the way gangsta with it, because these dudes out here will try you."

The loud sound of a click was heard as Daryl cocked his pistol. "Well I don't have to worry about nobody playing me for weak because I have no time for faking. I'll put a hole through a bamma that won't close up until he's cremated."

Tim realized that he had slipped back into his old ways. He had to be careful around Cliff and Daryl because they were capable of turning his criminal switches off and on.

"Since we're in the area I want to holler at my man real quick. He lives on F Street," Tim said purposely changing the subject. Tim gave Cliff the directions and they were off to Mike's house. Mike and Brenda were sitting on the porch when Tim, Cliff, and Daryl arrived.

Tim got out and greeted them both with open arms.

"You look good!" Mike said.

"What brings you through here?" Brenda asked.

Tim smiled and said, "Good friends can't be replaced."

Brenda and Mike smiled at each other in a suspicious way.

"What's wrong?" Tim asked.

"Should I tell him baby?" Brenda asked Mike.

"Nah, he should hear it from me," Mike said with a joyful smile on his face.

"Thanks to you road dog, I'll probably be walking again very soon."

Tim had gotten Mike one of the best physical trainers available in the area and evidently it paid off. They conversed awhile longer before Tim left. Tim told them about his new found freedom in life and promised to return soon so that he could treat them to dinner. He was happy for Mike, but he just couldn't get pass the guilt that tormented him every time he saw or thought about Mike being in a wheel chair.

Cliff took Daryl and Tim to a restaurant called Houston's in Georgetown. They joked and talked for hours. Cliff was interested in cleaning up his dirty money and he admired the way Tim set his businesses up. Cliff informed Tim of his drug operation in Southeast. Cliff wanted to close up the shop because of the drama that surrounded the drug game. Tim was ecstatic to hear that, but Daryl wasn't ready to give it up.

This is often the case, Tim thought to himself. Whenever you're in the game there are certain laws that one has to abide by. One of the laws is the mere fact that just because you want to give up the lifestyle doesn't mean that the people that have become dependent upon you will let you. Sometimes they'll rather kill you then allow you to throw the towel in." Tim realized that Cliff and Daryl were even closer than before after going through so much together. Therefore, Tim not only had to give Cliff the blueprint on making a business-oriented transformation, but he had to present it in a way that it would be appealing to Daryl as well.

"You have to find someone willing to open a business account for you so that the illegal money won't be questioned," Tim said. Tim was tapping his fork on the table. The sound wasn't loud but it was irritable to Daryl. However, Daryl ignored it. It wasn't until Tim explained the loan process and the reason for obtaining a loan that Cliff grabbed Tim's hand bringing a closure to the table tapping.

"You have to get into a business that's profitable. They offer franchises for subway, McDonalds and any other major businesses that you can think of," Tim explained.

"That sounds good. But suppose it doesn't work out?" Daryl said.

"If ya'll put the same effort into it that ya'll do the drug game, then it can't go wrong," Tim replied.

"Man…you make it sound real easy," Cliff stated.

"Nah man, nothing worth having comes easy. That's why my shit is out of order. I didn't take the time or put in the proper effort to make my empire work for me."

"Yeah, but you still came out with a nice piece of change," Cliff said.

"I didn't come out on top. I settled for less."

"Okay, I'll pay you to help me set everything up once I decide what I want to do."

"Just don't take forever, because there's a lot of money to be made the legal way," Tim said in a nonchalant tone.

As they were leaving, Tim noticed a familiar face eyeing him. It was Linda, and she was sitting with a male friend. She smiled then waved him over to her table.

"Hello," Linda said as she stared him up and down. Tim was awe struck as his resentment towards Linda subsided.

"How have you been?" Tim asked. Linda turned to her friend after he interrupted the moment by tapping her leg.

"Oh I'm sorry. This is my friend Tyrone. Tyrone this is my ex-boyfriend."

Tim noticed the emphasis that she put on the word boyfriend. Linda was unbelievably attractive Tim thought to himself.

"What's up slim?"

"Nothing much... Nice to meet you." Tim and Tyrone exchanged greetings. But Tyrone wasn't his name. In fact, he knew more about Tim than Tim would ever imagine. The male companion who accompanied Linda was a paid private investigator. Without his help, Linda would have had a lot more work to do to complete her Drama City files. Tim and Linda conversed and exchanged apologies for their destructive run-ins with each other. They contributed the fall out to the unpredictable manner of love and broken hearts. They also exchanged phone numbers, before Tim hugged her and left the restaurant.

The next few weeks came quickly and Tim was finished with the independent living phase of the program. Although, Tim knew that it was very crucial for him to continue with aftercare and one on one sessions with his drug treatment coordinator, he was content knowing that his movements would not be dictated.

Tim had packed most of his belongings a week in advance. Therefore, he didn't have much to pack as he gathered what was left of his personal items. His family and friends offered to help, but Tim insisted that he handled it alone.

For Tim this was what independent living was about.

Rhonda was expecting him at 11:00am, but it was 9:30am and Tim was heading out the door. He wanted to surprise her. Rhonda and Roland were staying at Tim's mother house temporarily. Tim was planning to buy a house. In fact, he had negotiated everything with a real estate broker. He just had to sign the contract to close the deal.

Tim inhaled the solid aroma of spring as he exited the apartment building. The insurance agency had covered the total cost of his truck repairs after the shooting. Tim was feeling as if his life was restored as he fumbled around in his truck looking for his favorite C.D.

Tim reached in the back seat and recovered the Chuck Brown C.D. that he was looking for. Nothing could have prepared him for the horror that he felt as he turned around to the screams of the drug enforcement agents.

"Freeze! Put your hands up. Place your hands where we can see them!" the agents demanded. They grabbed Tim and slammed him on the pavement.

"What's going on?" Tim asked.

"Shut up punk!" one of the agents replied.

"You have the right to remain silent. Anything that you say can and will be used against you in the court of law...!" The words of the Miranda rights cut into Tim like a sharp sword. He could no longer hear the agent reciting his rights to him. Instead, his thoughts were on trying to figure out what episode of his past had come back to haunt him.

"Pick him up," one of the agents demanded.

A short, stocky agent walked up to Tim.

"I'm D.E.A agent Anthony Scales. You and I have a lot of things to discuss."

Tim gritted his teeth. "I'm not discussing anything with you without my lawyer present!"

Mr. Scales laughed aloud. "I know all about you, Mr. Johnson. I know you're smart and I know that you've been dealing drugs for a long time. But I'm not out to get you. However, you do have something that I want."

"Yeah! And what is that?"

"You have all the answers to my many questions."

They both were silent momentarily.

"Take him to headquarters," Mr. Scales demanded.

As Tim sat in the unmarked police cruiser, his mind was racing with a lot of different thoughts. What could this possibly be about? Why him? Why now? He was no longer in control. This ordeal was out of Tim's hand. Therefore, he took a moment to pray so that he could put it in God's hands. When he reached the F.B.I headquarters in downtown D.C., Tim felt embarrassed as the curious onlookers eyed him. The interrogation room was almost like all the other ones that Tim had seen. It was furnished with a long table and three chairs. Other than that, his room was empty. However, it was one small detail that was a little different about the room.

The room was furnished with snacks and a television. Tim laughed because he knew that whenever there were snacks and comfort in an interrogation room, there were usually agents trying to manipulate the client into giving information.

"Have a seat, Mr. Johnson," agent Scales demanded. There were two other agents present as well.

"I understand that you want a lawyer Mr. Johnson, but there's no need to get hasty."

"What's this about?"

"Well, Mr. Johnson, I have a few things that concern you. I don't even need to ask you any questions at this point because my case is basically an open and close case."

Agent Scales opened the folder that he was holding then he placed some photos on the table.

"Take a good look, Mr. Johnson."

Tim was becoming ill as he focused on the picture of a dead body slumped over on the ground with a bullet wound to the head.

"You can barely tell who it is by that picture, but here's a picture of him before his life was taken."

Tim knew Rabbit's face all too well.

"That's what this is about?"

"Not quite, Mr. Johnson. Here are some more pictures."

Agent Scales had vivid pictures of Daryl pulling the trigger. However, the picture didn't give a clear view of Daryl's face. Tim continued to look through the pictures. There were pictures of Daryl, Cliff, and himself during the times that Cliff exchanged drugs for money from his runners.

Suddenly, Tim's stomach started to quiver. He had been in the game long enough to know where Agent Scales was getting at by showing him the pictures.

There was a federal law called conspiracy which enabled law enforcement officials to arrest a suspect based on his knowledge of a criminal act as well as his participation. Tim had known several people who were doing life in prison just for knowing about a drug transaction and not reporting it to the authorities. There were a stack of pictures that lie before Tim. It seemed as if the D.E.A had been investigating Cliff and Daryl for some time now, but that wasn't the case. It was Linda who had been investigating them in an attempt to find Tim.

Linda was in the grocery store one day when she saw Cliff. He didn't remember her, but she remembered him. After keeping close surveillance on Cliff, Daryl came into the picture which automatically made him a recipient of her surveillance.

Tim continued to look through the photos.

"Take your time, Mr. Johnson. I want you to absorb every detail."

Tim wasn't amused by Agent Scales antics. In fact, this whole ordeal was beginning to become a nightmare with each photo that Tim saw. It wasn't until Tim reached the photo with Rhonda and Cliff entering the hotel, that his entire mood changed. Agent Scales noticed the changed expression and immediately took advantage of it.

"I see you've entered the danger zone. That's your so called friend betraying you with your girlfriend."

"This shit is fake. You're trying to trick me."

"Hold on a minute, Mr. Johnson. I have plenty of ways to arrest you and make sure you're convicted. I would be doing society an injustice though."

Agent Scales flipped the photo over and revealed the next photo of Cliff and Rhonda leaving the hotel.

"There's a murdering drug dealer running the streets of D.C. and he banged your girl, but he's supposed to be your main man. There's many more just like him running around in the streets playing God, but right now I'm targeting him."

"I understand, but what does this have to do with me?"

Tim was fuming, but he did a good job at not allowing it to show.

"I'm not going to beat around the bush, Mr. Johnson. Cliff and Daryl are about to be indicted on charges of drug distribution, drug trafficking and conspiracy to murder," Agent Scales said. He sipped some water from the cup he was holding then continued.

"As it stands, you're included in this conspiracy just because of your association with these gentlemen. In which a conviction would put you in jail for the rest of your life. However, I can help you if you help me."

Tim knew how the game went. Agent Scales wanted him to be an informant for the government. Tim had never told on anyone in his life, and had talked against it with his life. The more he looked at the pictures of Rhonda and Cliff; he became so furious that he broke his own code. Tim told everything he knew about Rabbit's murder and the drug transactions. He even lied about other murders which Cliff and Daryl had no knowledge of. He contributed the murder of Corey and the attempted murder of himself and Mike to a feud and intimidation strategy by Cliff and Daryl.

"Will you be willing to testify before a grand jury?"

"Yeah, it's time to make those suckers pay."

Tim hated to involve Daryl, but he realized that life was a dirty game and his way of playing dirty was revenge without remorse.

"I'm going to put you on a twenty four hour witness watch," Agent Scales stated.

Tim thought about it for a minute. He didn't want to ride around with agents on his back all day. However, he realized that it didn't matter whether they were there or not because he wasn't doing anything illegal. Tim's cell phone rang. He thought about allowing his voice mail to pick the call up, but when he looked on the small screen that shows the number of the incoming call, his curiosity got the best of him.

"Excuse me," Tim said.

Tim answered the phone and to his surprise it was Linda. The conversation didn't last long, but he promised her that he would call her back in an hour.

"Mr. Johnson, I appreciate your cooperation. Now, all I have to do is get you over to the court house and have you sworn in. Then the grand jury will hear your statement," Agent Scales commented assertively.

The realization of what Tim was about to do really hit him. He was about to break the main code that he lived by but his reasons for doing so blinded him in such a way that it didn't matter to him.

"We'll have these guys in custody tonight. Therefore, you don't have to worry about your life being in jeopardy."

"You couldn't protect me if you tried your hardest. I don't live in fear. Life was a gift and death is an even greater gift."

"Haha. I like you Tim."

CHAPTER 26

Once he made the statements that got Cliff and Daryl indicted by the federal grand jury, Tim headed to his mother's house. He was informed that he would have to go before the grand jury in superior court for the murder of Rabbit.

Agent Scales knew that it would be hard for them to prove that Daryl and Cliff tried to kill Tim, Mike and Corey at the McDonalds. Therefore, he spared them on that one. Rhonda had called Tim several times, but Tim brushed her off with lies of where he was and what he was doing.

Agent Scales took the liberty of giving Tim the pictures that were taken of Rhonda and Cliff. Tim held the pictures tight in his grasp as he reached the street that his mother's house was on. He was furious, but Tim knew that this had to be done quietly. When he walked in the house Roland ran to him and jumped in his arms.

"Hey little man," Tim said as he rubbed Roland's head.

"My mommy was waiting for you," Roland uttered.

"Yeah, and just where is your mommy at?"

"In there," Roland pointed to the bathroom. Tim put Roland down and walked into the kitchen. Roland followed him, of course.

Tim was still furious, but the time that he had to travel to get to his mother's house gave him the delay that he needed to gather his wit. He looked in the refrigerator and grabbed some orange juice. As he poured the juice into the cup, he could feel the eyes of another watching him.

"Hey baby," Rhonda said. She walked towards him and caressed his shoulders.

Her hands felt dirty now that Tim knew her little secret. He began to feel as if he was a possession, rather than a man.

"What's up?" Tim replied in a low tone.

"What's wrong baby?" Rhonda asked. Tim paused and put his head down.

"Everything is fucked up," Tim whispered. Rhonda was shocked. Tim never used profanity around Roland.

"Go in the living room Roland. I'll be in there in a minute with a peanut butter and jelly sandwich," Rhonda said.

Rhonda rubbed Tim's hair. "Talk to me baby. What's going on?"

Tim was speechless as he reached in his pocket and handed Rhonda the pictures.

This was not the way that Tim originally planned to do it. He wanted to talk to her first. There were so many questions that remained unanswered. Rhonda couldn't prevent the tears from rolling down her face heavily.

"I have so much curiosity running through my mind, but I'm afraid to ask questions," Tim spoke gently. He paused for a moment before he continued.

"I do have one very important question. Did he manipulate you or cause you to feel as if you had to have sex with him?"

Rhonda wanted to tell him yes, if it was just for the purpose of making him feel a little at ease. Tim turned around in the chair. Rhonda put her head down to answer.

"No Tim, it wasn't like that," Tim's ego was crushed.

"Then what the fuck was it like?"

Rhonda was startled by Tim's mood change.

"You...you wouldn't understand."

"At this point, I can just about believe or try to understand anything I see or hear," Tim replied.

"Okay, okay," Rhonda took a deep breath before she began.

"While you were in recovery, I realized that I had acquired a sex habit. I didn't want to get it from just anybody or any place, so I convinced Cliff that we could have protected sex with no strings attached."

"And he agreed with this?"

"He wasn't comfortable with it. But I told him that I would probably get it from somewhere else."

Tim was caught off guard by her candid response. He almost choked. This information changes things. Even though Cliff went along with the charade, Tim felt as if Cliff was coerced.

"I want you to listen to me closely, Rhonda. I'm not coming home tonight and I think that you need to make arrangements for what best suits you because I can no longer be with you," the words were assertive as Tim continued.

"I'm not sure if I'll feel this way forever, but you crossed me in an unspeakable way, and right now, the sight of you feels like my eyes are being cut out by razor blades."

Tim stormed out of the house just as quick as he came in. When he got into his truck, he took a deep breath and dialed Linda's phone number. The phone rang a few times before she answered it.

"Hello...Linda where are you?" Do you have time to talk? Okay I'm on my way."

CHAPTER 27

Ring ...Ring...Ring. The sound of the alarm clock was more than enough to startled Tim.

"Turn that shit off baby," Tim whispered to Linda.

"You told me to set the alarm...It's time to get up," Linda responded.

Tim had been over Linda's house for an entire month waiting for the trial to begin with Daryl and Cliff. They had talked extensively about numerous subjects.

Tim had told her about his whole ordeal, but what he wasn't aware of was the fact that Linda probably knew more about the last year of his life than he did.

"So today is your big day huh!" Linda said.

"It may be. However, I may not be able to take the stand today if the other witnesses are called before me."

"But you are the prosecutor's trump card."

"Look I'm not trying to talk about that shit. I think I need to get dressed."

Tim went into the bathroom and took a shower. Although, he had taken plenty of showers in his life, there was something different about this shower. It seemed like the water from the shower head sprayed differently today. I guess it was the simple fact that Tim was about to commit himself to an unethical act. With all due respect, it just didn't sit well with him. As the water splashed against his skin, Tim's mind began to race. He thought of the many different moments of loyalty where Cliff and Daryl stood up as men.

Tim realized that he wasn't worthy of stealing the honor amongst gangstas. But he also realized that impulsiveness had allowed him to react in such a way that made it almost impossible to turn back. However, this was not his style. This was not how Tim wanted to be remembered.

Although, memories do fade away, Tim refused to let his memory fade with a cowardly essence.

After Tim finished taking his shower, Linda ran some water in the bath tub so that she could bathe. This was the perfect opportunity for Tim to take care of his business. He dialed a number on his cell phone quickly and waited for someone to answer.

"What's up Tee? Yeah it's Tim. I need you to meet me at Forestville Mall. I'll be in the arcade."

Tim quickly got dressed and left a note in Linda's coffee table. *Tim Johnson was back in action*, he thought, as he glided across the intersection of Walters Lane in Forestville Maryland, with the sounds of After Seven blasting from the speakers.

Tim had a lot of things on his mind, including a bag of heroin which told him that he needed to get an NA meeting.

CHAPTER 28

When Tim reached the mall, he browsed through a few of the stores before he went into the arcade. He was amazed at how advanced the features were in the arcade games. Tim hadn't played an arcade game in a long time. In fact, the games that he grew up on were much more basic than the games that currently exist. Tim walked pass a couple of punk rockers. One of them glanced at him and flashed a superficial smile. He ignored what he believed to be a hidden racial stare. He didn't have time to entertain any non-sense.

After waiting for what seemed like hours, Tee finally arrived. They greeted each other with warmth and sincerity.

"Hey what's up good looking?" Tee said as she squeezed his cheek.

"You don't look so bad yourself, killa!" Tim responded.

"I do what I can do when I can do it." Tim continued to look her up and down.

"I see, I see," he said in a flirting manner.

Tonya was an old girlfriend of Tim's. For years they went through the motions of separating and getting back together. When he got locked up, their friendship blossomed.

Tim learned the importance of true friendship, because most of the people who he thought were true turned out to be as fake as a million dollar bill.

Tonya looked into Tim's eyes. She saw something different. She didn't know whether it was fear or indifference. She didn't care. Her main concern was to assist him in any way that she could.

"So what's up?" she asked while staring at two kids who were fighting over a video game.

"I need a passport."

"What? Huh!" Tonya was caught off guard.

Tim looked away.

"Yeah, I need a passport because I can't stay here anymore. I've crossed a line and I don't have enough guts to undo what I've done."

They talked for hours. Tonya understood his plight and was willing to help him in any way she could.

"So what does this mean? Is this for...good? I mean you have people here who love you."

Tim gazed in her eyes. He saw something that he never saw before. He saw the way that she truly felt about him. Tim realized Tonya had used the word people in place of herself. Tim gently rubbed her face.

"Don't worry. The people who love me will most definitely see me again."

He smiled at her. "You never answered my question."

Tonya put her head down. "Of course I can. You know I can."

They walked through the mall talking for hours.

Tim had forgotten about his demise momentarily. However, the degree of his fate wouldn't let him forget for long. No one could imagine what he was feeling, Tim told himself. He had crossed the very line of loyalty that his foundation stood upon. Tim refused to get caught up in the ramifications of his demise. *Shit happens*, he reminded himself. However, he realized the mere truth. There was no way he could justify his act of disloyalty. Tim prided himself on the respect that his followers gave him when he showed them the in's and out's of the game. This respect would no longer be given to him, for he would now be known for going against the code.

A lot of hustler's knew what price they had to pay if they broke the code. Their name was tarnished, their reputation meant nothing, and they had to be very cautious with the neighborhoods they ventured into and the people they associated themselves with. It didn't matter how gangster they may have kept it, their existence suddenly meant nothing.

Tim gathered his belongings. He convinced himself that he wouldn't be able to live with the label of being a snitch. But, didn't he know that the damage was done?

He couldn't undo what was done. He wasn't sure if he would be viewed differently in the eyes of others, but at least he would be able to sleep at night knowing that he changed his original game plan.

Tim saw so many cases of disloyalty by others who claim that they would rather die than be dishonorable until the feds, D.E.A, or the A.T.F came knocking. Then it was every man for himself. Afterwards, a lot of lives changed. Some affiliates went home with their families, while the others went to do hard time, never to return to society.

The way Tim viewed it society had found a way to hold everyone affiliated accountable until they rooted out the big fish in the pond. In some cases, there had to be pawns or people who had minimal roles, but refused to cooperate so they received maximum time.

If Tim didn't know anything, he knew how to disappear whenever the butter had gotten to thick to cut through. As many different moments flashed through his mind, he pondered the thought of one day making his return. Years would pass and the world would forget about him. But it wasn't the entire world that he was concerned with....only the world that he knew to be Drama City...The Nation's Capital.

CHAPTER 29

Overlooking some documents, he seemed to be puzzled by the paperwork that he was viewing.

"Can you approach the bench council for the defendant?" his raspy voice uttered.

"Certainly your honor."

After exchanging a few words, the judge demanded that the case proceeded.

"Is the government ready to take this case to trial?"

"Uh …no…I mean yes…well…you see your honor, the government has a slight problem. We can't seem to locate the witness."

"What do you mean? He's your witness. He should be in your custody considering the seriousness of this case."

The District Attorney swallowed a glob of his own spit before speaking.

"The witness refused protective custody," he uttered.

"Well, I didn't know that they were given a choice nowadays."

The judge shook his head.

"I'm going to give this trial a recess… a thirty minute recess and if the government is not ready, then the case will be dismissed."

Cliff smirked while Daryl tried to hide his fear. Cliff knew that Tim wouldn't be able to go through with it once his conscience sat in.

CHAPTER 30

The cafeteria was crowded with hungry patrons, lawyers, policemen and court service providers.

"So do you think he got cold feet?" Daryl uttered.

"Nah! I think he realized what was at stake." Daryl smiled.

He was relieved at the thought of not having to be associated with the one person who had mentored him as being a snitch. He ordered his food. Cliff didn't want anything. He didn't have an appetite. After all, he never counted his chickens before they hatched.

He contemplated Tim walking through the doors of the court building any minute now.

Instead, his lawyer walked through the doors of the cafeteria. He hurried towards their table as a surge of fear engulfed Cliff.

"The Judge wants to see us," the lawyer said.

Cliff's heart was racing.

"I knew that nigga was going to sell us out," Cliff uttered.

When they reached the court room, there weren't as many people there as before, Therefore, the room was quiet. The judge tapped the gavel on the desk.

"This is the case of the United States Versus Mr. Daryl Jenkins and Cliff Porter." I hereby wish to declare all charges are dropped…you are free to go."

"Whew!" Cliff screamed.

"That's what I'm talking about," Daryl said.

They both hugged their lawyer. And before anyone could change their decision they were off.

EPILOGUE

The view was enchanting, Tim thought as the aircraft glided through the air. He would miss a lot of people, places, and things, but most of all, he would miss his family.

In the beginning, the glamour and glitz seem to outweigh any potential consequences that may lie ahead. But in the end, there was a much more delinquent price to pay for a game that never promised freedom from anything.

"Can I get you something to drink sir?" the pretty airline stewardess asked.

"Um...yes I'll have a sprite," Tim said in a low tone.

Tim felt more relaxed then he had felt in weeks...maybe months. As he reflected on his past, he realized how blessed he was. He had survived addiction and the criminal lifestyle in which he was living, but for some reason he didn't feel as if he had remained true to the game. Maybe in a few years, he could return to Washington D.C. with a whole new set of rules, but for now, he was headed somewhere where no one would know him. A place where the sunshine seem to be never ending and the people there were anonymous to him. The more he thought about it, maybe he could go to some self-help meetings and continue his recovery.

As everything changed around him, the one thing that remained the same was the fact that the drug game always ended two ways; jail or death.

"We're now arriving at the LAX airport please turn off all electronic devices," the voice in the overhead speaker announced.

******

WORDS FROM THE AUTHOR

Almost every state has a Drama City. The drug lifestyle and the many different faces that create the love, pain, loyalty, regret, and violence live in a world of its own. In the end, lives are shattered and it's impossible to replace the irreplaceable.

This book is dedicated in loving memory of Larry Moon Sr., Delores Hinnant, James Hinnant Sr.,Denise Moon and Sulaimon Yusif Malik. May you all rest in peace.

Larry Moon Jr.

Made in the USA
Middletown, DE
08 October 2022